THE KINDNESS
OF RAVENS

Frank Bardessono

Author contact:
Email: cabobard@yahoo.com
Facebook: https://www.facebook.com/Bardessono
Twitter: @RavenBard

ISBN-10: 0615649564
ISBN-13: 9780615649566

Library of Congress Control Number: 2012909959
CreateSpace, North Charleston, SC

For Elizabeth

I

My birthday would have been unremarkable save for the naked madman at the deli.

At the grand milestone of one point six decades of existence, smack dab in the heart of nineteen hundred and eighty-five, I'd crafted a montage of illuminati pretenses, seasoned with the buzz of pop culture white noise. Issued a standard issue five foot eight inches of whitebread, topped with curled, flaxen hair and dark copper eyes, the total package was by all trustworthy accounts too rough around the edges, too brazen with coarse commentary, and too susceptible to the usual delusions of teenage grandeur. Given a hinterland choice between Southern Cal suburban wrangler or new age preppie, I'd opted for a cheap department store version of the latter, with its garden-variety uniform of Levi 501s, polo oxfords (collar turned up), surf T-shirts, and Nike high-tops, accessorized with a maudlin superiority complex, and like many disenfranchised youths of minor intelligence and moderate savoir faire, I'd been an early starter in all the wrong areas, late in all the right ones.

After school that day, I walked to a nearby grocery store where I maintained an unenthusiastic modicum of employment bagging foodstuffs. Two hours passed in dreary bagboy monotony. I informed my manager I was taking my dinner break, stripped off my blue grocer's apron, and went down the block into a nearby deli. Aromas of cold cuts, mozzarella, and fresh-lit cigar wafted about as I nodded to the butcher behind the counter.

"Hello, my friend."

"'Allo, *paisan*. Your usual order? Coming right up. Let me tell you something. There are two great truths in life. Would you like to know what they are?" He grabbed a wedge of bread, sliced it in half, buttered it, and began sprinkling the dough with red peppers and garlic cloves. Rubio was his name, and he sliced bologna like a pro, both the sandwich and bullshit varieties, having the weary look of a man who was supposed to have done something important in his life but instead had resigned himself to menial citizenship, occasionally imparting dry Mediterranean wisdom. I knew the type. Heck, I was apprenticing to the type.

"Of course I would," I said, and prepared to listen to his earth-shattering revelations with private contempt, as I was oft known to do. I glanced at specials written on the chalkboard behind him (spinach ravioli and olive loaf by the pound) and feigned a façade of interest.

"The first is this...come here, *paisan*." He beckoned me closer, shushing. His eyebrows scurried, eyes darting, mischievous, to a young girl in line behind me, a knockout of a redhead. "Women are something beyond us," he whispered. "All lovers are but fools. The only reliables in this world are good dogs and old money." This produced polite chuckles out of a few customers in line, who were also following his parable.

"Yeah, I've heard that one," I replied.

"The second is this. Despite what many believe, red pepper, not garlic, is the better ingredient in any table-worthy marinara sauce."

He scooped my noodles and bread into a plastic container.

"I'll pass on that tip to my mother, though I'd hazard a guess she'll disagree."

He laughed, booming, and rang up my order as I paid for my food. The others floundered in the anticlimactic ending of his lecture. An elderly lady rolled her eyes, a Hispanic man with a handlebar moustache looked perplexed, the redhead pouted. A collegiate-type fellow wearing black, oblong glasses and sporting a nappy goatee tapped his foot, impatient. I took my pasta over to a table, sat down, and picked over my food. I chewed on a raw piece of garlic and thought about the redhead in a series of lascivious ways.

Then the crazed street druid came barreling in the front door. He was stark naked and filthy, his fingernails yellow and bleeding. He began bellowing, his gist, predictable to a fault, concerning end times. Homeless nomad, lost soul, inter-dimensional visitor, asylum escapee, acid flashback sufferer, or combinations thereof—whatever he was, he was quite a sight to see in an upscale Italian deli, much less in upscale Durango Bay.

I'm not certain when I started labeling the street culture folk as druids. Probably when I was a kid, after I'd read Tolkien's trilogy or some Asimov science fiction or something else fantastical, during one of my family's rare sojourns up or downstate to San Fran or LA and I'd first encountered some panhandling waif. I saw a newscast once wherein a reporter was conducting an interview with an advocate for the homeless in Los Angeles. Behind them, near the downtown Greyhound bus station and its shantytown maze of Skid Row alleys and streets outside, a large group of street folk gawked and shambled in the background. A grizzled bag lady burst through the front of the crowd, holding a square piece of plywood with the slogan *Will Fart for Food* emblazoned upon it. She was toothless, with sad, ancient eyes. Upon noticing the television crew, she ceased the promotion of her services, more fascinated with the cameras. I'd thought her hook was an original approach and would've gladly handed her some funds for a bit of inspired flatulent entertainment, had I been present.

I figured out pretty quickly as a kid how urban denizens of major world metropolises knew the drill of Big City doomsayers, dregs of society carrying placards and signs proclaiming *The End Is Near, Repent,* or *Ragnarok Approaches.* Often they seemed to wear raggedy trench coats (naturally indicating a hidden, awful Something underneath). They barred one's path, ominous, and quoted cryptic passages from a saint-like figure or another convenient source of dread, preaching about the errors of one's ways. Most of them were human beings suffering from mental illness or disability, post-traumatic vets, schizophrenics, and addicts whose families or social workers had either lost track of their charges or given up on them.

But I also noticed, among the herds of aimless wanderers, were some few who were other than they appeared, vagabonds of purpose, perhaps. They still stemmed from the stock of those who took it upon themselves to remind the masses how shit-out-of-luck we all were, but somehow those vibrant bedlamites were *more*—blessed, cursed, a dark light behind their eyes, a crazy understanding. Something fractured them. The pariah currently preaching to us deli patrons had been broken long ago. Whether he was one of the drifting elite remained to be seen.

Those observations in my youth had convinced me the *meshugganah* of our cities were testaments to the wayward infancy of communal spirit. As a result, I never crossed the street when they rambled toward me in nearby Santa Crisca, where they normally congregated. Durango Bay was far off limits, and it was boggling how this guy got to the middle of town in his birthday suit without being intercepted by our local boys in blue.

I often let them remind me of the underside. I gave them a few bucks if they asked, if I had some to spare, usually after a harrowing diatribe of providence due. I tried to share their pain for a brief moment, hoping it might lighten their load, and when they turned their attention to the next soul in need of spiritual rescue, I'd mutter some hack venerable words for them, like *Vaya Con Dios* or *Godspeed*. But really, deep within, while I would have liked to believe I was doing those things purely for goodness' sake, I had ulterior motives. I was afraid, not of the religious lecturing despite the withering Catholicism lingering within me. I feared that one day I too would devolve into a haggard, witless fool spouting Biblical prophecy, imposing my unhinged dementia on inconvenienced others. I figured if I understood them, if I embraced their presence, I might avoid their fates, which is why the druid in the deli was more intriguing than intimidating, and also why I wasn't pissing my friggin' pants.

The redhead ogled him, agape. The college boy stared, uncomprehending. The senior citizen and the Hispanic man cringed near a rack of potato chips.

"The end is at hand! Let the Lord cleanse you, or burn with the wicked!"

"Out! Out!" Rubio said. "I am calling the police!" He picked up a phone and dialed emergency services. I watched the deluded man preach to the terrified old lady cowering in a corner. Hounding the elderly with forceful threats of damnation didn't jibe with me, however well intended. Few Durango Bay souls in need of deliverance were about to convert via the berserk ravings of a dirty naked guy.

I stood up and approached him. He had reduced the poor octogenarian to tears.

"Knock it off," I said.

He spun around to me, a shower of dust falling to the floor. Pink blemishes and knobby scabs covered his body. His eyes were reddened and teary. He appraised me up and down, gauging my threat level. "I am delivering messages of Jehovah. Stand back, lest you suffer my Lord's wrath…wait. You. *You!* You have seen it, young one. How old are thee?"

"Actually, I'm sixteen just today. It's my birthday."

"Sixteen. Four years short of a score? And you saw it, you saw it, I see it in your soul; it taints your very essence as surely as sunlight and cabbages, I know you did."

"Um, I've seen what?"

"Ah, but you know. You may know it in a different form than its manifestation to Joshua the Son, but you've seen it. I know it too well. It has been my companion for so long in the shadow. You are one of its children. Everyone is, but only some of us see its face. Only days and nights and one turn of a corner separate you and me, brother."

"What are you talking about?"

"Tell me when it happened. Tell me now!"

I knew of what he spoke. Red shift. He likely called it something different, but it was red shift all the same.

"Let's find you some clothing, I'll buy you a cup of coffee, and…"

"Tell me!"

"Just humor him!" the redhead hissed from her corner.

"OK, fine." I supposed I could try to distract him until the gendarmes showed up. The druid plopped on the floor, crossed his legs

Indian style, squashing his unmentionables with little notice, and closed his eyes as if to meditate. "Well…a few years back, me and my friend Alex, as kids we spent our downtime during summers playing in the backcountry near my family's ranch, exploring hills and creek beds, swimming in fishing holes, building tree forts, hunting for tarantulas and alligator lizards. You know, boys' stuff."

"Mmm," the druid murmured.

"Well, uh…at the end of an engagement involving a pretty annoyed king snake we'd been trying to wrangle…"

"Aha! Serpent in the garden," he mused. "Did the beast succumb to your combined might and tactics? Or did it elude your best efforts of capture?"

"It got away. It slithered down a gopher hole."

"And?"

I paused, looking at the immobile customers and Rubio, who had hung up the phone and was backed against the freezer behind the counter. "And, uh, then, well…Alex changed. He was winded from our run chasing after the snake. He was breathing hard. So was I. His face was flushed with sunburn, probably adrenalin too."

"Chockfull of robust tomorrows, no doubt. And then?"

Hesitant, fearful the deli folk would soon consider me as nutter-butter as the naked fellow on the floor, I went on.

"Then a dark cloud…no, not totally black; it had red fringes. Like black cherries. It engulfed him."

"The shadow, cheerless apathy, silent thief, yes, yes, yes! Giving no quarter as it conquered his bastion, yes?"

"Yeah, I guess. His face became a silhouette through the murk of the thing. But what was most unsettling was Alex seemed resolute, as if he'd known all along a turn of the worm had been coming. His eyes flickered, for a second, through the fog, and then…um…well, he morphed from what he'd been to something else. It found me next. It's hard to describe. Oily, blood-tinted tendrils, but they were see-through, transparent. It made me nauseated, kind of a null void, there and yet not there."

"It is omniscient, isn't it? And it ushered each of you to your new long term residences, teeming dens of inequity, turbulent with endless disarray and television and plastic foods."

"That's maybe a little dramatic."

"Alas, young one, you have my pities. You'd never have witnessed the transition had you not been harboring a certain quality."

"I don't know what you mean by that."

"Then you have yet to recognize it, but it shines like a beacon, rest assured."

"Er...whatever."

"Your friend, he noted the event not?"

"No, I don't think so. He's never told me if he did."

"And you never discussed it with him?"

"No. I thought it was a trick of the sun, or haze mirage, heat exhaustion maybe. I didn't want him to razz me."

"But the entity, you know now, was no trick. It crept. It stalked you and your friend. It pounced. It lurks still. Yes?"

"I, uh...maybe, yeah. I don't know." I took stock of our captive audience, whom as I'd expected, by the looks on their faces, had lumped me in with the naked man as promising candidates for the nearest rubber room.

"What do you deem the intruder?"

"Red shift," I mumbled.

"An apt classification. She is an efficient lioness, intimidating prey into submission with nary a claw lifted, is she not?" He rose from the floor, took me by the shoulders. His fingers were strong, digging into my arms like vice grips. "I must resume delivering the Word, brother."

"No offense, but the only thing you're delivering is the creeps to everybody in here. Probably me too, by now."

"You can say that again," the redhead said.

"You dare doubt the Word of God?" he demanded, his tone accusing her of horrid blasphemy. He turned back to me and said, "You, who hath seen the machination of the world asunder, tell this recreant bimbo the urgency of my task."

"I'm presuming God would not want you to speak to people in this manner. Fear is no way to spread hope."

"You do not heed the warning, though you've been shown the way and the light. You will suffer the holy vengeance."

"Vengeance isn't holy."

He raced to the counter, and Rubio recoiled. The crazed karmic messenger picked up a ballpoint pen and brandished it toward me. "Stay away!"

"Do you really want to end up in a jail cell? Come on, man."

"You do not believe the end is near," he said, crestfallen.

I shrugged. "Long odds, I'm wagering."

He gagged and began to sputter and spit, stomping his feet like a child in the midst of a tantrum, his shrunken, dusty genitals flapping up and down, long victimized to gravity and heaven only knew what else. His muddy, bare feet left brown smears on the white vinyl floor.

Then I saw him as he *really* was, only for a split second. I knew not how, and it was a frightening thing. His nude form coalesced into a knight of singular repute, tarnished armor splendorous, blazing sword of light and fire, steel blue eyes, wanton and beautiful. As quick as he'd appeared, the strange royal warrior transmogrified back to his former desperate, naked state, a crumbling underworld jester.

Without hesitation he thrust the pen into his right eyeball. Goop and viscous flesh splattered across his face. The redhead screamed in horror. The college boy bolted out the backdoor. The butcher cried out, as did I. The street druid, ignoring the pain such an act should have warranted, did not seem fazed in the slightest. His one good eye glared at me.

"I will no longer bear witness to that minion of *Eblis*. I will not watch it take one more soul into its bosom. Do as you will, young seer."

He raised the pen again. "No!" I yelled. I lunged for him, trying to grab his arm, but it was too late. The pen punctured his remaining eye. Blood gushed down his cheeks. He slid to the floor, the pen clattered away across the vinyl. Then he covered his gory sockets with his hands, mucous fluids dribbling through his fingers.

I stood over him in shock, wondering how I had gotten involved in this imbroglio on my half hour break from work. How impossible it was for this to occur in the sheltered haven of Durango Bay. How very possible it was that I was dreaming, must be dreaming.

Rubio was aghast, unable to process what had just occurred in his deli. I barked at him to toss me some towels. He found some cloth handkerchiefs and brought them to me. I tried to stem the blood flow.

There was a lot less than I thought there'd be. A couple of policemen came barging in. Paramedics arrived soon after, and they carted away the blinded man, surely off to the psych ward in Santa Crisca. The street druid was silent and *smiling*, exuding a macabre calm that was far more alarming than his ruined face. The police took statements from all who had observed the incident. I rinsed my hands in the deli's restroom and became melancholy as the druid's blood trickled down the drain. I walked back to work and told my manager I was going home, ignoring his requests to explain the need.

Alex called later, expecting birthday hoopla, which I deferred, much to his confusion. At the dinner table, my mother cut me a piece of chocolate birthday cake, and I ate it, dutiful, grateful. My father and I discussed my impending DMV appointment to acquire my driver's license. I didn't tell them about the deli. They would read about it in the paper soon enough.

I found a new place for my meal breaks. It was my first extended communion with a street prophet. It would not be the last. I knew in my heart he'd been correct, about red shift and also about my inclusion in a roughshod circle of witnesses to a portion of that which is unseen. They were my brethren, twice removed only by luck and the graces of gods, our mutuality as real as, to wit, sunlight and cabbages.

2

Happenings like the deli fiasco were as foreign to an orthodox Durango Bay citizen as a Thai whore might be announcing her candidacy for mayor of our pleasant Gold Coast borough.

Durango Bay lies north of Los Angeles, two hours or so as the crow flies. It is a veritable Shangri-La, an outlying extension of the American Riviera, golden hills laced in manzanita shrub, majestic oaks and pepper tree orchards, sprawling equestrian ranches housing sheep and cattle, exotic ostrich farms, Arabian and Peruvian show horses, occasional herds of domesticated bison. It is country to raise children in; settling down is not only a way of life, it is an expected mandate. In the markets everyone knows your name, when you were born, and to what political platform you owe allegiance. Durango Bay didn't get its first McDonald's until 1981, and its first movie theater arrived a year after that. Dreamy weather year round, no modern decay to spoil youthful impressions, quaint festivals and picnics and Scout jamborees, pep rallies and Little League, the usual men's clubs designed to escape the doldrums of domestic stagnation by drinking beer, grilling meat, and talking shop and sports. Lions, Elks, and Shriners, oh my.

My father was a good man, an Old World Catholic-Italian, a New Jersey native, Republican, ultra-conservative. Against all odds he escaped the Jersey temper that should have followed him from the Eastern Seaboard to California. Pleasant to a fault and nose perpetually held to the grindstone, the man defined the meaning of the word *work*. It's a foregone conclusion I will never sweat and toil as much as he did. He was employed at an Air Force base about thirty miles west of Durango Bay, where he applied his radar specialist skills he'd picked up while stationed in Seoul during the Korean War. A jack-of-all-trades, he was an expert in all things electronic and just about every other handyman skill. Carpentry. Plumbing. Farming, ranching, livestock breeding. Never a single repairman or contractor on premises, no sir.

He took great care of his gardens every spring, back when he still had the attention spans of his sons, me and my younger brother Jim, eager to help forage acres of hay for the horses and cattle, rows of corn and endless mutant zucchini, mini-orchards of stone fruit trees and wild grape vineyards. We loved riding his antiquated tractor, a huge contraption with numerous mad scientist-type lubed moving parts. We sat up by our father's side perched like cockatoos on a lumbering iron birdcage, giant metal fenders sheathing massive tires crushing all in their path, churning earth flying with each stroke of the tiller.

Late summer chores included mowing and reaping meadows of barley on the southern end of the ranch. The fields of reeds grew long each year and concealed Jim and me for hours in hide-and-seek games. The tractor cut through these pristine meadows like butter. Its mower was a vicious, menacing apparatus not to be taken lightly, utilizing grating teeth that grinded back and forth across a chain-axle rod. One day I was pitching hay with a fork into a wagon when I heard a sudden shriek and the horrific sound of something fleshy being shredded between blades. The mower had caught a jackrabbit in mid-flight between its shears and sheared off the poor critter's back legs.

Have you ever heard a rabbit scream?

It's quite disturbing.

My father, ever the pragmatist, instructed me to put the thing out of its misery. From atop his tractor he tossed me a heavy crescent wrench. I raced after the mutilated rabbit. It was dragging its bleeding half-body across the shorn grasses with its front legs. The only right thing to do was to whomp the rodent with the wrench, crush the skull, and end the rabbit's suffering. I raised the wrench, wishing the bunny would stop its undying screams on its own. My father gazed at me, glowering with disappointment. I couldn't bring myself to do it. He turned off the tractor, jumped down, and grabbed the wrench from me. I turned away. The rabbit's skull cracked like a walnut. As my brother jeered and my father scolded me, I wondered why I'd been so terrified to strike the dying rabbit, why I'd failed to do that which was necessary, something as obvious as putting down a terminally suffering animal. The shame was potent.

But too, there was admiration of my father. He didn't think about the Zen of things, the endless scope of decisions and their repercussions, actions and reactions and the flow and ebb of being, the near exact opposite approach of his eldest son. Even at the bourgeoning entry unto adolescence, I was already imposing on myself a cluster-fucking mess of lazy cerebration. My father acted upon instinct, as many of his traditionalist generation did, the ones who'd come of age under the umbrella of the Good War, forged from sacrifice and fortitude, emerging from the fifties with the hard-boiled wherewithal of post-Depression Americana. Much to my dismay, more so for him, I was not my father's son. In addition to my child-of-privilege liberal disposition, I was about as athletically coordinated as a three-legged duck. And Jim was already showing telltale signs of punk rebellion: earrings, experimental Mohawks, morbid poetry. When it came to neighborly bragging rights and vicarious All-American living through football trophies or wrestling championships, Dad was batting 0 for 2.

As for my mother, in Durango Bay there were few men who thought their mother was anything less than a latter-day Virgin Mary. I was no exception. Yet she and I had our issues. She grew up in Kansas. We rented an RV each year to facilitate cross-country trips to see her relatives; her bloodline had owned their huge plantation-style casa and its thousand acres for the last century. She left home when she was eighteen and met my dad at the University of Kansas when he was en route to California. The visits to her childhood home gave her a kind of solace, as such sojourns are meant to convey, but those hot drives through the southwest were hellish. No air conditioning. KOA campgrounds. Infrequent splurges on a Motel Six. Dad knew how to stretch a dime. To me, the Midwest was endless, a limbo of plains covered in corn and wheat stretching out unceasing, broken up by rickety fences of untended barbed wire. Huge barns long abandoned stood in memoriam of rich beginnings and humble ends. Ponds dotted the flat country, peppered in moss and thirsty cattle and warbling frogs. Water towers emblazoned with local co-op advertising slogans broke the horizons, along with towering concrete grain silos that only slightly reminded one of Minuteman missiles laden underground throughout the heartland.

Culture there seemed to digress into blue-collar conglomerates of rodeo, demolition derby, and farming. Maintaining the world's breadbasket takes a certain breed. The communities were haphazard mélanges of hole-in-the-wall bars brimming with Old Milwaukee neon, John Deere dealerships, Circle K gas stations, VFW halls, and trailer parks. Houses were solid, founded, reinforced brick and stone. That tornado thing. We'd stay with my grandparents, whose massive house was borderline derelict, creaky wooden stairs leading up three stories that howled when stepped upon, kitchen shelves lined with Mason jars full of every imaginable homegrown herb known to man, a deep pantry in a dirt-floored basement, dry-weed and dust and mud hornets' nests seeping in each available crack, crocheted afghans draped over antique furniture, a snowy black-and-white TV, older than time itself, tuned to soap operas, farm reports, and *Wheel of Fortune*, brass country crockery, cowboy paintings, assorted pix of multiple grandchildren. My grandparents were amiable folk, bingo on Thursdays and bowling on Saturdays and bridge games on Sundays. They always told Jim and me how we'd grown, they talked about foreclosures on neighbors' properties, the pitch game Grandpa won a hundred bucks in, and which friends had recently died. They still called black people "darkies." Wacky.

We had uncles there, Unca Joe and Unca James, the latter Jim's namesake, who let Jim and me take our first peeks at *Playboy*, gave us our first sips of beer. Their rusty Fords and Chevy pickups were always loaded with mangy, loyal dogs. Unca Joe was the supposed black sheep in Mom's family because he'd voted for Carter and listened to FM radio. He took us to the local Circle K a lot to get candy bars and play Donkey Kong. Unca James was a true farmer: dressed in overalls and straw hat, covered head to toe in grease and hayseeds and chiggers, chugging any and all cheap beer in reach—Pabst Blue Ribbon, Old Milwaukee, Schlitz. He competitively raced wheeled farm machinery, combines, tractors, and lawn mowers. Some people really do that. He could have squeezed my head like a zit if he'd had the desire. Huge guy. Not Californian in any way. I realized my world was just that when I first met my uncles. *My* world, my teeny-tiny world. Regionalism is a tough bastard to beat.

Several months after I witnessed the deli druid's mutilation, my family returned from the annual Kansas pilgrimage a few days before Easter. My mother was frantic because our house was the place dozens of people came to depend on during holidays. She only had seventy-two hours or so to organize the grand spread. She threw us into preparations, relentless. It was the last thing I wanted to do, having just gotten back from another venture through purple mountains' majesty sans air conditioning and a private bedroom. I grumbled my way through my assigned task, polishing the crockery and silverware.

"Why say you're going to do it and then bitch about it?" Mom asked.

"All I asked was if I have to do the crystal too."

"If it's such a hassle, I'll do it myself."

Holidays were nonnegotiable at my house. My mother cooked ten-course feasts that fed extended family and half of the surrounding neighborhood. My father carved the roast, my mother never ate a damned thing, sipping wine throughout the meal, while everybody else present wolfed down the wide array of vittles. Old folks around the table raved about this casserole and that entrée. The TV blasted from the living room. Dogs under the table took scraps from our hands. Dysfunction set in as with most upper-middle class Durango Bay, and we became accustomed to the mesh: Dad the Workaholic, Mom the Alcoholic, Jim the Blue Collar Punk Rebel, and me, the Aspiring White Collar College Boy. Add water and stir.

I continued polishing silver. Nineteen place settings this year. I watched Mom salt the top of her scalloped potatoes. Too much salt, but that was the way we boys liked it. She put down the saltshaker and took a drink of wine. She had perfected the quiet denial phase of the addict. She got a lot of hell for it from our father, and from her boys too, me more than anyone.

She didn't deserve it. She was a compassionate woman, showing boundless generosity with resources to back it up. Geriatric nursing was her life. We had taken in a few bedridden family members over the years, and she worked her fingers to the bone providing care for them until their usually hard ends. The geezers' demands had been high, and the alcohol took some of the edge off for her. I romanticized her as much as any kid would, though my canonization had dark undertones. The only difference between "normal" romantics and dark romantics is this: the romantics will eat life up with a silver spoon, relishing every taste, enjoying every sunset, smelling every rose, and the dark romantics will do the precisely the same except they'll take the time to complain about how the spoon isn't shiny enough. We went head to head countless times, running around the circular loops of an alcoholic's denial and an enabler's pleading. I wanted June Cleaver and told her so. One night she'd told me, after several glasses of cabernet, she'd always wanted to open an Italian restaurant of her own. I asked her why she hadn't. Tears in her eyes, she refused to respond, and we watched *Starsky and Hutch* in silence. After that, in private, I often mourned an unopened ravioli factory.

Roasted turkey gravy and spicy pumpkin pie taunted me from the oven burners. "More wine?" a brittle voice called from the patio. The Geritol set usually basked on the deck outside until the meal was served at two o'clock on the dot. Mom grabbed a bottle of merlot and headed out. I watched her through the screen door, nodding to one of my great aunts, well into her nineties, as Mom filled her glass. Healthy lifestyle paradigms were unknown to the holiday troops. Most of the clan smoked, drank, and ate loads of salty red meat all the livelong day. The old biddies and coots were hardier than stone. The extra effort required in entertaining the semi-senile elders was exasperating. I found excuses to leave the table when cornered with another endless story about prohibition or horse-and-buggy pointers. My impatience and boredom, however, didn't blind me from the fact my mother respected the wisdom of elders. Her ability to endure lengthy anecdotes laced with sudden memory lapses was extraordinary. I knew she touched the blood of the world in that way. She walked back in the kitchen with the empty merlot bottle, tossed it into the trash, and sat down. She lit a Pall Mall and hacked on the first drag. Television had told me mothers in general weren't like this, the drinking and the smoking and the desperate silence. Laundry detergent commercials in particular, it seemed. I believed the TV. The TV told me much. There was leeway though; I was no dope to presume generalizations, and via a bit of research through Al-Anon and other such organizations, plus my own intuition, I'd concluded that when alcoholics looked in the bottom of their glass, it only showed them a mirror, and they'd fill the glass once more to cover a reflection. I understood, and there was empathy, young and untested as it was.

But sometimes there was anger nonetheless.

"You should take it easy on the vino today. I'm not really up for the usual slurring and slopping after supper. Wait until everyone goes home, OK?" I spat it out like a viper. I was of the opinion that consequences of words were never as dire as fear of saying them. Rude sumbitch, was I.

Her faded azure eyes flashed. "I won't be talked to in such a manner."

"You never care about how it affects us all, do you? You're my mother. Just once I'd love to have one goddamned sober day." I headed outside. I almost made it to the door before I heard her sobbing. We'd been there before, ugly expectations intruding once again into a rare attempt at harmony. Not to mention marring the celebration of the resurrection of Christ, I guess. Chocolate bunnies and the dead rising, let's bake a ham and look for painted eggs. Whatever.

I was subdued during dinner, thinking of reasons why I needed to blame her. Many justifications came to mind, as long as I didn't look in the mirror at the bottom of her glass. My glass. *Our* glass.

3

The long strip of beach loomed, daring me to tread upon it, taunting with smooth sands. Logic had taken a back seat in my mind. My inner child was uneasy with its newfound freedom. I was a magenta-toned phantom, psilocybin oozing through my pores, my skin taking on the purple color of the recently devoured mushrooms.

I looked skyward with obsidian eyes. A jigsaw splash of faces peered down at me, passing judgments, the heavens themselves holding high court. I wandered over to a wall of beachside cliffs, where various lines of erosion and ridges of sandstone reared above, crisscrossing in myriads of patterns, a maddening flurry of direction. I debated scaling one of the shale bluffs, unsure whether my depth perception was too impaired to succeed.

Alex burst into my bubbled world from around the bend. It was an abrupt intrusion, although we couldn't have been separated for more than ten minutes. His shirt and jeans were soiled from whatever adventures he'd been having. He came up too quick, larger than life, corny as a cartoon. He ran around me twice and dove into the sand, digging into a dune, pawing fistfuls of sand and throwing them up in the air.

"Breathe it in, man! Taste it!" he gasped, hyperventilating.

"What was that anyway?" I asked.

"What was what?"

What was what. Exactly.

"That whole spaz-out in the sand bit."

"Um," Alex said.

"Yep," I said.

I thought we were being sort of strange.

"Sort of strange," Alex echoed.

Whoa!

Suddenly the world flowed over, and soon we were helpless, sobbing and twitching on the sand, laughing as tears streamed down our red, red faces.

"Let's smoke a bowl. Over there," Alex said, pointing at a nearby niche in the cliffs. We walked into a secluded enclave separating two large boulders of limestone. Inside the confined hollow, it was quiet, jarring in its immutability, our ears accustomed to crashing waves of beach break. The air was moist and stale, like inside an old plastic bread wrapper. We surveyed the surroundings. The back wall was a massive lime formation, shaped by runoff water streams and the tides, coated with moss and algae. The colors were magnificent: crimson reds, clover greens, sunflower yellows, oozing blacks, and alkali whites. The molds overlapped one another, making an organic quilt of beach turf. The holes and crevices of the formation, accentuated with algae crusts, turned the structure into a veritable Golgotha, severed heads and soulless faces peering back at us.

"The Abyss," I said, offering a definition.

"Infinity," Alex countered.

I had met Alex through childhood sports, AYSO soccer and Little League, long before we started partying, before girls, before hierarchal rankings and high school class warfare, when we were wee lads on a ball field looking to impress our fathers on the sidelines. Alex shared the non-sporto flaw with me, further adding to our progenitors' disappointment (that, however, didn't stop our parents from signing us up to every seasonal kids' sport organization available, in the hope that we might break out of our girly-boy brackets by force). While we warmed benches and sucked on orange slices, we established an underdog bond 'twixt each other, which led to a tight-knit friendship. Action figures and make-believe gave way to juvenile weaponry and petty theft, then to the pandering anxieties of latter day adolescence.

At an unhealthy sixteen, Alex was tall, six feet and inches, and had an orange-blonde mop top, olive skin, and lime-green eyes that always appeared as if they were laying odds. His pretty boy looks and charm had landed him quite the ladies' man rep, having slept with just about every Betty in our sophomore class worthy of the effort. He was the bitter comic to my aloof scholar, the id to my super-ego. We drank our first hard liquor together (apricot brandy) and smoked our first smoke (Pall Malls, unfiltered). Boyhood chums, Tom and Huck, attached at the hip, and we knew all too well what types of dogs and ponies were being showcased in each other's homes. Our separate domestications were a matter of degrees. Alex's parents were wound tight as drums, their uber-evangelical, right-wing prattle and hum making my Italian-Catholic upbringing seem like elective yoga. Going to hell had been a constant pending fate for Alex, and often he'd lament—with no small amount of sarcasm—his heathen preclusions in seeking the pleasures of the flesh, of which, he had little to no limit, or for having the gall to order blasphemous, adultery-promoting Push-Ups instead of plain Jane Astro-Pops from the ice cream man, insisting it'd be a lot easier to accept Jesus Christ as his personal savior if the Son of God embraced his Afro roots and shimmy-shammed the gospels instead of putting the fear of Great White Father into everyone. It was little wonder Alex had blossomed like a weed both in sexual conquest and illicit substance abuse once he'd discovered life was not as simple as a nativity manger scene, nor was it full of mystical commonplaces like global floods occurring via divine directive, immaculate conceptions, or virginal married women. I had similar revelations concerning organized religion but didn't embrace the yoke's release as triumphantly as he did. That was Alex all over: *fuck your five and dime, Jimmy Dean, get outta my way.*

We smoked weed in the hollow grotto.

After a long silence, we moved on.

For a time we walked, and it was good.

"The fungus shrine. It was a message," Alex said.

"Really. What was the message?"

"It said 'Ditch the cast of thousands.'"

"Cast of thousands. Like the old movie headlines for *The Ten Commandments* or *The King of Kings*? *See Moses part the Red Sea! See cast of thousands!*"

"No, not that kind of cast of thousands, you dork. Goddamn, you watch too much television. All *those* voices, man."

"Which voices?"

"The voices that say 'Don't do that.' 'Don't risk it.' 'Get a real job.' 'Wife and two point five kids, a station wagon, the picket fence.' The rule makers, the money takers, Billy Bob and John Doe, Slick Slim and Betty Sue and Kitty Kat, the presidents and the pimps and the corporate execs. *Those* voices, man. All of them. The mainstream, boss. The cast of thousands. It's large, it's loud, and we always have to listen. It follows us everywhere. It watches our lives like a perverted voyeur."

"Where are they now?" I asked, amused.

"They're right there." He gestured back to the empty, sandy plain behind us. A single pelican glided overhead. The beach was desolate, deserted. "They're right fucking there."

I *did* see them. A living mass of memories, my life and its supporting characters: my third grade teacher telling me I had to learn to write cursive with my right hand instead of my left, Jim telling me my Transformer wasn't as good as *his* Transformer, my father admonishing me when I wouldn't hit the rabbit with the wrench, my soccer coach imploring me to pass off the ball when I wanted to take the shot, celebrity personalities advising me on where to buy from, what to ignore, and whom to idolize.

But most of my cast of thousands seemed to have *my* face.

Surprised? Not really.

Alex's hallucinatory epiphany wasn't that contrived, I thought, as I alternated between stupor and lucidity. Perhaps getting reared within a sheltered haven of prospering suburbanites who took for granted their elevated position on the planetary eco-scale wasn't all cookies and milk. Sure, folks starving in Ethiopian deserts or braving landmines hidden in Asian rice paddies would scoff at such an audacious assertion. Only a people who banked on the certainty that the fast-food drive-thru would still be there come sunup could craft boogeyman claptrap like a cast of thousands. My father, utilitarian that he was, would've said my half-cocked analysis had only come about because I could afford it. The rest of the world was too busy putting food on their plates to waste time with idle mind games. Point, set, and match.

Yet the old cliché rang true, regardless of the fortune of being born within a select longitude and latitude. Wherever you is, there you are, fiddle-dee-dee, said Scarlet. On the other hand, I was sure some one-legged child in Cambodia would switch places with me in a heartbeat. Was I pretentious enough to compare the sterilized facade of the West to the horrendous plights of genocidal third world regimes?

I managed to humble myself. Barely.

Nevertheless, a cast of thousands will be heard.

The 'shrooms were high grade. I didn't slip back into normal space until after-school rehearsal the next day. It was aggravation that kick-started reality again, due to my irksome windbag of a dramatic arts teacher.

"That was bad acting, Moon," Mr. Wyke said. "Bold, awful, plain bad acting." He rose from a last-row seat in the auditorium and came down to center stage. The target of his anathema, a trio of teen thespians including Keith, Moon, and myself, stood there sweating in starchy, itchy suits and gowns, miserable under hot rainbows of stage lights. Costume makers stitched and fitted in the first few rows of the theater. Set designers argued backstage about paint colors. Supporting cast members ran lines in corners. With an awkward lack of enthusiasm, people continued to polish up the play before opening night, forty-eight hours away. *Charley's Aunt* was an easy enough three-act comedy, British man-in-drag Pythonesque slapstick humor, yet Wyke was demanding we treat the script like Shakespeare.

"I was doing the best I could," Moon said. She trailed off, looking at me, eyes pleading, for help. I shrugged in sympathy. She wasn't an abysmal actress by any means, and a lovely specimen of womanhood to boot, with droopy, hazelnut eyes; long, straw-colored hair; and hourglass curves. Her name was her sole drawback, usually a deterrent to our apple-pie, boy-scout filters, but Alex was actively appreciating her attributes, star-child retro-sixties moniker and all.

Reggie Wyke, classic community theater director. Shoddy Cal State undergrad who majored in a going-nowhere humanities degree, got the teaching credential as a backup, settled in a backwater town directing horrible renditions of thespian standards during the school year with unmotivated elective students, then community productions during the summer break coordinating the chaos of amateur children and their overbearing parents, bored retirees, and aspiring twenty-something actors stuck in local jobs hoping to break out of Durango Bay's quicksand, off to Hollywood and silver screen glory.

Art for art's sake. Righteous craft, it wasn't.

"How was the fry?" Keith whispered.

"Out of hand. I'm still sorta buzzing."

"Need I remind you that we've been working on this simple little skit for three months now? You were supposed to have had this scene down two weeks ago. We're opening IN TWO DAYS!" Wyke raved, pacing in front of the stage. One of his patented tizzy fits was about to begin, entailing outrage and contempt at our low-level investment in the mostly awful spectacle of high school theater.

Keith had completed our triumvirate in seventh grade, when we'd interrupted his solo smoke-out session behind the bleachers of the elementary school's football field. He'd passed his joint, cracked a joke about the typing teacher's fabulous breasts, and that had been that. He had long, blonde hair atop a short, lean build. He was lantern-jawed, tanned to a sienna-black shade, a consummate beach bum, and he boinked beach bunny teenyboppers as if they were going out of style. Musically he was brilliant, played drums and guitar like they were appendages. Rare was the occasion when he'd be caught in a group gathering without an instrument of some kind at the ready. It's always important to have a minstrel in a crew. He chain-smoked Marlboro Lights between bouts of sucking regular air.

Keith was a quintessential SoCal surfcat, not as dull as Spicoli from *Fast Times*, not as hardcore as Bohdi in *Point Break*, but somewhere in between. Alex and I lambasted his lackadaisical attitude, as he cared not one iota about our respective angst and spared no feelings

in belittling our darker ruminations. He scoffed at the esoteric, anthro-
pomorphized notions of red-cloaked clouds and casts of thousands. It
was one of the reasons why we loved him. Keith was happy just being.
He didn't need to think about every goddamned thing in the universe.
He could breathe. He lived in the moment. I envied him for a great
many things—the girls, the musician prowess—but his innate ability
to accept things as they were was a most powerful thing, a handy trait
at our age, and I tried to emulate it time and again without much success. He tried on a monthly basis to get me back into surfing; I'd quit
after a rookie mistake, riding my board in too far, coming down on
a rock and splintering my board, a long shard running through my
leg, the exquisite searing pain effectively ending my surf hobby. That
didn't stop Keith from always begging me to get back on the horse, or
for Alex to even hop on in the first place (no wavebreaker was Alex, he
had enough adrenalin rushes to consider, thanks very much). Keith
constantly encouraged us to attend his pilgrimages with fellow surf
brethren to nearby Rincon or Jalama, or down south to Huntington or
Seal Beach, or long weekends up north at Maverick's, the latter amus-
ing as not once had I ever known the semi-bonzo saltwater swami to
actually attempt the big wave death gambit north of Santa Cruz upon
arrival. He'd end up 'shrooming at the Mystery Spot or cruising the
boardwalk for babes, lamenting the notorious break's lack of laidback
vibe, and he'd return back down PCH through Big Sur and smoke the
rest of his road trip weed in the redwoods.

At our bequest, he had diverted his musical interests long enough
to try out for the play, landed a leading role, and had already divided
and conquered a bevy of drama babes. Alex and I had long been a
part of our local hick theater troupe, having landed there in earlier
years thanks to our inept bungling in the athletic arenas, and kept it
as a summer side hobby when we came of post-shifted age. These days
we were mostly stoned out of our gourds at rehearsals, laughing at
our fellow hokey thespians, dismissing the ironic frailty of our glass
house. Alex had been banished from this particular production due to
creative differences with the director, a polite way of terming simple,
small town pecking orders. He told Wyke to fuck himself when he
didn't get cast for any of the leads.

"I'll be damned if I'm going to sit here and listen to ad-libbing. If you can't remember the line, then you call for line. That's why it's called dress rehearsal," Wyke continued. I'd already tuned out of his speech, and Keith looked ready to fall asleep even with the pouring stage sweat running down his neck.

What do you expect? Sir Laurence Olivier? This is Durango Bay's podunk high school theater, not Carnegie Hall.

He winded down as he trudged up the aisle back to his seat, muttering, "God knows what Principal Weiss will think of such an abomination of a play. He'll want the five hundred back for the set costs. I'll have to teach remedial again next quarter."

For years I'd cherished the child movie star dream. I convinced my parents to pony up for a portfolio of black-and-whites submitted to a central coast talent agency. I'd been on the stardom track. Mom had been supportive, Dad less so. They would have preferred a doctor-lawyer-priest ambition for their eldest.

But I'd given up pursuing the actor's path. I was only doing it now for a lark and because I wasn't half bad at it, and it was something to do in the wasteland of Durango Bay doings. Prestige acting would require working one's way to the very top of the field, where one could pick his projects, a privilege delegated to a very small margin of the SAG card-holding populace. I really didn't want to scrounge around the LA basin for years begging for dog food commercials. Yeah, there were the rags-to-riches fairy-tales of those scant few who'd found fame and notoriety, and also there were tens of thousands of career waiters and waitresses throughout Los Angeles who hadn't come to California for the oranges.

Moon began running her lines once more. A hasty correction came from the depths of the back row. "Louder!"

"Asshole," Keith mumbled. A pregnant pause followed. The costumer designers looked up, eyes wide, preparing for another unleashing of hot air.

"That silence you hear, Keith, is the same one the audience will be giving you on Friday night!" Wyke roared. He stomped out the back door, off to smoke a cigarette.

Keith grinned. "We're never going to make it."

"Who cares," I replied.

"You passed over the 'don't give a shit' attitude when you persuaded me to try out."

"All for one and one for all."

"D'Artagnan, you traitorous bastard."

"Ah, relax. Knocking boots with Nancy Rothchild in the green room last week couldn't have been torture."

"Granted."

"Are we starting from the top, or what?" Moon demanded. She'd been testy ever since Wyke had refused to allow Alex entry in the building while she'd been entrenched in rehearsals with her squeeze's goon squad.

"You tell us, sweetheart. Alex never kisses and tells," Keith said.

"God, you're so gross," Moon replied, and harrumphed her way offstage.

"Time for a doob," Keith said.

"Right behind you."

4

I am not sure how it is possible I am invisible to the two figures before me. They are sunning themselves, carefree, at the edge of a cabana on some paradise's golden sands. What's odder than my apparent transparency is that one of them is me, a little older, a bit heavier. I am able to read some of his thoughts, feel some of his feelings. It's a wonderful sensation.

The other person is difficult to see. A woman, but her features, no matter how I move around her, stay hidden in shadow. No, it's not shadow. Stranger still than the invisibility or the telepathy, segments of a huge bird's wing encircle her from all angles. Black, shiny feathers make gentle rustling noises, letting only the tiniest of appearances peek through—a blood-red lip here, a sculpted eyebrow there. Somehow I understand the mystery is a purposeful thing, and I endure the anomaly as it becomes evident that it is not going to subside.

A local vendor approaches them. Then I—he—speaks: "Ah...no, senor, we don' wan anytheeng," he says in a lame Scarface Cuban accent, as if that will help the fellow understand. What a moron this "me" is. The vendor scowls, surely more for the inane, politically incorrect lingo than the failed sale. He shrugs and moves on.

"I think you have a fine grasp of the language, gringo," the woman says. Her voice is mellifluous, soft rain and vanilla cream.

"Why, thank you, senora," he replies, "and now, for my encore, I will attempt to ascertain the actual price on these hats coming our way."

Another vendor approaches, hucstering wares with all the enthusiasm that continual rejection can muster. He is selling woven straw hats with colorful bands and painted feathers.

"I don't think I'd wear one of those," the woman says, "because I'm not really into making a fashion idiot of myself."

"Don't sell yourself short, honey. Those hats are just crying out for an elegant fit, and I think London's calling, if you know what I mean."

"Babe…if you buy one of those monstrosities…"

But the other me is already up and gone, the Latin vendor rushing up from the breakwater to greet him. The salesman puts out several examples of his merchandise on the sand.

"You like? For the lady? How 'bout two?"

Gullibility reeks off this stupid turista. The hats aren't that bad. Maybe five bucks apiece, no more.

"How much?"

A sly grin creeps across the vendor's sun-blemished face. Shiny white choppers, several trimmed in gold, glint in the sun. "For you, senor, only twenty-five…buy two, only forty."

I sigh. So does the other me.

"Ten dollars for one." He is smug. I know how long that will last. Three minutes and twenty-five dollars later, it's over.

The woman addresses him with utmost amusement. "Well, how'd it go? And if you think that thing is going to even touch the top of my head, think again."

He sits down in a beach chair and takes a swig of warm Corona. "C'mon, at least try it on." He digs out a soggy lime wedge in the bottleneck and bites into it.

"How much? I have to know, babe. What'd you pay? Thirty? Forty? Do we have to go get more traveler's checks?" She laughs. Like wind chimes tinkling.

"Just put it on."

"Well…if I must. Perhaps I owe you for the moonlight gymnastics last night."

"That's the spirit," he says.

She flops the straw hat on her head. "Well?"

He snickers. "You look like an albino Pollyanna."

"Your wasted tax dollars at work, not mine. But I thank you for the thought, Lamb Chops." She smacks a long, warm, wet kiss on his lips. "That's for upholding the white knight banner you carry on the inside."

Cool enough, *he thinks, and I agree.*

The sun drops into a waiting silver sea. Swaths of the woman's hair have partly emerged from behind the shuffling wings. She has a beautiful calico mane. In the setting twilight, it turns into a blazing mist of gold and copper.

I probe further into this guy's thoughts. Sensations come to me: the toots and squawks of a mariachi band at a dinner table loaded with shrimp and mango, the sour-sweet tang of margaritas, the stubborn ambience of local taxi drivers, the glitter of high-rise glow dancing on a tropical bay, but he's mostly thinking of her. He is completely in love with this woman, but he's also frightened of something, and I cannot determine what that fear entails. I want to know. I try harder to pry. No dice. He's got it buried but good.

Yet I am envious.

Whoever he was—or whenever I was—I want to be him, or there. I wake up, the vivid dream leaving behind a considerable weight of intrigue.

5

Tweakers lived there, that was clear. Black-light Zeppelin and Hendrix posters, an antiquated, long-dry aquarium, old, musty couches confiscated from dormitory dumpsters, coffee tables cluttered with empty wine cooler bottles, overflowing ashtrays, dirty laundry stench. Walls covered with lusty rock-and-roll carnival mirrors and strip-mall, deco-shop, neon pop art, Motley Crue's *Shout At The Devil* shrieking from a monster stereo system. Tweaker 101.

We went inside, cautious, as if we were navigating a trail laden with bear traps. Derrick, our hook, said not a word as he went to his bedroom to get his stash and a scale. He didn't want to screw around and small talk with the kiddie parade. The night before, Alex and I had consumed an entire case of Corona I'd stolen from my place of employment. A serious hangover had refused to go away, which was why I'd agreed to Alex's request to score some coke. I was hopeful a line or two—or three or four—might aid my aches and pains.

Two young men, disheveled and sweaty, sat at a yellow kitchen table nearby. One of them used a razor blade to cut up a pile of cocaine.

"What's up?" Keith asked, but they paid him no heed.

The guy who was cutting blurted out, "How long d'ya think you can go through a coupla eights a day and keep snorting? Stupid. For rookies, dude. I just cook the shit now. I mean, what's the use, if you're going for the buzz, why do it half-ass, you know?" The free-basing Chatty Kathy was freaking Keith out a little bit. This would be Keith's first time doing blow. I was an old hand at skiing the slopes. I'd snorted coke two times before. Fucking A. The rambling dude applied the razor blade across a Jack Daniel's carnie mirror with the finesse of a Japanese chef. He scooped up half of the pile with a tiny spoon and held a lighter underneath it. The coke began melting, bubbling, fateful. He was gaunt, sweating bullets, drumming his legs under the table in that nervous way of a coke fiend. He was on, way on, so on that he'd be on until his cash ran out. He'd become a husk, empty and dry and brittle. Light of the soul doesn't take well to amphetamines.

"Probably debating whether to sell us the baking soda or the rat poison," Alex whispered as we heard Derrick rummaging around in his bedroom. The cutter's partner, a lanky Latino, dipped a cigarette into the pile of cut coke, lit the cocoa puff, and commenced a spectacular series of coughing and hacking.

Derrick returned. "So how much is it you guys want?"

"Um. A gram?" I said.

The kitchen guys chortled. Derrick looked at me like I was an exotic toad. "*A gram*? Gimme a break. You'll be back here in ten minutes. I got a better idea. You give me your money for a *gram*, and I'll spot you an eight ball 'til the next time I see you. A good deal because I trust the guy who sent you here."

I looked at Keith and Alex, who lowered their eyes in confusion, bowing out of the decision. I was the middleman, inexperienced as I was.

"Yeah, sure," I said.

Derrick promptly pulled a sack from his pocket. He had already weighed it out for us. *That was nice of him.* I took it and handed him a fifty. "I'll settle up next time."

"I know you will. Gotta go now."

"Hey, you mind if we use the coffee table?"

"Go for it," Derrick said. Then he was gone. The Latino dude resumed smoking his cocoa puff. The freebaser leaned back in his chair, zoned out, riding his rush. Keith and Alex flopped on a couch spotted with cigarette burns. I sat in an armchair opposite them and dumped a quarter gram out of the bindle onto a mirror with a Harley Davidson logo etched on its surface. I took my driver's license out of my wallet and started cutting up the coke with the ID's edge. The powder was fine, and it separated easy. I edged the pile into three long lines as Alex rolled up a five-dollar bill for a tooter. I wondered if Keith's mind was frenzied, as mine had been the first time I did coke. *What's it cut with? Sugar? Aspirin? Talcum powder? DDT? How many hands has this passed through to get to my nose? Will I do it right?*

"You only live once, right?" Keith said, nervous. Ah, that enduring tenet of teenage invulnerability, always when we tried something new, usually something hazardous. Drugs. High speeds. Unprotected sex. Bungee jumping. What-have-you. Uttering that one little icebreaking statement made all potential dangers of the risk null and void. Sure.

I took the rolled bill from Alex and bent down over the coke. My sweaty face, the Harley Davidson logo superimposed over my reflection, was an unpleasant visage, the green tooter shoved halfway up my nose, eyes wide with dread anticipation. Some of the line blew apart. I was blowing out instead of snorting up.

"No, you idiot, you gotta inhale, not exhale!" Alex said.

"I know, I know." I tooted the rest of the line. Powder fluttered out of my nose. I wasn't seasoned enough to know for sure, but maybe it *had* been cut with something less than desirable. My nasal passages felt soaked with lighter fluid.

Alex leaned over and hoover'ed his line with a graceful swoop and tuck. He took another deep snort to absorb the full hit. His eyes bulged and took on a deep, green-black dilation.

Keith took the tooter from Alex and leaned down. He snorted the whole line without pause. After a minute he said, "Right. Let's do more."

"And Bingo was his name-o," Alex said.

Two hours later we were strung out. They wanted to go walk a mile or ten, expend mass ratio energy, shoulder-tap someone to buy us some booze, kick on a beach somewhere. Not me. I was not looking forward to a shift at work later. We left Derrick's apartment; the tweaker duo was zoned on WWF bouts. It was hot outside. Keith and Alex ran down the stairs. They were wired. I'd smoked too many cocoa puffs. I hacked up a gooey blob of phlegm and spat it over the stair railing. It fell in slow motion, hitting a child's pink bicycle with a wet splotch. *That was pretty*. I considered asking my guardian angels for a boon, if they would be so kind as to wipe my mind of the speedy vomit coating each passing thought. A reckless fancy, as if The Forces That Be had time to guide ne'er-do-well, middle-class kids getting high for the sole purpose of getting high. As if they had nothing better to do. *Mass starvation? Ethnic cleansing? Holocaust? Not today. We have to direct hosts of seraphim to protect and inspire the youth of American drug culture.*

We cruised in my VW cranking tunes, scoping the limited scene available (zero happenings, a few callous babes at the pizza parlor, dippy nerds at the arcade). A rough comedown ensued. Keith was sick from the cocoa puffs and Alex was bug-eyed and comatose when I dropped them off and proceeded to my evening shift, whereupon my manager cornered me. "Lot duty," he said, "is a luxury among box boys at this market. Instead of bagging or stocking, tonight you see to it that no concertgoers park in our lot. Otherwise we lose customers. Tell them if they park here, they will be towed. Think you can handle that?" He had a greasy white mustache with cracker crumbs stuck in it, which almost made me dry retch. I told him I could handle lot duty. He stomped off, dragging his candy ass behind him. Career grocers. I knew them well. Everyone's gotta eat.

I'd forgotten about the show. Everybody had been talking about it all week at school. Alice Cooper in Durango Bay. Who'da thunk it. Our local chamber of commerce had decided get with the times. By and large our small auditorium was reserved for country music gigs and square dances. Good for Durango Bay, obviously not great for Alice's continued mass appeal if he'd been reduced to thousand-seat vet halls. Yet the local teen populace was pumped for the sake of variety, though I doubted one in a hundred could name a single song by the B-list rocker other than *School's Out* (me and mine weren't huge Coop fans, or we might have gotten tickets).

Outside the market, a cold draft pushed through my shirt. It was a fair, brisk evening, the moon full and blue. I shivered. I felt like cooked roadkill. I did not want to be at work. People should never be at work when a thousand tiny snakes are crawling over their bodies and a thousand tiny hammers are driving tiny nails into their tiny brains. I trawled the lot and listened to Alice's roadies tune the instruments at sound check in the hall next door. I was a meter maid for Alice Cooper, strung out and coming down hard, Yosemite Sam's gruff bluster echoing inside my head: *rassafrassafrickaseein'tarnation!*

A blue Toyota Corolla careened into the lot, its insides brimming with intoxicated concert attendees. I mustered my best authoritative face. Two frat boys in the back seat, likely from the university in nearby Santa Crisca, began to chant out the back windows. "Alice Cooper rocks!" they yelled in unison to a shocked elderly couple carrying out their groceries.

"Um, you can't park here," I said, shrugged, and rolled my eyes, trying to give an appearance of sympathy. "Sorry, dudes. You'll get towed."

The driver leaned out his window and beckoned. "Listen, pal, we've been driving around this shitty little 'burg forever. Couldn't we work something out?"

I smiled, the added incentives of "lot duty" now coming to light. "Like what?"

He pulled out a joint. "Only the best Humboldt this year, and this fat bomber is all yours for that spot right over there."

Maybe the jay will help me sleep. "Sure."

He dropped the joint in my hand and swung into the parking space. Twenty minutes later I'd accumulated two small bindles of coke, an eighth-ounce baggie of gray mushrooms, half a dozen joints, a sheet of cheap Grateful Dead acid—the kind with top hats on the dancing bears—and a handful of black beauties.

A sputtering VW camper pulled up. Three gals were inside, collegiates, head to toe in leather and studs, death babes with black makeup, black clothes, black everything, wasted. The driver was a luscious brunette, clad in a funeral shroud and loops of dark red rosaries, batting a pair of battleship-sinking blue eyes. Her two friends, blondes with red eye shadow and spiked heels, tittered in the back seat of the van. The brunette leaned out her window, whiskey-slick. "Like, uh…can we park here?"

"I'm not supposed to let any concert people park in the market lot, miss."

The brunette smiled. "Maybe we can work a deal."

I was making a killing. "Let's hear it."

"How about a hand job?"

Here's something new. "Really." I stopped cold. After a fumbling pause, broken by the sudden laughter of the goth gals, I said, "Well, I can do that myself, you know." *OK! The cool answer! Good one!*

"Take it or leave it." She reached under her seat and—*no fucking way*—brought out a jar of Vaseline.

"You always carry around a handy-dandy jar of that?"

"No, junior. It comes in *handy-dandy* for the roadies who won't let us backstage on our good looks alone. You can be a warm-up."

The blondes brayed and cawed.

Gosh, this is just little old DeeBee, not the LA Coliseum, girls.

I looked inside the VW at the girls in the back seat. "All of you have jars of lube?"

The one on the left said, "I wanna meet the guy who bites chickens' heads off."

"I think that's Ozzy Ozbourne. And it's bats. Or doves. But Alice does gross stuff too," I said, and decided to push the envelope. "A blowjob's out of the question?"

The brunette groaned. "As in, totally."

The girl who thought they were going to see Ozzy taunted me. "What's the matter? You got something against orgasms?"

"Fine. Let's do it. Pull over to that stall by the tree." They parked. I climbed in the back of the van. The two blondes crowded up front, and the brunette settled on the back seat next to me. She dipped her hand in the Vaseline jar, coating her fingers with the yellowy grease.

"OK, let's get a move-on."

I looked at her friends, who were gulping down last minute shots of whiskey. "In front of them?"

She yawned, bored. "They couldn't care less."

I unbuttoned my pants, dropped my boxers around my ankles, and off she went. The blondes watched, amused, drunk, and jaded. I was a pawn. After a while, her grip tightened and gained in speed, and her goal became manifest. The girls up front cackled, leathers creaking. I pulled up my pants, urgent in my need to vacate the vehicle, thinking the day couldn't possibly get filthier. The brunette, unfazed, wiped her hands with a napkin. "Damn, I got some on my new skirt," she said, as if it were a drop of ketchup or salsa, and not at all like, say, my life-giving seed. They shuffled and I broke for open air. The lot was jammed full of Alice Cooper fans clamoring for empty spaces. *Crap.*

"Thanks for the spot," the brunette said, and they vanished into the assembling throngs.

The spot in the lot? Or the spot on your skirt?

My pockets full of drugs, I resumed patrol. So much for my assiduous guard of the market's precious parking spaces. Not to mention my dignity.

6

The biker lifted the poor guy off the ground, his balled fists holding the pimply-faced fellow by the lapels of a pressed navy-blue jacket. The kid was far out of his league, his paltry armory consisting of a walkie-talkie and a small tube of mace. He was shitting bricks. There was no way the county was paying the fair's personnel enough to deal with stuff like this.

"Ten bucks says he throws him in the trash can," Alex said, striking the head of a wooden match on the top button of his 501s, then lighting a Marlboro Red.

The biker screamed in the kid's face, spewing a number of colorful obscenities. Spittle flew from deep inside the gnarled, tattooed giant's beard, dousing the young man in a spray of beer-flavored saliva.

"I wonder what he told that guy," I said.

"Coulda been anything. Chopper-boy's skunky drunk," Alex said.

"Maybe the kid takes his job too seriously," I said.

"I bet he reminded the big guy he couldn't drink outside the beer tent," Keith said.

The biker roared something about God-given rights of Americans and then one-armed the blubbering guard over a shoulder into the trash, just as Alex had predicted. The biker's friends cheered him, and he bowed with drunken grace. The kid spilled himself out of the refuse, grabbed his walkie-talkie, and began babbling panicky blurbs into it. The bikers laughed and stumbled toward the fair exit.

"Told ya," Alex said. "Probably does that every time he has a sixer and an audience. Thumping on security guards is a drinking outlet only when you're seven feet tall."

Fairgoers swarmed around us, pushing baby strollers, buying ride tickets, eating corndogs. Our county fair was like anywhere else in rural America, a testament to regional pride, the chance for local gardeners and ranchers and craft makers to compete in blue-ribbon competitions, all in tandem with the annual arrival of the traveling carnival, that weird, cheapo, rusted conglomeration of amusements, a time-honored opportunity to flirt and grope unseen in the dark recesses of the House of Mirrors.

We wove through the campy booths of the midway alley, having prepared for boys' night out by ingesting generous helpings of moonshine en route. I'd downed a pint of Southern Comfort, Keith had finished a flask filled with peppermint schnapps, and Alex had polished off two pints of Johnny Walker, one red label and one black label. He was *El Blotto*. He struck a teetering path through the crowds. A long, fiery cherry on his cigarette glowed in the vaudeville haze of the games. Alex always sucked on his smoke as if it were the last one he'd ever have.

We waded through swamps of mud and scattered straw, wandering the exhibitioners' mazes of trucks, RVs, Jacuzzis, and boats, ignoring the wheedling propositions of wiry carnies selling rigged contests of chance. I took in the musty odors of barn and pen, the rattle, hum, and crackle of carnival machinery and accompanying screams.

"All this commotion is making me sick looking at it," Keith said, gazing green at a Ferris wheel overhead, the bumper cars, the Skydiver, the Himalaya, the Zipper.

"Look at that," Alex said, pointing out a family of four laden down with pinwheels, pennants, and cotton candy. "Fucking Rockwells."

"Lighten up, Jeeves. It's only the fair, OK?" Keith said. He could stand a dark romantic bent for only so long. Alex and I could go on for hours if left unhindered.

"Besides, you're being too nice," I added. "The guy probably ties her up at night or fucks her sister or whacks off to granny beaver shots or something. Or the kids already have probation officers. Nobody's a Rockwell."

"No?" He posed in disbelief, and in that moment his half-lidded eyes, emerald smoldering coals, belied criminal mastermind genius. Besotted, I wondered if Alex was like Doyle's Moriarty, ever scheming and plotting, complicit in the corruption of many a young wench, and then I worried I'd have a sudden psychotic break when my friend turned into a three-dimensional construct of Boris Badenov from *Rocky and Bullwinkle*, sporting a dark handlebar mustachio, and as soon as he twirled its ends with a thumb and forefinger, emanating a sinister cackle to punctuate a dastardly scheme, I would plunge over the nearest psychic cliff. Shaking off that Southern dis-Comfort, I figured his ne'er-do-well abandon was more like a hair metal version of Kerouac's Moriarty (well-read was I, sure, a geek captain of bookworm industry). He was easier to contemplate that way, an Epicurean head-banging hedonist worshipping the likes of Bruce Dickinson and Rob Halford instead of Charlie Parker and Dizzy Gillespie, London hard rock blitz in place of smooth 'Frisco jazz. And not unlike the beat poets in Jack's magnum opus, Alex was on a similar quest searching for It…whatever It was…wherever It might be.

"Let's check out the animals," I said.

We headed to the livestock barns. The 4-H kids were trimming and shearing their lambs. Cattle shuffled and shat, fowl clucked, pigs grunted. I was into it. I used to be in 4-H too. Raised a lamb of my own. It was a bittersweet memory. The lamb's name was Dusty. She followed me without leashes or halters. The damned thing adored me. Domestic critters and me, we always got along. Growing up on the ranch, with an All-Father of goods, trade, and outdoorsman aptitude, I'd been an apprentice to a wide manner of animal husbandry, including bovine, equestrian, and general barn and shepherd proficiency. The penultimate conclusion of the 4-H animal deal is entering your stock in competitions. Dusty was in perfect shape by the time I took her to that same county fair several years before. I won Best of Show. We went to auction, and I guess I'd assumed some jerkweed would buy her for his private petting zoo. She sold for nineteen dollars a pound, a good price for a young loin destined for spitting, roasting, and mint jelly. I was supposed to be proud. I had achieved my goal of raising a lamb for show and received a nice profit to boot. When I watched her getting herded into the truck that would take her to the slaughterhouse, my bowels turned to lead, and an agonizing guilt came over me. I heard her bleating, scared, maybe even calling out for me, her pal, her buddy, the guy who had cared for her and fed her and walked her and enjoyed merriment with her, much as one would with a dog. I let her go. That was the deal. That was the program. Had to get with the program. So I'd been instructed. So I'd followed the program. Blind, lemming-like, duteous, just like the rest of the...sheep. Irony. You betcha. Bittersweet.

"I'm hungry," Keith said.

"We should bail soon. We need to get up early for the long haul tomorrow. And I'm gonna be hung like a bitch if I don't get some sleep," Alex said.

"You're already hung like a bitch," I muttered.

"Hardly har har," Alex replied.

I rubbed a black lamb's head. It blinked and chewed cud, unaware of its pending fate. We hit the food courts, gobbled churros and fried Twinkies, then piled into the VW. I drove the back roads home at the posted speed limits (the drunken detour). Vineyards and grazing pastures passed by, one second lit ablaze in my headlights, the next fallen into craggy shadow.

"Think I'm gonna..." Alex gurgled from the back seat, and he didn't need to finish for me to know what was coming. I braked hard and pulled over. He lurched out of the car and began heaving spurts and streams of Johnny Walker-Twinkie punch. Keith and I smoked cigarettes in the squareback while we waited. Time passed as the dreadful, wet gagging devolved into dry heaves. I scoped the horizons for constabulary. There was little need; it was late, and we were deep in the back forty of Durango Bay. I leaned out my window, took in a few cold breaths of night. I looked up at distant dying red suns and colliding sapphire galaxies. It sobered me some. Not much. But some.

"He's on the edge, you know. By my count there's near a dozen different substances in his bloodstream this week alone, and that's not even including the booze or the weed," I said.

"You need to talk with him," Keith replied.

"Why me?"

"That's why we love you. You say the things other people only think."

"That only means I'm crude and socially inept."

"Yeah, that you are, for sure. Even so, it's gotta be you."

"Maybe we're splitting hairs. Are any of us poster boys for rehab?"

Alex crawled in the passenger side, sullen, disoriented, wiping his chin. He groaned and rubbed his stomach and passed out. I fired up the VW and drove on. Not two miles later, Keith dozed as well. Four more miles after that, I reached my home's driveway and keyed off the ignition. My buddies snored as I cried for Dusty, wiping away tears with a sleeve still stinking of fresh lamb's wool.

Fucking Southern Comfort. They'll get ya, those sweet liqueurs, every goddamned time.

7

I estimated long odds on our timely arrival back home. The old gal was grumbling but steady. The squareback never left us anywhere stranded, despite plenty of close calls while we figured out which wire to cross or which cylinder to kick.

The return from the barren Nevada 'scape east of Laughlin was as tedious as I'd feared. The desert rock festival had been worth it, but it was a near thing. We'd rocked out to a full day's worth of indie bands followed by headliners Santana, the Steve Miller Band, and Bob Dylan. It was a good show, tiresome, hot as hell. Were it not for the fire hoses being turned on the crowd by the management, some of the sunstroke cases might have turned terminal. We were crispy-fried. My head throbbed. No sleep for forty-eight hours, lots of dope and beer and smoke and sapping, dreary heat.

Keith smoked a Marlboro, eyes closed, warm winds scattering his long, red-brown bangs. In the back seat Alex cranked Y&T on a Walkman full blast. Alex did not practice auditory TLC after loud rock shows. I was a big fan of post-gig Golden Silence. His bottom lip puffed out with a big dip of Copenhagen chew. He spat a gooey mouthful into an empty can of Coors.

"I need coffee. I know we agreed we weren't going to stop, but I'm burnt." I said.

"I'll drive if you want," Keith offered, but he was super baked. Not that I wasn't.

"No. I'll be all right. I just need a cuppa coffee."

I took the next off-ramp. A lonely pit stop beckoned. As I parked, I remembered the crowd energy, so many individual souls in proximity, bonding on the same medium, dancing, singing, raving. When the masses grew louder than the vast array of amps and speakers onstage, it became an intense experience, like when I saw the Stones, where under cloudy skies in a sprawling, fat crowd of one hundred thousand rained-on rockers, all the lighters, umbrellas, and tears during *Angie* had been a sight to behold.

Alex and Keith went inside to use the restroom. I got out and stretched, joints popping, and appraised the ramshackle truck stop. Flashes of pink peeked through Venetian blinds covering the diner's windows. A blinking neon sign over the door established the place as "Jack's." An adjacent gas station was caked black with diesel smoke and oil slick, and a mini gift shop within offered gaudy turquoise Indian jewelry in display racks. When I opened the diner door, tiny red dust devils swirled at my feet and a blast of grease-spoon fumes smacked me in the face. Pink booths lined concrete walls. Most tables sat unattended, littered with cloudy salt-and-pepper shakers, sticky syrup jars, and clotted ketchup bottles. Chrome stools slouched at the counter. I picked a booth and collapsed. Alex and Keith took the other side of the booth. We surveyed the clientele of the desert diner's three a.m. rush. An old man sat at the counter, mumbling, smoking Kents, and slurping coffee. A strawberry-blonde woman sat in a booth alone, humming and reading a Nevada travel guide, nibbling at a pastry. Powdered sugar smeared her upper lip. A dark man of Native American descent fingered a pendant around his neck. A fat truck driver devoured a plate of fried chicken. Behind piles of iron skillets and crusty cookware, the graveyard chef flipped pancakes. He was bald and grizzled and was wearing soiled aprons. I wondered if he was Jack.

A waitress ambled over. Her blotchy red-checkered uniform hung loose on her, and she wore thick blue eyeliner under a beehive hairdo, two-inch fake nails glittering with candy-apple-red polish. She looked twenty, forty, and sixty all at the same time. She slapped down greasy laminated menus.

"That's OK, we know what we want. We'll have coffee all around and slices of lemon pie, if you got 'em," Keith said.

"We got 'em," she said, and returned to the counter and grabbed a pot of coffee.

Then the diner changed. A curtain drew, as in Rubio's delicatessen, and the displacement was again unsettling. Alex and Keith faded away. I saw the haven as it was…elsewhere, or when, or in what light or from what perspective (I knew not which). Not just a temporary respite for wandering flotsam and jetsam of the desert, a rural oasis, sanctuary for interstate roadway travelers. The desert outside cooked dreams and moods into a festering brine, and this air-conditioned shack was a common ground collecting ragtag messiahs and peasants, a measly coffeehouse turned celestial pantheon. And light everywhere, beautiful, translucent, pearly-blue light! True light. Other realities, they were right there next to us. Other times, other levels of existence, otherness, and I was a part of it. We all were. *We all are.* The waitress stood before me as the questing angel she really was, in that *other,* clad in silver skin and brandishing a brilliant shining spear (no longer a mere coffee pot). Iron fury poured forth from her. The rest—the chef, the old man, the dark man, the strawberry blonde—young, vibrant, golden and so very bright. Was I was seeing their souls? I dared not gaze at Alex or Keith; if I saw their true natures, I might go mad. No man should know his best friends that well. Not in this world. It was exhausting. It took everything I had not to bolt from the diner.

My head ached with sharp pain, and then the diner shifted back. I blinked and brought my eyes to bear across the table. Keith stirred his coffee. Alex scraped off his pie's meringue layer with a knife. The waitress popped gum. I was disoriented and must have looked it too, as Alex regarded me suspiciously. I sucked in air, pretending my coffee had been too hot.

I was melancholy when we walked out later, after several cups of java, and not because of the driving hours ahead. Another glimpse of hyper-reality, this time more vivid; this vision had *hurt,* like the feeling solitary hermits might experience after decades in a self-imposed, cave-dwelling exile, if they suddenly found themselves transported to the middle of a Russian bathhouse seething with dozens of Mafiya coupling with their concubines. Or maybe I was just a crackpot destined to crack open a Pandora's box of psychosis. I pondered the likelihood of the latter all the way back to DeeBee.

The next day we were out of weed, so Keith and I cruised over to our illustrious dealer Jethro, always sitting in front of his big-screen projection TV and offering color commentary on the programs to a crimson Macaw parrot named Perry. A pack of yapping, ill-kempt poodles announced our arrival. Keith and I took in greedy gulps of air before entering, knowing we'd reemerge with the heebie-jeebies from braving the wonders inside Jethro's drug emporium.

"You wanna know what life is, man? I'll tell you what life is," Jethro drawled as he weighed out a quarter-ounce, an old scale balanced in his lap. Perry bobbed his head up and down from atop his perch on a gruesome and pungent guano-catching towel covering Jethro's shoulder. Jethro had been drinking jugs of cheap Gallo wine. Empty, bulbous bottles littered the room like little glass pigs. The TV was tuned to a *Cheers* rerun.

"OK, Jethro," Keith said, indulging the roly-poly drug dealer, "Tell us—but only if you also share where you got your guru's license."

"That s'posed to be some kinda joke, boy? Some dumb-fuck, rich brat like you has to remind me why I can't get a real job after I watched guys' fucking guts spray all over me..."

"Yeah, yeah, Jethro, after guys' guts sprayed all over you when that tank dropped in your trench at the divide, meridian, thirty-eighth parallel, the line between north and south, whatever. You've told us this before, ya know," Keith said as he handed Jethro a couple of twenties and took the bag from the scale. Little bits of bud slipped off the scale plate and landed in the soiled carpet. Perry cocked his head and eyed the extraneous morsels.

Jethro looked confused. Suddenly he grabbed Keith's wrist. I thought about all those cliched psycho war veteran movies and wondered if I had the stones to hurl myself through the living room's window should he whip out an AK-47 from under his easy chair. "If you ever wanna scrag here again, you gotta listen to my stories. House etiquette," he said.

"OK, I want to hear what life really is," Keith replied, unfazed by Jethro's aggression, ever the mellow surfcat. *You never know who could be God, incognito, crawling in the muck among us unwashed masses. Perhaps Jethro is Jehovah or Joshua in disguise. Maybe he'll divulge an answer or two.*

"Life is all this," Jethro said, releasing Keith's arm. He shut his eyes and spoke all in one breath: "Lemon rinds and tiger jade, and orange spice tea, a bride's veil, and Spanish missions, lost civilizations and religious wars, cold iced lemonade on hot southern days, New York bagels, tears and laughter and restless sleep, skinned chickens hanging in Chinese pharmacies, terrorism and Viking ships, oppression and lies and greed and oil and bars, igloos and teepees, redwood trees and horses and dog biscuits and the sweet smell of a woman satisfied, grapes and bread...and drunk drivers, and little boys riding bikes..."

He trailed off, choking and sobbing.

"Hey, man, don't stress. It's all OK," Keith said, trying to cheer him up.

Cheers *isn't cheering him up*, I thought.

Jethro fell silent, watching Carla belittle Cliff. Keith and I slipped out the front door. We hopped in Keith's Camaro and drove.

"Do you know if he was the drunk guy or the kid's father?" Keith asked.

"Does it matter?"

"Point. Maybe we should get a new hook."

"Good idea. That parrot stinks like hell anyway."

We picked up Alex and reached our ultimate destination, a party at a ranch in DeeBee's boondocks, an elaborate kegger thrown by Durango High's water polo crew. In the car we smoked a good portion of our begotten baggie and poured mucho Cuervo down our gullets. We went inside, and they split off to schmooze while I wandered in a tequila-fueled daze. I bumped into Mandy, a cute, perky blonde who was rumored to have lips of extraordinary ability. A while later, perhaps because of my pity play in relaying my regrets regarding Dusty the lost lamb, I found out Mandy's reputation was well deserved as we rolled around on some absent child's pristine, unsoiled linens. She assured me there would be no intercourse—she claimed she was saving herself (as if)—but tended to my own needs with expert aplomb. However, the consequences of trysting with Mandy revealed themselves in the morning when my privates took on a noticeable indigo shade. *Bruised penis? Are you kidding?* Nobody ever told me oral sex could be so vigorous. I was in serious pain. Alex and Keith picked me up for lunch, and I whined about my lingering ache. They didn't have much commiseration for me.

We headed to the school theater afterward. I had no desire to audition for any roles in that summer's community theater production, but my friends, citing the lack of other preoccupations, had talked me into joining them as stagehand lackeys for Mr. Wyke's attempt at a hack production of *Oklahoma!* Keith disappeared into the gathering throng of auditioning amateurs. Alex and I took a couple seats in the last row of the theater, assessing the crowd. A usual turnout: scores of Dungeons-and-Dragons nerds looking for excuses to dress up, old geezers wanting a late-life hobby, assorted suburban moms preening their child stars.

"Look at 'em all. They're so serious. It's a halfwit 'Bay play. Wyke will be hawking tickets at the supermarkets and liquor stores," Alex said, rolling his eyes. "Wait a sec…who is that with Keith?"

I looked down to the stage, where Keith seemed to be demonstrating an aerobic maneuver to a gaggle of females in dancing gear. I hoped he wasn't actually doing so.

"Which one?"

"The brunette, dude. See her?"

I leaned forward to get a better look and grimaced when my groin protested. As I continued scanning the stage, I heard tinkling musical laughter, the song of the raven, for the first time. I looked for the source. It was coming from one of the dancers. A vision. Her long, wavy mane of black tresses and copper frostings fell upon alabaster shoulders. Her lips were exquisite, pursed, and blood red. She had a small, angular nose and a dimpled chin. She stood on long dancer's legs that could've wrapped around me twice. She wore loose-fitting clothes, a white, long-sleeved shirt two sizes too big for her, black, baggy cargo pants tucked into knee-high leather boots, a red sash at her waist. I recognized her; in a couple of past productions, she had turned in excellent performances as Snoopy in *You're a Good Man Charlie Brown* and as Helena in *A Midsummer Night's Dream*. She had to be in her early to mid-twenties by now. I didn't know her name. She had ethereal poise and innocence. Her chocolate Tootsie-pop eyes darted to and fro. It was as if she were performing perpetually. She was a woman out of time, a displaced Victorian paramour of impeccable allure.

I thought her the loveliest woman I had ever laid eyes on.

"Yeah, I see her," I replied to Alex, uttering the understatement of my life.

Alex was equally enticed. "She shore is purty," he said in a faux western drawl.

"Too good for us. Too old for us."

"Maybe Keith should introduce us to his new friend."

"Ask and ye shall receive. Here they come," I said. Keith led her up toward us, chatting away. "Dancer's rags. I hate 'em. Too many layers and folds, all that room to move and padding for protection. Wonder what she looks like underneath."

"Think she's new?" Alex asked.

"No. I've seen her in stuff before, a few years back."

"I've known these guys forever," Keith was saying as they reached our upper loge station. "This is Alex, penned with red ink inside Mister Wyke's black book, banished to a techie underling post."

"Nice to meet you," Alex mumbled.

"And you," she replied and turned to me. "And you must be the one with the...*injury*."

"Um...I guess I am. I'm also wondering why my friend here would tell you that," I said, glowering at Keith.

He grinned. "Well, you two were up here watching everyone, and she wanted to know why you were looking even more constipated than usual, so I debriefed her on your...debriefing."

"Hilarious," I groused.

"There's really no need to be embarrassed. I know how young love is," she said.

"Do you now?" I replied.

"I do."

"It was a quick but interesting fling," I said.

"One of the best kinds," she said.

"Sort of one-sided, though."

"But the goods tipped in your favor, at least."

Her eyes dancing, her everything dancing.

"Yes, aside from the wear and tear," I admitted.

"Obviously she wasn't doing it correctly," she said. At this, even the usually unflappable Keith dropped his jaw.

"Ah…yeah, probably," I stuttered.

"With age comes wisdom," she cracked, with a dreamy-creamy smile.

If I didn't blink soon, she would discover me for the forgery I was.

"Actually," Alex said, "we were just talking about you."

"Really?"

"Shut up, Alex," I said.

"Go ahead, tell her," Alex said.

I sighed. "I was just commenting on your dancing gear."

"What about it?"

"I tend not to like that stuff on a woman."

"Why? Because you can't tell if I have a tight ass or a nice rack?"

"Precisely."

"You were looking at me that close?"

"Just like every other man in this room. You're quite striking."

She reddened. "Aw, thanks. That's very nice of you to say, though you might be exaggerating a tad. And I'll let you continue using your imagination."

"I'm using it this very moment, in fact."

"You're a different sort of breed, kid stuff," she mused, smirking.

"You don't know the half of it," Alex said.

"I don't think I caught your name," I said in a daze.

"I'm Lee. And you are?"

"Daren."

She regarded me for a moment, amused yet sagacious. It was a Herculean task to keep steady eye contact with her. "Nice to meet you, Daren. And you, Alex, and thanks for the tips, Keith. I'm sure I'll see you boys around." She fluttered away, a playful bounce in her step as she rejoined the crowd onstage.

"Now that is a woman with presence," Alex said.

She's the woman behind the dark wings in the dream.

The dream!

My blood pounded, my groin ached, my mind raced.

In her eyes I had seen something impossible. Incredible as it seemed, I thought it had been a mutual exchange. Pure crap, of course it was, fruitcake wishful thinking. I was sixteen. She was approaching the quarter-century mark at the least. Pure crap. Duh.

8

I reclined in the back seat of Lee's Buick sedan, smoking a clove cigarette. Alex passed me a flask of apple schnapps, and I waved it off.
The cast was convening at DeeBee's one late-night eatery after the evening performance, which had gone as well as it could. Standing ova-
tions from parents and friends, a few awkward silences and forgotten
lines. A local reviewer for the Durango Star promised only a mediocre
review, though he did mention that Lee, having landed the lead role of
Laurey Williams, would be singled out as the one redeeming factor in
Wyke's tactless rendition of a Rodgers and Hammerstein classic.

Lee abstained from the boozing almost without fail, never imbib-
ing when we teens were present. We'd kept a small semblance of honor
by not asking her to buy for us yet were dumb enough to ignore the
potential consequences for her should we minors be discovered drinking in her immediate vicinity. She'd had little exposure to party scenes
such as ours and exhibited a cautious, sorrowful fascination with our
bad habits. She was untainted. Red shift seemed to have passed her
over. Apparently there were exceptions to the cherry cloud general
rule of law.

After java and sundaes, Alex and Keith climbed into someone else's car in search of a post-show gathering already in progress at a set designer's house. Lee and I dropped by Mariah's, a fellow cast member big on red wine and the Moody Blues. Inside Mariah's pad a stoned group of thespians listened to the B-52s, toking on a hookah. Mariah asked us if we wanted to partake in some wine tasting, and we accepted. She and her boyfriend Fred led us downstairs and outside into a bona fide retro love van, its exterior painted with sunflowers and rainbows, plastered in Grateful Dead stickers and Rastafarian symbols. We settled on the van's floor among worn beanbags and Mexican throw rugs. The seventies ambience was quaint and a little sad. Mariah was one of those gals who believed she was born a decade too late. She uncorked a bottle of cabernet and passed it around. Lee splurged and took a couple of swallows. The four of us bantered for a while, then it became evident the bacchanal couple had been on the hunt for two suckers willing to indulge their swinger voyeurism, which we roundly trounced in unison. Mariah and Fred shrugged, told us we didn't know what we were missing, and crawled to the van's far corner, shuffling under a large pile of ratty blankets, and soon enough they were screwing, uncaring of our presence only a few feet away. We giggled through the first few moans and groans. But then we talked, real and fluid talk, for hours, all night, long after the other duo had finished and fallen asleep.

She was twenty-four and still lived with her parents. Her family had migrated to DeeBee from La Jolla when she was ten years old. She worked as a receptionist for the local branch of a national architect company and was saving up money to move to Los Angeles, as serious aspiring Californian actresses were required to do. Her father was a decorated war hero, a marine in Vietnam currently fighting another one-sided battle, this time with bone cancer. She loved him deeply. Her cat Simon stole her breath while she slept. She listened to Peter Gabriel and Genesis under her bed covers at night. She hated Pink Floyd. She didn't own one Van Halen album (this, I assured her, was not going to be the case much longer). A dance instructor once tried to get her to join his "nude" class, and she clocked him. She was liberal on the far left side of the spectrum, deriding all policies, idioms, and platitudes harkening from the right. She'd been performing in one sense or another since the day she could walk, singing and dancing; taking ballet, tap, and swing classes; joining choirs; and anything else DeeBee could offer in preparing her for the Big Time.

Dozens of other small and integral pieces of who she was came forth. I absorbed them, eager, voracious, hungry, until she insisted I begin reciprocating the flow of information, and so I confided in her a variety of adventures and aspirations. It was easy to share with her, so natural. I talked about my mother. Carefully. The shadow of tradition from my father, my casual sibling distance with my brother. The two other members of my trio, the nature and extent of our excess, at which she reprimanded me, claiming I was too smart for such mud, and in turn I assured her I was more than adept in colossal wastes of time and energy. Then I relayed my unwanted glimpses of beyond, the druid, the diner, and my theories on red-shifted phenomena. I wasn't entirely surprised to find she accepted the surreal as conventional. She warned me about defining such incidences while under the influence of mind-altering substances.

We talked about our first orgasms. We hated how the cherry blossoms brought out everyone's allergies in the spring, how we loathed walking through the supermarkets to the tune of a hundred sneezing, Kleenex-dripping DeeBee folk. We discussed our dramatic interests, how mine had petered out, how hers was a wildfire that would never die. We traded rapid-fire snippets like those back and forth, immensely satisfying small talk, the bread and butter of bonding. It's always the stuff in between that counts.

She seemed happy as she rested her head against my shoulder. A sliver of sunrise broke through cold morning mist into the van interior. We had neglected to note time's passage; if pressed, I'd have said we'd crawled into the van five minutes before. It had been six hours. She turned to me and stared into my eyes for what seemed like a long and uncomfortable time.

"What?" I finally asked.

"How old are you, again?"

"You know how old I am. Something on your mind concerning that?"

"You're so direct. You make sense. None of the guys my age I've known say anything that matters." She reached her fingers through the front of my half-unbuttoned shirt to my bare chest, tracing little circles there. I twitched, involuntary, scared to death. "You don't just hear me, you listen to me. And when I look in your eyes..."

"I know," I said. *Unbelievable. She feels it too.*

"It's like, I have to spend more time with you. Like I'm *supposed* to know you."

"Sure you're not just a cradle-robber?" I joked, trembling.

"I know what I know. And you're no kid."

"You'd be surprised..."

"Shut up," she whispered, and doused in orange rays of dawn, we kissed. I was too amazed to initiate anything more, which she seemed to appreciate. We held each other, wordless. Mariah and Fred were dead to the world. Soon we heard other people who had crashed upstairs at Mariah's getting in their cars and going home. Drowsy, we primped our appearances. "I want you to know that I've never done anything like this before. I don't care what people think. I mean, besides the possibility of arrest, I suppose. Maybe we shouldn't say anything...revelatory...until we figure it out ourselves."

"Makes sense to me," I agreed. Her stipulations were unnecessary. At that moment I would have signed over my eternal soul if she'd asked. We slipped out of the van without disturbing the proponents of free love. When she dropped me off, I considered kissing her goodbye and thought better of it. I told her I'd see her that night at the theater and watched her drive away, musing on cloud nine. How she was drawn to me was an enigma and stating the obvious, that she danced to a different beat, wasn't enough. Disillusionment with her own generation had something to do with it, and it was possible she was partially infected with Peter Pan syndrome. I was somewhat intelligent, and not entirely unattractive, but nothing in my possession was, in my perhaps-not-so-humble opinion, seemingly powerful enough to override the usual ordained guidelines and taboos.

We gathered later, for *Oklahoma's* fourth performance, in the men's dressing room backstage. The room was small, a counter littered with makeup kits and props and costume accessories and a large mirror framed with round fluorescent bulbs, a toilet and sink in a rear cubicle. Lee winked at me as she laced up her costume cowgirl boots. We were her only morale boosters now that the rest of the cast had shunned her, imposing isolation on the star of the show. The saga continued to unfold. Our strange entourage had ascended to Priority Level One within the gossiping ranks of drama minions, and thus out to DeeBee's main grapevine. Unfortunately, it wasn't due to fallout from the local rag extolling Lee's contributions to the otherwise lacking ensemble. It began, of course, when Lee chose to start associating with us kiddies instead of her age-appropriate peer group within the play's troupe. The backlash resulted in predictable reactions. Wyke, several condescending mothers, and assorted older male cast members had approached Lee and discussed at length the impropriety of canoodling, however platonic, with sixteen-year-old boys. She told them to mind their own business and was summarily banned from the women's dressing room for her *faux pas*.

Alex threw a rouge pad, horsing around, and it hit the side of my cheek, leaving a red, powdery smear. "Let me get that," Lee said. She finished lacing her boots, pulled a tissue from a box on the counter, wet it with the tip of her tongue, and wiped my cheek. She was close to me, and I loved it. Her scent always held blackberries, jasmine, and cinnamon.

"*The horror*," Alex prompted.

"*Let me tell you about...my mother*," I replied.

"Excuse me?" Lee asked.

"Oy," Keith said.

"Am I missing something here?" Lee prodded.

Keith groaned. "You shouldn't encourage them. They'll go on for a million years. Alex's favorite movie is *Apocalypse Now*, and Daren's is *Blade Runner*, and they'll argue about which is the better movie until, evidently, the end of time."

"Do tell," Lee said. "And what's the consensus?"

"*Apocalypse*," Alex said.

"*Blade*," I insisted.

"Like when Robert Duvall orders the surfer grunts to catch waves on Charlie's point, and they do, dodging mortar blasts and shrapnel flak. Like the casual indifference of men deep in blood and despair, like the insane yet human things men do in wartime, how ideas of normalcy are shaped by circumstance and fear," Alex said.

"I *get* it. I have seen the movie, Alexander my dear," Lee said. She finished swabbing my face and peered at me, mercurial. *Uh oh. Cool the jets, they're watching.*

Alex bristled. "*Anyway*, as I was saying, scenes like the one with Duvall make *Apocalypse* the darker film."

"Yeah, and *Blade Runner*'s a G-rated flick because of family-friendly fare like greenhouse effects, android sex and murder, and urban dystopia," I countered.

"*Ten minutes to curtain!*" a stagehand whispered outside.

"The surefire teller of a movie's message is the ending, right?" Lee posed.

"Yes, indeedio!" Alex exclaimed. "Harrison Ford and Sean Young live happily ever after, leaving the dark dystopia of future LA into lush green forests. And then there's Martin Sheen hacking up Marlon Brando with an machete somewhere in a Cambodian hellhole. I win."

"Sounds darker to me," Lee said.

"OK, maybe mine has a little hope at the end," I murmured.

The door opened. Missy, a blonde ditz with a freckled face and no talent whatsoever, stuck her head in. "Dorian says you have extra blue eyeliner, Lee."

"Here," Alex said. He picked up a makeup tube and tossed it. "So, Missy, is Dorian still trying to get down your pants?" She huffed and left without answering. Alex chuckled. "Are we that ostracized? Lee, you certainly have panache. We used to be popular here."

"For whatever that's worth," I said.

"Sorry if I've damaged your reputations," Lee said.

"Think that's the other way around. We've destroyed yours. Let's hit it, boys," Keith said, leaving the dressing room. It was time to retire to the tech booth, dim the house lights, return to our dramaturgic positions. "See you at intermission, babe. Break a leg."

Alex jumped down from the counter and cocked a wary eye at us as we held back. I wished she'd dial it back some; Alex was scrutinizing, and we were strutting around like kittens full of canaries.

"OK, come on, Daren," Alex said.

"I'll be there in a sec," I said.

Lee faced the mirror, brushing her hair. Impatient, Alex looked at me, then to her, then back to me. "What…" he began, but then clamped his mouth shut. "Whatever." He disappeared into backstage darkness. The door shut with a hiss of hydraulics.

"You told him, didn't you?" Lee demanded.

"No. He's figuring it out."

"Figuring *what* out? There's nothing to figure out!" she said, storming. Her temper was making her all the more exquisite.

"You're right. There's nothing to figure out."

"We kissed. That's all. They can't lock me up for that, can they?"

I laughed. "I think if they suspected, and somebody wanted to, they could try. But I promise I won't tell."

She stood nose to nose with me. "We just kissed." She brushed her lips over mine.

"Right. We just kissed," I agreed, nuzzling her nose.

"Why is it that all I can think about is rolling around a Volkswagen bus with you?"

"For the same reason I've been waiting for those guys to leave so that I could do this."

I pulled her to me, and we kissed, and it was fiery and urgent. I pushed her up against the door. Frantic, groping, moaning, we started taking off each other's clothes. Our bodies strained, writhing. She looked lost. I wondered whose disbelief was more. I felt the curtain drawing yet again. It was different. It didn't hurt, quite the opposite. This was no mere transition to the next phase. We shared soul, two as one. No kidding. Have you ever *really* shared soul? It is beyond the stuff of this life, surpassing marriage and family, friendship and community.

"I want you. Right. Now," Lee said, unbuttoning my pants.

"Two minutes to curtain," I mumbled, slipping off her bra and sliding my hands around her small, firm breasts. She sighed and shuddered.

The door started to open, stopped dead by the weight of our embrace. "What's the deal?" a male voice asked. We scrambled; she fumbled with her bra as I buttoned my jeans and wedged my foot against the door so it wouldn't open further. "Open the door, Daren. Why are you blocking it?" It was Walter, a D&D wastoid who happened to have a decent set of song pipes.

"Half a minute, Walt. The star of the show is changing into her costume."

"In front of *you*?"

"No, Walt. My back's turned. It's civil in here. Try not to get too excited."

"Lee, could you hurry it up?" Walter asked.

"Who are you?" I whispered to Lee, mischievous.

"No one of particular note," she said, throwing the door wide and striding past Walter, who gave her a frowning once-over and pushed his way in.

"Just because Lee and her little minions have taken over this room doesn't mean you own it," Walter snapped.

"Screw you, Walt," I said in a euphoric dream state surpassing any highs I'd ever known, and I'd known more than a few. Rationality set in as I made my way around the building to the tech booth up above the lobby foyer. I had to tell the guys soon, whether Lee liked it or not. They were bound to discover us anyway; they knew something was up, especially Alex, who was waiting, albeit with grit teeth, for confirmation.

A week passed. One day we hiked down to the Durango Bay River and smoked a joint and sunned our bodies like lizards on water-smoothened boulders of granite. *Fuck it.* Red-eyed and stoned, I just told them.

Alex was infuriated, dumbfounded.

"What do you mean, you're *hanging out*?"

"You know."

"No, we don't know, Daren. Enlighten us," Keith said.

"Have you fucked her?" Alex demanded.

"No. I don't think it's like that. Not yet, anyway."

"Yet? Whaddya mean? What *is* it like?' Keith asked.

"Look, I'm not trying to kiss and tell. I wanted you guys to know because I like her. A whole lot. So if we cut out sometimes from the gang, you know what's up. OK?"

"You *kissed* her?" Alex asked, stupefied.

"Can you get past this?" I replied.

"Dude, you're turning seventeen in a month. What is she thinking? She must be more deranged than she looks. You'd think she'd be more discriminating or something. Um, no offense, but she's toeing a line," Alex said.

"None taken, asshole. Don't start something you can't finish."

He puffed up his chest. "Is that what I think it was?"

"OK, OK, dick measuring contests not required," Keith said, keeping the peace. "He just means it's kind of weird, man. Yeah, you're not your average DeeBee kid. Hell, we all know that, but what are her parents going to think? More importantly, what are *your* parents going to say? Your Mom is gonna shut it down pronto. Might even call the cops."

"It's not at the meeting-the-parents point."

"But she'll find out. You know this 'burg. Everyone's saying…"

"I know what people are saying. They'll have to deal. I like being with her."

"Well, no shit. Who wouldn't?" Alex said.

"I'd prefer to keep this in confidence for as long as possible."

"Uh, yeah, OK," Keith said. Alex said nothing. I didn't expect them to hold their tongues for long. DeeBee was no place for secrets.

The ripples began sooner than I had expected. My friends' reactions were not unlike many others who'd heard or suspected. Lee was confronted several times by inquisitive, disbelieving personages. It was distressing because no one would talk to *me* about it. I had somewhat of an argumentative side, and not many people liked to fire it up. Nobody was using the statutory rape term…yet. The fact we hadn't slept together was unknown. One night we split our sides laughing when Lee suggested our situation was like one of those old Joan Collins soft-porn movies, *The Bitch* or *The Stud* or whatever, in which the vivacious Miss Collins gets it on with her pool boys, plumbers, and the like. The *Dynasty* vixen had nothing on Lee in my opinion, but we both knew DeeBee, true to form, would make the comparison more real than it was. It was only a matter of time before some nosey housewife ran into one of our mothers at market.

9

Santa Crisca roared.

City of leisure and Spanish conquistador spoils, its lifeblood was tourism and prime oceanfront real estate. Its beaches and boulevards were decorated with queen palms and latticed patios thick with purple bougainvillea ivy. The surrounding foothills were foliated patchworks of yucca plant and dogwood, glens of oak and eucalyptus, lemon groves and olive orchards, stilted mansions and lavish estates crowning the coveted Riviera district, its red tile roofs and white adobe architecture rearing up steep slopes of the Durango mountain range, overpriced monuments to Old California. Dense fogbanks settled over the city throughout long Indian summers, blanketing the exclusive fertile strip of land between mountains and sea. It was a frequent destination, only a half-hour drive from DeeBee through a notoriously dangerous mountain highway pass. Its main thoroughfare of movie theaters and pubs and trendy surf shops, arcades and art galleries, seaside piers and sands provided many a setting for our misadventures. Santa Criscans knew how to beat the drum, and they never needed an excuse to throw a party. They'd lionize just about anything, anywhere, anytime—assorted ethnic and cultural festivals, its biggest annual soirees including a Summer Solstice celebration, the Fourth of July, a late summer Old Spanish Days Fiesta, and Halloween at the university.

As we'd learned years before, our underage anonymity was lost in the squalor hosted by Santa Criscans, a good portion of which now spread before us in a heaving mass. Burton Beach, a popular tanning spot and surf point, was once again transformed on the Fourth of July. Locals had a longstanding tradition of digging hundreds of deep pits all about the beach, setting up grills and coolers and kegs within, many sponsored by the university's fraternities and sororities, and under the sham of toasting the anniversary of our nation's independence, before the nine p.m. fireworks show over the nearby harbor, thousands of Santa Criscans would revel in a volley of coastline shenanigans, hot dogs and burgers and warm potato salad, popsicles and flat beer and sharp whiskey.

People *had* to dig the pits deep, for cover. Burton Beach became a war zone once twilight arrived. Personal fireworks were prohibited within the city's jurisdiction, but it was easy enough to jaunt up to the next county for combustible party favors. Each year we attended, it was anyone's guess whether one might come home with first-degree burns on fingertips or other body parts as a result of frat boys and teenagers lighting off colorful snapdragons and roman candles, blazing flowers and M-80's, firecrackers and pinwheels. The real danger was the bottle rockets. Thirty thousand ragers, drinking all day in the sun, armed to the teeth with point-and-aim explosive devices. Hundreds of bottle rockets were shot between pits during the pre-gala tension. People got hurt. The small army of local law enforcement, on horses and ATVs, patrolled to break up fights and prevent total anarchy, but there were too many people to issue citations for the illegal fireworks, and they had plenty to do in limiting the underage drinking, which was next to impossible after dark. We'd been regulars at the Burton Beach hoopla for a few years, long before we got our driver's licenses, hitching rides over the hill thanks to older friends, so we were versed in exploring the mazes of dunes and pits looking for free kegs, scoping Santa Criscan chicks, and dodging angry, buzzing tracers.

A section of the crowd roared again in response to a great, bright-blue peacock's tail blooming and sputtering within a group of half-naked teenagers. Lee had accompanied Keith and me down to Santa Crisca for the Fourth. Keith tried to talk me out of letting her tag along, thinking she would be way out of her element. I considered his acute observation, ignored it, and now was regretting said decision. On the way down, I tried to describe the chaos, especially the bottle rocket danger, and she scoffed and told me to relax.

Alex declined. He planned to head up to Pismo Beach near San Luis Obispo with some of his acid buddies. My brother decided to go with him. I told Jim about Lee not long after Alex and Keith, and all he'd said was, "Typical Daren. Mom's gonna have a cow."

"My God," Lee muttered as we leaned on a fence overlooking the north end of the beach. A young boy ran on top of gangplanks between two neighboring pits, sparklers in hand, dodging bottle rockets left and right. Many of the collegiate Greek pits had raised their respective fraternities' banners, charging fees and "drink penalties" for crossing their pits' dune bridges and catwalks. These same flags were inspiring play conflicts with other pit factions, crazed drunken members filling empty beer bottles with bottle rocket stems and shooting them at one another. Lee gasped as we looked at one unfortunate fellow run into the beach break screaming and laughing, his pants on fire. It seemed to be the biggest year yet, well over fifty thousand people squeezed together on the quarter-mile stretch of sand.

"It's pretty intense, isn't it?" I said.

"Intense is a word. *That* is sheer stupidity." She pointed at a topless woman on stilts who tried to navigate the unwieldy extensions between spinning cracker-flowers in the sand and then fell on them, squealing in pain.

"It looks worse than it is," I said.

"Yeah, right. Don't listen to him, Lee. It's exactly what it looks like," Keith said.

"I got it covered. She's gonna wear shades and her hood."

"I am?"

"You are. Can't have your eye popped out. I couldn't live with it. More importantly, your mother couldn't live with it."

"But I won't be able to see with sunglasses on."

"They're not that dark. It's OK. I'll hold your hand."

She smiled. "OK then."

"Oh boy, that was sweet," Keith said.

"Lead on, Macduff," I said.

Keith struck forward. We followed hand in hand, weaving through the crowd.

"Why are you dating me?" I asked.

"I'm very particular."

"That seems contrary to my query."

"Ha, ha. So we're dating now?"

"We spend a lot of time together. We make out a lot. We've almost done the nasty several times. I think about doing you every second of every day. Feels like dating to me."

"Subtle you aren't, Lamb Chop. I suppose we *are* dating because I have the very same feelings, which means I am as mad as the Mad Hatter or you are an extraordinary young man."

Lamb Chop. And I haven't even told her yet about Dusty. Serendipity...up or flippity.

"Well, it can't be that last bit. You're probably off your rocker, Alice."

"Everyone seems to think so."

"Does it matter?"

"My family will not be supportive."

"Mine, either. Maybe they'll call the cops."

"*What*? You think so?"

"We can always claim we're just friends."

"You're not that good an actor."

"Ouch. When the police arrive, I'll let you do the talking."

"It's only funny because it's not," she huffed.

We came upon a pit adjacent to the walkway. Half of its occupants were passed out on beach towels, the other half tossed cherry bombs at passersby. We ducked under a few of the smoking marbles as I gave the nearest offender a dirty look. It was a madhouse. Bringing Lee was a mistake. It wasn't that she was too delicate. Extreme hedonism just wasn't her bag.

"Put the hood on. And the shades. We'll go down near the beach break. It's safer by the water. People don't want to waste their fireworks by shooting them into the ocean," I said.

Everyone was setting off the last pieces of their arsenals before the big show started. The air reeked of flash powder and vomit. A swarm of bottle rockets flew overhead. A few of them landed in front of Keith, exploding in snaps of sand and powder. Another one whizzed by my ear. The line to get by the next pit was backed up, and as a result, we were easy targets for a nearby pit full of drunken jocks.

"Down in the pit and around!" I yelled to Keith. "That way, Lee."

"That thing almost hit you."

"Yeah. Let's go."

"Maybe this wasn't such a great idea."

"Nearly there." We tiptoed past a couple making out, a tender moment amid the mob.

Lee giggled. "How can they do that in this mess?"

"People can do *anything* in this mess."

A bottle rocket sizzled, smacking my forearm in a shower of sparks, bouncing off and hitting the sand in front of me before it exploded. A piece of smoldering flak burned my arm. I slapped it out. It burned.

"Dude! Are you OK?" Keith called back.

"Let me see, Daren," Lee said.

"It's OK. Keep going, gotta keep moving; it's crazy in the center here."

"Let me see," Lee insisted, examining the small welt. My frizzled arm hair stank.

"It happens. Let's go."

We scurried across pit holes and dune bridges, coming out on the far south side. A poor fellow was bent over in the water, puking in the sea. Keith asked him if he was OK, and the guy heaved again.

"That guy has had too much. He'll miss the show. Too bad," Keith said.

I squinted through the haze and spied a familiar face. He was in a pit marked with a flag of Durango Bay High's sports insignia (a charging horse framed by spurs). It was Alex.

"The DeeBee pit is over there, Keith. Alex and Jim are here."

"How do you know?"

"I saw Alex."

"But they said they were going to Pismo."

"Indeed."

"OK, well, I'm going where the action is," Keith said.

"We'll stay. Tell Alex I said hi," I said, acerbic. He ran off, barefoot and fancy-free.

"He just does whatever," Lee observed.

"One of his many charms."

The fireworks show began with an earsplitting boom. We sat in the sand, arms wrapped around each other. As the ensuing pyrotechnics commenced and raucous thunder and rainbow blooms filling a clouded, marine-layered sky, we kissed. All we saw of the grandiose display were the changing colors of the glow on each other's faces.

A mass exodus to parking lots and hilltop roads followed the finale. We decided to wait until it had thinned out. I looked for Keith in the swirling masses.

"Hey," a voice said behind us. It was Jim.

"You've been here the whole time?" I asked.

"Yeah, we blew off Pismo. Hitched a ride with McGee and his crew. People are wasted." He stumbled. "Including me."

"This is Lee, by the way," I said.

"Good to meet you finally," Jim said.

"And you," Lee said.

"Hope my brother's not being too much of his pain-in-the-ass self around you."

"I'm learning how to cope," Lee replied.

"I like her already," Jim said.

I gave him a cagey look. "Blew off Pismo."

"Yeah, bro."

"What *is* his problem?"

"I don't know. He's a bitch sometimes."

"You don't say."

"Sorry. I gotta meet them at the car. Keith said to tell you he's going with us. Just wanted to say hi. Later, man." Then my brother disappeared into the smoke.

"What was that about?" Lee asked.

"I'll tell you on the way home. Let's roll."

We made it back to her Buick without seeing them. I *wanted* to see them. I wanted to give Alex a heaping pile of shit for lying to me. We chatted amiably as we drove back to DeeBee. The burn on my forearm stung like hell. When we reached my house a half hour later, scattered hoots and whistles and the rat-tat-tat of firecrackers rose from the surrounding suburbs.

I felt like walking off the evening's smoke and vibe, so we left her car in the driveway and walked to The Ponds, a section of backcountry just west of my parents' ranch, several hundred square acres of oaks and cattle-grazing pasture, gullies full of horse trails and sage, rolling hills of yellow timothy. It was where red shift had first found Alex, then me. A trio of watering holes dotted the expanse, the first at the north end of the property doubling as a private trout farm, its well-stocked pond full of big-mouth bass, bluegill and catfish, where in my youth I'd fished late summer evenings with Dad and Jim, watching bats flutter above while cleaning our catches. Two more ponds in westward succession lay beyond the trout farm, one primarily a rainwater-catch and breeding ground for hibernating crawdads, the other a combination of cattle drinking trough and kids' swimming hole, complete with a makeshift jetty of rafts, inner tube floats, and canoes. We'd added our own contribution to the flotilla long ago, a monster raft constructed out of plywood sheets and two-by-fours hauled from the ranch with great effort.

Much of my childhood was spent at The Ponds, out of sight of society. Riding horses, fishing and chumming and fighting, exploring and pillaging and hunting, Truth-or-Dare make-out sessions with neighborhood girls. It was a safe place, barring the occasional coyote or rattlesnake, and we could be as loud as we wanted while we foraged for wildlife critters and adventures galore. It was a place of great magic. Something there became a founded part of me, for it would draw me to its borders time and again.

I lifted up a strand of barbed wire for Lee to slip through. She scampered under, agile and playful. A crescent moon arced through black sky. Stars blazed above. Squirming crawdads clawed and scratched in mud at the second waterhole. Frogs chirped and crickets cheeped, falling silent as we approached.

"It's beautiful back here," Lee said.

We ambled by the third pond. Lee executed a graceful ballet jump over a fallen tree trunk, sodden with pond water, recently having been used as a rough canoe. Assorted rafts lined the shore, still in use by the next generations having inherited our scrubby wooden legacies, and there were newer flotation devices, colorful, modern, plastic buoys and pontoons and swim toys. It wasn't hard to find our old raft, an ancient, hulking giant among the kiddie armada beached at an overgrown mooring point. It was sagging and hardly seaworthy, laden in moss and wood rot. We stepped onto it, in the shallows, and it took on algae-crusted water under our weight.

"OK, so tell me about Alex now," Lee said.

"Nothing important," I muttered.

"Tell me anyway."

"It doesn't matter."

"You've been irritated ever since we left the fireworks."

"I'm fine, babe."

"I'd appreciate a little more candor."

"Let's climb that hill. There's a decent view there."

"Daren…"

"He's jealous, all right?"

"Jealous?"

"Sure. All the guys in the theater are. The ones your age are livid."

"I suppose I should be flattered. I don't get that feeling when they're around."

"That's 'cause they're too busy being mad at me."

"You and Alex aren't speaking?"

"We're speaking, just not very nice. It'll pass."

We scaled the hill, groping in the dark through green thistles and mustard weed.

"I'm about done with people judging us," Lee said.

"Ditto that, sweetheart."

We reached the top of the crest. On the other side, a vast horse ranch sat on a wide plateau, with gigantic barns and equestrian arenas.

Arabians and quarter breeds and Andalusians rustled in their corrals. The night air grew redolent with odors of leather tack, hay bales, and sweet manure. We threw our jackets down under a black walnut tree and sat back to catch our breath. Beyond the ranch was the river, its dry bed of bleached stones visible in the moonlight. I was at peace. I had brought a powerful raven to my sacred place. If a man cannot be right with the world at such a time, he is no man at all. Even a dumb country boy mystic like me knew that much.

"There's something I've been meaning to tell you all night. Yesterday was strange. Your mother called me at work," Lee said.

I winced. All pleasantries aside, my mother could be one serious bitch to people when she didn't agree with something, as any member of my grade school's PTA might affirm. With a few drinks down the drain, Joan Crawford and Bing Crosby themselves might tiptoe around her.

"She wanted to have lunch," Lee went on.

"And you agreed?"

"Of course."

"You waited to tell me this until *now?*"

"I needed to process."

"So when are you having lunch?"

"We already did. Same day."

So much for running interference.

"I see. What did she have to say?"

"What any worried mother would say if her teenage son was dating a twenty-four-year-old woman."

"And what would that be?"

"Oh, you know, *what was I doing,* and *are you sure you know how old he is,* and *what are your intentions.* She was pretty cordial, all things considered. Nothing you wouldn't say to your own son, had he been involved with a temptress like me."

"I would trust the way I raised my kids."

"Easy for you to say…kiddo." She tickled me.

"You're taking this awfully well," I said, tickling her back. She wiggled on the jackets, grass crunching beneath us.

"I was terrified. I figured I'd just tell her like it is. She seemed to respect that."

"What exactly did you tell her?"

"The truth. Her oldest son is extraordinary to me, and I would do nothing to hurt him or his success, and that when her son speaks to me it is with sincerity and compassion, and that he makes me feel good about being alive."

"Um..."

"And she said that she could see what I was talking about, that you'd always been more...advanced...than your peers. She was worried I was playing with your mind. I reassured her I was not that kind of person, that I didn't have a pedophiliac fetish for young boys, and that you and I were basically on the same level, improbable as it might be, crazy as it might sound."

I was *pissed*.

"She had no right to do that."

"She's your mother. She has every right. Really, it turned out to be a nice conversation. I'd have been a lot harsher to me if I'd been her. She loves you dearly, you know."

"Did she tell you who told her about us?"

"Daren, you're just going to grill her whenever you see her next, so why not wait and ask her then? Now I have to break it to my parents. And pray some busybody doesn't make an anonymous call to the sheriff."

"Your parents won't call me up for an impromptu Q and A," I said, sulking.

"Are you sad? Are you grumpy now?" she asked, rolling on top of me. "I think you'll be fine. Maybe you *should* feel a little heat for once. Along with everyone thinking I'm a pervert babysitter, I'm sure your contemporaries think you're in high heaven getting your rocks off... and to be honest, there's more than a little swagger in your step lately."

She gave me a long, exploring kiss. I rolled her over, burying my head in her shoulder, nibbling the tender skin around her neck. "It would be stupid to think I'm *not* in high heaven," I murmured. "But I'm better equipped than most at determining my own destiny."

"So arrogant," Lee whispered. She moaned as I slid between her legs, her back arching, her hands pulling at me.

"Any fool can tell," I whispered.

"I'm any fool," Lee moaned. She stripped off her blouse. Her naked porcelain body glimmered in moonlight.

I reared up on my knees, fumbling with my belt, kicking my sneakers away. As I perched on one leg to slip my jeans off, my foot caught on something behind me, and I fell backward on my ass. Lee burst out in laughter. "Damn, now that's romantic. Nothing like a little slapstick to get the mood rolling," I said, rising, picking at burrs and cockles. She laughed and laughed, her ravensong too rich and sweet.

"Are you all right?"

"I tripped on something." I crouched down, squatting in my boxers, squinting in the night. Beneath the black walnut tree, between two large roots, stood a small cross leaning to one side. Somebody had nailed a couple of wooden tent stakes together and carved a rough etching on the horizontal bar: "**SCRUFFY—R.I.P. 1972—197**." The last number of the epitaph was blurred from exposure to the elements.

"Oh, great. I tripped over a grave."

"Excuse me?"

"Somebody buried a pet up here. Something named Scruffy."

"*Now* this is romantic."

"All the make-out points in DeeBee, and I pick the one with the shrine to a dead cat," I groused as I crawled back to her. She wrapped her arms around me. We looked at the drooping cross. "We can go somewhere else, you know."

"No," Lee said, reaching into my boxers.

As we touched each other, our thoughts and fears melted away into nothingness. We rocked back and forth. Our souls met, our bodies along for the ride, and as we bared the sheer force of each other to each other, we loved. I'd had sex before, the bump-and-grind caliber. This was something else, far beyond. We cried as we climaxed together, energies expanding, contracting, releasing.

"Daren…oh, God, Daren…I love you. I *know* I love you."

"I love you too, Lee."

We bundled under our jackets. My boxers hung, gregarious, on Scruffy's slapdash headstone. It may have been disrespectful to leave my underwear draped over a gravesite, but at the moment forbiddances were far from my mind. Lee cuddled in the crook of my arm.

Her blackberry-cinnamon scent filled the moonshadow showcasing our union.

"Do you think Scruffy was a cat or a dog?" I posed.

"Why couldn't it be a turtle, or a goldfish? Or a hamster?"

"Who's gonna go to this much trouble, hike all the way out here, for a varmint?"

"Always with you it's black or white."

"Not always. Telling a woman I'm in love with her for the first time in my life is not very black or white. It's a whole lotta wonderful gray."

"Can't argue with that," she replied sleepily.

I spent the next half hour watching her doze, wanting to keep awake, to stay present in a night of paroxysm, but soon I was too tired to keep my eyes open.

10

A muted ZZ Top video played on the tube, long legs and long beards, red muscle cars and furry guitars. Downstairs I heard Jim getting ready for work, cranking Kiss far too loud for seven a.m. On the weekends he picked up part-time cash tending grounds at a golf course. Me, I was blowing off my grocery gig more and more.

I lay on top of my sheets, exhausted, joyous.

I loved her. She loved me. God was good.

The aroma of frying bacon came from below. A shower was running. The immediate family members were early risers. I wasn't. But I couldn't sleep. Too jacked up. I put on a beaten terry robe, lit a smoke, and hacked up half a lung. I descended the narrow stairway from my attic enclave and shuffled to Jim's room. He stood in front of a mirror, slicking back his platinum mane with gel.

"Morning. Late one last night, eh? Heard you crawling in a couple hours ago."

"Yeah," I croaked.

"Crazy this year, huh? The DeeBee pit was out of hand. Alex was gone, man."

"I believe it."

"Your girl seemed a little scared. Not exactly a date scene."

"I know."

"She's smokin'."

"Yes."

"Ah, you should know I heard Mom on the phone the other day making a play date with her. Didn't sound like she got your permission."

"I just heard last night. Why didn't you tell me?"

"None of my beeswax, I guess."

I stubbed out the butt in an ashtray on Jim's dresser. "I need to speak with her."

"Good luck with that. I'm out of here."

I followed him to the kitchen, where Mom scrambled eggs in a plastic bowl. A greasy crisp pile of bacon layered with paper towels sat on the kitchen table. "See ya, Mom," Jim said, and turned to me and wagged a finger. "Don't be a dick, dude. It's a trippy thing even for a freak like you." He winked and left.

"You're up earlier than you have been in years," Mom said.

"So what?" I snapped.

"Don't you work today?"

"Let's cut the crap. What were you thinking?"

"It was a pleasant luncheon, nothing more. Don't worry. I picked up the tab. She's charming, isn't she?"

"I don't recall your having any say in who I choose to associate with."

"I'm your mother. I don't need your say-so, particularly when you're still a minor and someone else…is not."

"You're not qualified to judge me, or her."

"Let's not start this right now."

"*You* started it when you decided to call her up and ask her things that are none of your fucking business."

"Watch your language. Do you want potatoes with your eggs?"

"Don't change the subject. I don't want anything to eat."

"I'm your mother. She's in her twenties, Daren. What do you suppose *her* mother thinks, her beautiful daughter dating a junior in high school? Hmm? Have you thought of what it will do to her name around this town?"

"I couldn't care less what people think, and neither does she."

"I'm not sure you should continue to see her."

"Good thing that I'm sure, then."

"Think of her, for crying out loud. You understand I could involve the authorities."

"But you won't."

"No?"

"No."

"Breakfast!" Mom barked out to my father.

"I know what I'm doing. She is not a pedophile. I am not a child."

"I don't think you realize what…"

"*Do you understand?*"

She sipped a cup of coffee, silent.

"Mom, this is important to me."

"You don't know what you're doing."

"I know when something's real and when something isn't."

"Sometimes I doubt that."

"Doubt away. It's not open for debate."

"It's strange. I don't have to agree with it."

"That's fine, but you have to live with it."

"I *will* say she's a nice woman, though she's a bit quirky for not recognizing this is highly inappropriate."

"It's…more than you think."

"Is it now?"

"Yes."

"Hmm."

"Funny thing…you mentioned something to her about understanding."

She sighed. "I wish she hadn't told you that. We don't need you cockle-doodle-dooing anymore than you already do."

My father walked in. "You're up early, son. Let me guess. You and your mother are arguing about something."

"No, I'm enlightening her."

"About that girl Lee?"

"Dad, leave it alone."

"She's too old, Daren."

"Shut up, Dad."

"Respect for your elders is too much to ask?"

"I've never been very good at that."

He chuckled. "Ya don't say."

I slunk upstairs and sacked out until late afternoon, when my mother roused me with a call from Lee. She had talked to her family. A woman her age usually wouldn't have had to explain herself; but since she was still under her parents' roof, she felt it necessary if we were going to keep seeing each other. Half-hearted, she maintained it went better than she thought it would. It didn't take a mind reader to hear the words unsaid. Lee's own cast of thousands had to be calling for blood.

Weeks went by. The play ended, summer waned. After many more arguments both passive and aggressive, I persuaded my reluctant guardians to let me make my own designs on love, after they realized I was dead set. A more accurate observation might have been they tolerated my stance enough not to involve the police or child protective services once it became clear Lee wasn't going to kidnap me and toss me in a gutter, or far more important to my parents, talk me out of the college track and saddle my ass down with two or three brats before I was old enough to legally buy a drink.

Lee's parents were less brazen, more standoffish. A few awkward dinners at their house ensued. Her mother was graceful and elegant and an old soul, only wanting the best for her daughter. It made for interesting across-table vibes, as I tried to exude suave demeanor while her mother determined whether I was a young smitten delinquent who had bewitched her daughter. Her father, a polite and direct man, balding and emaciated from recent bouts with chemotherapy, expressed valid concerns about both my motives and the potential consequences for his daughter. During those first few troublesome interactions, Lee was fervent, her explanations of the nature of our relationship spotty yet earnest, rational and matter-of-fact. Against both our expectations, she began to convince them I wasn't your average adolescent and she hadn't lost her mind. After a while it became casual, even pleasant. Her father's recent travails with cancer had weathered him. When I talked with him, it was in awe. He was a worldly man, much like my father, only he was living with undeserved, extreme physical pain. Lee adored him. She sang to him at night, songs she had memorized from Broadway musicals, when he was reeling from treatments. She was a daddy's girl through and through.

The uproar died after the play ended. DeeBee's rumor machine shifted its emphasis as it became clear its inane chatter had failed in changing our course or proving the truth outright. We never became publicly torrid enough for anybody to point fingers. People moved on to the next sordid circumstance, which as it happened concerned a member of our local PTA in high standing and her adopted Korean daughter and how she might have purchased the child through a black market baby mill. So it goes with small-town, domesticated Anglophiliac hype. The average DeeBee citizen could tend to grapevines only so many times before becoming bored, succumbing to the hunger of fresher tabloid scandal.

I entered my senior year with a raven roosted on one arm and several crutches under the other. I became a double agent of sorts, flipping a weighted karmic coin, balancing my prodigious life with Lee and my continued trespasses with the two other musketeers. Lee and I could scarcely stand to be apart; however, our mettle was about to be tested. She was notified her application for a dramatic internship at an exclusive theater company in London had been accepted. Jubilant about the once-in-a-lifetime chance, she reassured me that it was only three months she'd be gone. I held back my observation that raven-folk attracted opportunity like flies to honey and instead I was supportive, insisting she'd rock the English riff-raff. She packed, and I drove her to LAX and kissed her good-bye and wished her luck, all the while thinking about European men.

My insecurities hadn't subsided a week later as I sat in economics class. The real possibility of Euro-trash on the make for her made me cringe, with their pastel-colored cigarettes and white slacks and Italian shades and cocksure magnetic accents. I trusted Lee. Trusting *them* was another matter. I imagined scenarios of a luscious yet impressionable brunette drinking at jolly old pubs, day trips to the cliffs of Dover and weekending in France, my imagination's attention to detail the worst form of sadomasochism.

My dowdy teacher Mrs. Reynolds chattered at her podium about the continuing success of Reaganomics, praising the fortitude of our current president. School was easy for me. While many of my contemporaries struggled with making the grade while within the party scene, I breezed through curricula with little effort due to a couple of interrelated dynamics: the first a recessive geek gene manifested in bibliophile fashion, the second my hubris in making a neo-career of working the loopholes in established systems. I was a scholastic trapeze artist, adept at finding the weak links in old chains. I managed to keep a 3.7 average without busting balls.

I yawned, stretched my arms backward, glanced at Alex. He continued changing grades for some of our peers in Mrs. Reynolds' record book. She knew business but not kids, as was apparent in the selection of Alex as her afternoon TA. Tabitha, a slender Greek goddess with deep olive skin and black, wavy curls, sat in front of me. We talked once in a while at lunch and the occasional DeeBee high school wingding, having bonded when she revealed, under a haze of brandy, that she too had enjoyed bowls of Count Chocula while watching Saturday morning cartoons not long before our ascendancy unto young adulthood. Keith sat behind me. The reek of cannabis was absolute. He'd taken an extended lunch break.

Alex leaned over, whispering, "We're a go tonight, right?"

"We're there," Keith whispered back. "How much?"

"What are you guys talking about?" Tabitha asked.

"Twenty a hit," Alex said.

"We're X'ing tonight," Keith murmured to Tabitha.

"We are? I didn't get that memo," I said.

"Oh, cool. X is so fun. Do you have any more?" she asked.

"Sort of a guys-only thing, Tabby. You know," Alex said.

"I see," she said coolly, and turned away.

"Guys-only things are generally mistrusted by the fairer sex," I murmured.

"She needs to cool it anyway. She was at the last X party at Johnson's place and knocked knees with some football bozo she shouldn't have," Keith whispered.

"Say it ain't so," I said. Keith laughed, prompting a stern look from Mrs. Reynolds. "Ecstasy? Seriously? We're doing this?" Alex had been popping the stuff for the better part of a month, with his Maiden cronies and the water polo crew.

"It's time you two were initiated," Alex said.

"What's it like?" Keith said.

"You'll see, man. We'll be tripping for a while. I got a thousand tabs of the stuff. Let's camp at the beach tonight."

"Geez, when did you win the lotto?" I asked.

"Shut up. Bring wood, booze, and smokes. You know where to meet me." He went back to altering the grade book. I wondered if my own grade from the last test could use a tweaking, then changed my mind. An A-minus to an A was splitting hairs. The ex-Catholic in me reared its ugly head for even considering the option.

The Roman Catholic Church and all its outdated stony ethics had been a gloomy companion of mine since my christening. Aside from its niceties like guilt beyond forgiveness and that whole lake of fire bit, its bad rep might be a bit overblown. Too formal and stodgy, and of course all that sexual repression horseshit, but like the rest of the dogmas in the world, it holds certain aspects of truth and light. Love thy neighbor, do unto others, yada yada yada. Don't get me wrong; there's nothing like a good Catholic girl, and I mean that in the good way. Conversely, there's no such thing as a good Catholic boy. Trust me, I know. I did the whole shebang as a kid, having one of California's more majestic missions in the center of Durango Bay, Mass every Sunday, Baptism, First Communion, Seven Sacraments, Confirmation, the works. I was an altar boy for several years, during which I attended Catechism every Thursday night at the local mission where my fellow cohorts in God and I would sneak pubescent Catholic girlies up to the old Chumash ruins around the back of the mission and make out. Catholicism instilled in me a morbid fascination with the afterlife. It gave my conscience the definitions of original sin. To date, both tenets have been difficult to shake off. You Catholics understand, don't ya. Once, shortly before my departure from the faith, I asked the presiding father of our congregation to tell me the reason why women could not be priests. He'd given me the stock answer of tradition. I said it was ridiculous to assume God would designate men only as the purveyors of faith, and it seemed to me given their life-giving prestige, women were more in tune with a Creator than men could ever hope to be, which provoked statuesque placidity from my spiritual mentor. Pressing on, I wondered aloud how an organization as vast as the Vatican with its huge fortune could proclaim to protect the downtrodden while hoarding such levels of materialism. He told me it took resources to meet all the needs of the people they served. Then I asked if he thought the ways in which resources had been allocated would all line up with the teachings of Christ. He harrumphed and hemmed and hawed and accused me of having the tone of one who had lost his way. He then attempted to recite the Lord's Prayer with me. I almost brought up the involuntary conscription of the local Chumash tribe's ancestors, heathens all before the colonization of California via their misfortune of not ever having *heard* of the Big Kahuna before the missionaries arrived, to build the same mission we stood within. But the poor man's already beet-red face convinced me to drop it.

The sixth-period bell rang, and Reynolds's econ class filed out into the hall. I bolted for home. I loaded the back of the VW (I didn't have to purchase firewood, as the ranch stocked dozens of cords of red oak and raw pine thanks to—you guessed it—the most self-reliant man in the world). Avoiding my mother, who was glued to the tube in the living room, I snuck out some inebriants stored up in my room I had absconded from the grocery store—B&J wine coolers, a liter of Bacardi Dark, and a carton of Camels. I drove to Keith's place. Keith climbed in and said little at first, handing me one of the aspirin-like white pills Alex had given him. He popped one himself, grinning. I swallowed mine.

Off we went, both of us nervous about the unknown high coming soon to a theater near us. We drank lightly, sips of wine cooler, not wanting to spoil the pending rush of the X. Zeppelin sounded more amazing than usual as the drugs started to kick in. The high was exhilarating, a combination of amphetamine-like snap and the clarity of hallucinogens minus the hallucinations. Alex had told us to expect a cap of euphoria, acute awareness, and an irresistible desire to reveal *anything* to the closest person. The need to talk and share personal revelations was supposedly profound. In addition, he'd said, should we ever choose to participate in a couples' X night, a growing movement within high school ranks, we should prepare ourselves for a no-holds-barred session of swapping depravity. As we'd exited econ class earlier, Alex had relayed a few tales of moribund proportions, rather shocking anecdotes in our red neck of the woods. I often wondered how much larger the dark underbelly of Durango Bay might be than my estimates and concluded, long overdue, that what I didn't know was probably a lot.

I took the off ramp exit to the campground, beyond which laid the big blue sea and a setting sun. I pulled up to a ranger kiosk at the entrance, my eyes black and dilated. Keith pulled out dough for the camping fee, muttering under his breath, "Don't know how you're doing this 'cause all I want to do is run away screaming from this spud."

"Don't say that. You're my support system. Get a grip."

"I'm trying," Keith said, tearing up with mirth.

The ranger took the money and gave us a hard look, and Keith turned his head to the side window, shoulders trembling from suppressed laughter. I sweated. The ranger made change and dropped it into my hand along with a small map of the park. "Number fifteen's down that road. Can't miss it."

"Thanks. Have a good one, my man," I said.

"*My man?*" Keith said.

"My main fucking man," I said.

Keith lost it. I followed suit.

We drove into the campsite. Alex's white Ford van gleamed in the middle of a roundabout. Alex stood by a smoking grill, downing the last of a Dos Equis, a pitched tent standing crooked behind him. He smiled as he saw Keith and me laughing. I shut off the ignition and gasped, tiny white stars flashing in front of my eyes. The shit was heady, strong and disorienting, a construct of manmade Eros and Ethos, a Nirvana hit, a seeing drug.

Alex leaned in the window. A menthol cigarette drooped from his lips. His eyes were toasted, charcoal black irises with green tincture. "Looks like you guys already popped."

"Yeah, we did. Daren here decided on the way in that it'd be cool to jive-talk the ranger, though," Keith said, and that sent us rolling again. Keith jumped out of the car, giggling like mad, and lunged into the tent.

"He's on. I'm on, too. Whew. This stuff always make everything so happy-wacky?"

"Among other things. Come grab a seat by the pit."

A strong breeze blew, full with tar and salt. Grey clouds flew inland from the sea, faster than they were really moving, leaving smudgy trails in a darkening sky. Rain was forthcoming. We adjourned to the fire pit. Keith joined us and asked Alex, "So what did Valerie say about boys' night out?"

"She said we were a bunch of sissy boys. She's ticked. She wanted to trip with us."

"She's X'ed plenty with you and your other cronies," Keith said.

"That's what I told her. She wanted to be here for the virgins' first time."

Valerie was Alex's new flavor of the month, a recent transplant from the City of Angels, blonde and buxom and brimming with tragic glamour, sex and booze and hot dark blood. She was not a trifling woman. I already liked her immensely; she was a cognate to our order.

"How you feeling?" Keith asked.

"It's…interesting," I said.

"Other words will come to mind soon," Alex said.

"I told you not to drink too much, dude. You're not gonna come on if you keep drinking that Mexican shitcan brew," Keith said to Alex.

"I *always* come on."

My hands seemed to need something to do, so I took initiative and unloaded the firewood and built a fire in spite of the coming rain. Burning pinewood mixed with the pre-storm humidity. We smiled about nothing and everything. The world was good. Nothing was impossible. Then hail came, unrelenting. The fire hissed and smoldered. Ice nuggets the size of nickels pelted us. We took refuge in Alex's van and sat in powwow mode. The rapping of hail became louder on the van's metal roof, like a tommy gun. Alex began sharing intimate details on Valerie's prowess in the sack.

"A really high-pitched kind of moan. The bite-the-pillow kind," he said.

"Sure, Alex. The other night when we fried you told us Valerie was into a threesome with Samantha. Last week you claimed she was so horny she blew you right in the football bleachers. She sure seems to be liberated for someone who claims she lost her virginity to you just last month," Keith said.

"Yeah...maybe I was misinformed on the truth of that matter," Alex admitted.

I guffawed. "Ya think?"

"I loves me my blondes, but I gotta tell ya, bud, that babe would eat me alive and leave my bones for the hyenas. I dunno how you do it," Keith said.

"Well...I *am* a lion tamer," Alex said.

"Is that what she tells you?" I asked.

"It's what I tell myself," Alex shot back, eyes glowing, too much like fallout, full of emerald gloom. "Tell us of Lee's skills in the boudoir, Daren."

"A gentleman doesn't discuss such things."

"You, my friend, are no gentle man."

"I bet she's a jungle cat," Keith said.

"If I need to come over there and slap the two of you around, I will," I said.

"Dudes, we have known each other for like, so friggin' long, man!" Keith exclaimed.

"Yeah, we have," Alex affirmed with a huge Cheshire cat grin.

"Have I ever told you how much I love you?" Keith said to Alex, beaming.

"Yep, that's what Val thinks. We're out here fucking each other," Alex said.

"THE WORLD IS A GOOD PLACE!" Keith yelled. "IT'S NOT SO BAD! WE DON'T HAVE TO THINK EVERYTHING SUCKS, DO WE? I LOVE THE WORLD! IS THERE SOMETHING WRONG WITH A LITTLE HAPPINESS? NO WAY DUDES!"

"You're fucking right, Keith! It's *not* so bad, is it?" I joined in, his joy, however synthetic, infectious.

"Yikes. The testosterone in here is getting low," Alex said.

Keith passed me a smoking bowl. I toked on it and handed it to Alex. The thundering hail suddenly stopped dead. The silence was almost as deafening. As if on cue, Alex bolted out the driver's side, lumbering toward the campsite picnic table.

"He's gonna puke," I said.

"Too much shitty beer on top of the designer drugs," Keith said.

"I'll check on him. Need some air anyway."

"While you're at it, maybe you might rap about…"

"Yeah, yeah." The air was icy and invigorating. I walked to Alex, feet drifting through rivers of melting hailstones. He stood by the now-defunct fire pit, grim yet coherent, not at all like someone who was supposed to be, well…ecstatic.

"You doing all right?"

"You always take care of us, don't you?"

"Yeah, most of the time."

"You mean *all* of the time."

"Much of the time."

"I was getting dizzy in there. Tell me, have we ever had the pleasure of taking care of you when you've had too much?"

"You guys usually get more loaded than me, I suppose."

"But ever?"

I had to think about it. "At one of O'Mallory's parties I drank too much tequila and passed out, and when I woke up it was four in the morning, the party was over, and you'd left without me. That *did* irk me a little, actually."

"Oh. Yeah. I remember. Keith asked where you were. We thought you'd bailed."

"Nope. Unconscious on O'Mallory's sister's bed."

"Sorry."

"I probably think about that kind of thing more."

"What you mean is that you think about who you're with when you're out, more so than what you're doing. Not very high school, Daren, but then, you're *not* very high school, are you? Nor were you ever very grade school. Hell, I'm not entirely convinced you really had a childhood, and I was *there* for it."

"You're high, man. Chill with the Freudian shit."

He pulled out a couple of bent menthols, cupping his hands and lighting them. He handed one to me, and we smoked.

"Most people don't get you," Alex said.

"No? It's all there for the taking."

"I guess Lee can see it."

"Oh my, we DO gots our thinking cap on tonight."

"And what's she think about your life in the fast lane, anyway? She can't be too thrilled, I imagine."

I frowned. "No, she's not. But all of life is balance, bud."

"Life is balance, or life is a balancing act?"

"Is there a difference?"

"Damn straight there is."

"Good and evil, white and black, yin and yang, town and country, matter and energy, time and dimension, earth, wind, water, and fire, sun and moon, life and death, man and woman, old and young. Balance."

"But it's not all *balanced*," Alex said moodily. Behind him, fluttering in the winds, a cherry wine-colored eidolon manifested, spiteful and menacing. It looked different this time. It had a green, irradiated trim at its edges.

Keith burst out of the van, eyes bulging, white teeth chomping. He whooped, dashed across the clearing, and jumped atop a slick picnic table at an adjacent site. He ran back and forth on the tabletop, sliding through the slush in mock surf fashion.

"I don't think that table's very stable!" Alex yelled.

"You mean it's an unstable table?" Keith hollered back, and fell to the ground in fits of laughter. Alex didn't laugh. He tossed his cig into the wet ash pit.

The ecstasy trip sparked an epoch of degeneracy. We drank, smoked, snorted, and ingested whatever we laid hands on, acquiring illicit substances one after the other with our parents' handouts or the meager earnings from our part-time jobs. We established a regular presence at the single head shop in Santa Crisca, making connections among the curios of a standard mid-eighties underground hemp establishment: colorful plastic bongs and ceramic wizard-dragon-skull water pipes, peace symbol stickers, rock logo sew-on patches, tiger jade crystals and beeswax candles, pewter figurines and black light posters, all lorded over by the touchstone presence of The Dread-Locked White Dude, complete with red, yellow, and green-striped Rasta beanie and baked ennui, forever keeping an eye out for undercover DEA when a rookie customer referred to his wares as anything other than tobacco paraphernalia.

In that grubby place, we found a buffet of offerings. Mushrooms, acid, ecstasy, cocaine, crystal meth, speed. An eclectic menu of Mary Jane ranging from African Blackweed to Humboldt's Finest Chronic, Hawaiian *Pakalolo*, Panamanian Red, Kentucky Blue, Mexican Brick. Opium—both the cheap, green, glassy kind and the authentic Katmandu spongy stuff, blonde hash, nitrous oxide. We dabbled in mescaline and discovered Gonzo-Thompson levels of endurance wasn't among our strengths. Peyote was a disappointment as none of us experienced Castaneda-grade visions (though our skills in the black arts of projectile vomiting were dramatically heightened). An elder to whom I could apprentice, an old sage versed in reckless exploration of consciousness, someone I might hold palaver with on the rhyme and reason of my occasional lapses in reality, would've been ideal. Unfortunately I knew no Yaqui shamans to guide me through the dreamtime.

And as always, our constant booster at the forefront of our adventures…booze, and lots of it—gallons, kegs, fifths, liters, tubs, pints and half-pints, shots and snifters and bottles of firewater. Three months flew by in a blurry whirlwind of altered states.

Lee arrived home from England. I was late picking her up at LAX because I'd been up until six a.m. drinking vodka shooters. I woke on Alex's Jacuzzi deck, decaying like a fermenting compost pile in the morning sun, the boys sprawled out around me, zonked, Alex's parents having vacated for the week to an Aspen getaway. I jumped up, groggy and shaky, and drove straight to the airport. She was not impressed when I showed two hours late stinking of Popov. I relayed apologies. She only nodded, silent all the way home. I dropped her off and left with my tail between my legs. Not quite the homecoming we'd expected.

Valerie called me later, looking for Alex, whom I presumed was still crashed. She invited me to a late lunch. I showered and met her at a café famous for killing hangovers with strong coffee and biscuits and gravy.

"I just don't see it. Sorry, honeycakes. She's a weirdo," Val said, washing her lunch (four Virginia Slims and half a croissant) down with iced tea.

"You don't know squat," I replied. It was interesting that the people most incredulous about my relationship with Lee were women. Interesting, not surprising. What men, even DeeBee's elder patriarchs, were really going to condemn such a thing in their heart of hearts? The sexist ugly truth was, few swinging cocks on planet Earth would pass on the option.

"Hangover helper?" She reached in her purse and brought out a flask. I looked around for adult busybodies, found nobody caring in the cafe, took it, screwed off the lid, and sniffed…high-proof German peppermint schnapps, nasty stuff, extremely unwise after my long Russian night. German and Russian booze mixed about as well as their origin countries. I chugged a couple of deep draughts anyway and passed it back to her.

"Daren, how long have we known each other?" Val asked. She sipped at the flask, lit another brown Virginia Slim, her fifth inside of an hour. Most of us were frequent smokers; I was a pack-a-day fool, Alex and Keith too, but Val was a chain-lightning pro.

"Not long."

"I think I know you well enough."

"Do you now."

"I do. You were a dumbshit. You were late. You're a boy…a *boy*, Daren. Yes, a loveable one, with half a brain in that mop head, OK. But come on." She snorted in contempt as her crystal-blue eyes danced. She fingered long bangs away from her face and drew deep on her smoke. Ash fell over crumbs of buttery croissant.

"Let it go, Val. I've heard it all before. I don't need it from you."

In the months Lee was in London, Valerie and I had become fast friends. Whereas Lee was beautiful in a goddess-of-Venus sort of way, Val's blonde bombshell bit was outrageously Marilyn. She was a child of alcoholism just as I; the irony of this discovery came about via the assistance of whiskey and stout Irish beer and tequila. I suspected her childhood travails made mine look like dinnertime on Walton's mountain. When she drank, it wasn't like us, with our sport binging and drinking contests, our blind, merry gluttony. She wasn't partying, not really. When Valerie drank, she put it down. And rarely, if ever, was Valerie *drunk*. I never once saw her stumble or puke or pass out or slur a single word. She never got the spins, never weaved or wobbled. She could outdo any of us, no matter the type or amount of elixir. She knew, far too well, about the mirror at the bottom of the glass.

With no provocation she said: "When I was a child, I spoke as a child—I understood as a child, I thought as a child, but when I became a woman, I put away childish things. For now we see through a glass, darkly..."

She smiled and blinked her Sinatra blues at me, took a long swig of schnapps. I was surprised. Quoting biblical scripture was a skill I'd not attributed to Valerie.

"Corinthians, thirteen eight," I replied.

"Is that right? Just something I remembered from a long time ago, before...well, before. You smarty-pants Catholic boys are so yummy. You have the Bible memorized?"

"Just the parts that make you look good if you say 'em in public. And I think the exact quote is 'when I became a man,' not 'when I became a woman.'"

"Yeah, well, we vagina people adjust a lot of dick-speak. Even divine dick-speak."

"I suppose you do."

Valerie imbibed for sustenance, survival, under a yoke slung on her shoulders from a hard-boiled Angel-City existence. She'd already lived lifetimes by seventeen years of age, an archetypal force, a Neo-platonist *daimon*, a succubus of the middle realms shaped to bruised, exhausted form by something black and liquid in an abusive wasteland recess of the San Fernando Valley (*anima mundi*, the imps of the perverse, causality-scoffing, chaos-reveling, guise-taking bastard stepchildren of the mercurial, had not escaped my attention in my readings).

"She was easy on you. If you'd made me wait for two hours holding three bags at LAX, I would have cut your fucking balls off. Not to mention she hadn't seen you for three months and you had a hangover when you picked her up."

"I guess you and Alex have it all figured out."

"You've got me there. Seriously, you're still in high school, for God's sake, just like us. She's a *woman*."

"I love her."

"I know you do. I don't want to see you get hurt."

"You're starting to sound like my mother."

"We vagina-people tend to make sense, sorry."

"Gawd, will you stop calling women that?"

"Maidens of the clam?" Eyes darkling, coy.

"If you refer to my mother again as a maiden of the clam, I'll do something drastic."

"Cooter kitties?"

"Knock it off."

"Bitches of the beaver?"

"Crass."

"Keepers of the honey pot?"

"OK, that one's not bad."

I left a twenty on the table for lunch. We vacated the restaurant patio. Valerie stretched, her contoured body drawn inside a form-fitting jumpsuit, and I couldn't help but look. "Let's go get fudge," she said. I followed her to a candy store on the next block.

"I dunno about any more impromptu lunches. Alex gets sort of funny about these things," I said.

"Oh, relax. You're, like, married."

"Yeah, but you shouldn't go around with your boyfriend's friends like…"

"Like what? Like they were my friends too?"

"I know I wouldn't want Lee to just carouse whenever with my friends."

"Even Alex and Keith?"

"There have been issues about that in the past."

"Why? 'Cause Alex wanted to fuck Lee and you want to fuck me?"

"I don't wanna fuck you."

"Ha! You'd pay good money to fuck me, don't kid yourself."

"My, somebody's full of croissant and ego today."

"It's true. I warn you, I'm not cheap."

"Val..."

"All I'm saying is it's OK for your precious girlfriend to have guy friends."

"I know that."

"Oh my God, you DeeBee boys are sooooooo insecure. If it weren't for the fact they're attached, you'd bronze your dicks and display them on the mantel to worship."

"Pshaw. Nothing less than gold-plate for me."

We laughed as we hit the candy store and took stock. I popped a couple of pieces of saltwater taffy in my mouth, swiping them from overflowing barrels of the bulk candy. Val bought a few slices of rocky road fudge. We sat outside the store on a planter, snacking on the rich, sweet fudge. A white van roared into view, screeching tires, Keith and Alex inside the cab. Keith climbed out the passenger side, sat on the window's edge, and spread his hands on the top of the roof. "I figured you guys went for omelets. We're headed to the Rock, gonna sweat some of last night out. Let's go, Val. Coming, Daren?" Blue Rock was a local waterhole, filled each winter from mountain stream runoff, algae-green by summer, a biker cow-kickin' camping ground with an arrant reputation for drowning kids and general pandemonium.

"He's not. He's off to kiss his girlfriend's ass," Valerie said.

"Shocking," Alex murmured.

Val squeezed into the cab between them, and they were gone. I went home. Lee called and invited me over for dinner with her parents, wanting to show me pictures of her trip. I was on my way out when my mother peppered me with a barrage of college queries. I made my common mistake of engaging her in her inebriated state. After two hours of circling wagons, I extricated myself from the familiar roundabout and drove to Lee's house, irritable, weary, pushing the VW up to eighty. At one point the car hurled itself over a cattle guard, and I heard the muffler pipe clatter on the road behind me. The engine, minus its silencer, bleated like a mechanical goat. At Lee's, I cut the engine, popped the shift into neutral, and glided to a quiet halt. I popped a breath mint in my mouth. I was more than late. All lights were off. I clambered over the gate to the house and crept by the pool to her bedroom's glass entry. I tried the slider door, and it eased open. I smiled. The fact she still expected my arrival pleased me. I slid the door shut, took off my sneakers, and crawled on top of her. She mumbled, waking, putting her arms around me, her mouth flowering open under mine.

"You're very late."

"I'm sorry. My mother was being difficult."

"You mean *you* were being difficult."

"Probably."

"Two mothers you upset tonight."

"Great. She was mad?"

"Of course. You're a bastard. But I missed you anyway."

"I missed you too."

I lifted her nightshirt and buried my head in her shoulder, and I remembered what we were, and we cried and loved for a time.

Later, snuggled in the crux of my arm, she squirmed and tossed and turned. "You should have called."

"I know. I'm sorry. It won't happen again."

Promises, promises.

"I hope I'm not sounding like it's not a big deal. Because it is."

"I know."

"Do you?"

"Do we have to talk about this right now?"

She rolled away from me, grabbed her robe, stood up, and paced angrily to her bathroom doorway. "Yes, we do. This isn't Romper Room. Missing scheduled dinners and appointments, like picking up your girlfriend at the airport, is immature."

"I told you I was sorry about that."

"We didn't talk all the way home."

"I figured you were too upset."

"How gallant. How respectful. I'd accept that excuse except for the fact you smelled like a brewery."

"I'm sorry that…"

"You're sorry that what? That you hadn't seen me for three months and that you forgot? You overslept because you were hung over? Am I supposed to be OK with that?"

"Shh. Your parents are going to hear us."

I felt her powerful anger.

Cross ravens are formidable.

"It's OK for them to hear my boyfriend sneaking in their house in the middle of the night to screw their daughter, but not OK for them to hear me yelling at you?"

"Is that what I did? Sneak up here to screw you?"

"Maybe you should go."

I began to toss on clothes. "Why did we sleep together if you're mad at me?"

"That was a stupid thing to say. You're drinking too much. I don't like it. You haven't even asked me about the school in England, or about any of my adventures. Nothing!"

"I was getting to that."

"But only *after* you got laid, right?"

"That's not true."

"Do you want to know what I thought when you found me at the terminal yesterday?"

"What's that?"

"I thought, 'There's a mother's son.'"

Cut to the quick. Ouch.

"How profound."

"If the shoe fits."

"I *am* my mother's son. Rocket science it ain't. See ya."

I left, infuriated. I revved up the car, and its exhaust pipe, sans muffler, roared. I no longer cared about masking my presence. The VW left a trail of smoke in its wake. Dawn crested on the eastern horizon, illuminating a gray plume drifting upward, marking my bitter passage across DeeBee.

II

"Fred was doing Daphne, just like Shaggy was doing Velma. Everyone knows that."

Our faces were pink, the backs of our T-shirts ripe and damp. My room was a sauna. Alex had brought over a fifth of Bacardi 151, wicked octane. The bottle stood empty on my desk. We were seriously fucked up.

"Velma's gross. Dumpy, four eyes. Shag's got more class than that," Alex replied.

"You think?"

"I *know*." Why our analysis of Scooby Doo was so funny had everything to do with the gasoline we'd consumed. I was so drunk I didn't even remember how we had gotten on the subject of that comforting, predictable cartoon with the four whitebread teens and their speech-impeded dog and the accompanying laugh track, to which Scoob and company would solve less-than-complex hoaxes with the greatest of ease.

"Give her a break. She grows her hair long, gets some contacts, works out a little, shows a little cleavage instead of that turtleneck, she could be a hottie," I said.

The TV was tuned to local news. Bacardi sat like turpentine in my gut. My head spun. Three anxiety-ridden days since Lee booted me out of her bedroom. We hadn't spoken.

"Remember the one with the ghost of the miner forty-niner?" Alex asked.

"And the one with the undersea diver ghost?"

"Oh, yeah! And the swamp witch."

"Yeah, and the Tiki god ghost on that island. But see, that's the thing. None of 'em were real ghosts. Every single case was always some old man or a couple crooks pulling a scam. You'd think once, just once, they'd find like the Loch Ness monster, or Bigfoot, or a real ghost, you know? All that time cruising around in the Mystery Machine..."

"The Mystery Machine ROCKS! Groovy psychedelic airbrushing on the sides, green and red love flowers. It was grooooovy," Alex said.

"You'd think all those guys they busted, one of them would've caught up with them someday after getting out of jail and kakked 'em for blowing his chance at big bucks."

"No grudges in Scoobland," Alex replied.

We roared with laughter.

"The classic episodes had a cool seventies groove for the chase. When the gang ran from the ghost, there'd be a disco rock diddy, with songs that sounded like, I don't know, some dudes paid to sound like Buffalo Springfield, or David Cassidy, or ELO or whatever," I said.

"It tanked with Scrappy Doo."

"Actually, it was before that. When they started having special guest stars like Batman and Robin, Phyllis Diller, and Don Knotts. That was bad."

"Zoinks."

In fact (I mused in my drunken state), Alex had become a hard-core Shaggy, an avant-garde bum extraordinaire with a bitter streak. He'd been experimenting with heroin, crank, and crack, atypical city gutter swag difficult to locate in Durango Bay. We born-and-bred Dee-Bee boys had little exposure to horse. It's hard to be junkie-chic-sleek when bake sale fundraisers and Santa Maria tri-tip are integral components of one's upbringing. I'd thought we had enough inbred country yokel in us to fear syringes and track marks, but Alex, like clockwork, had busted another bubble. I was glad it seemed to be mere experimentation; he wasn't diving in full bore and continued to prefer old standbys within the tried-and-true hierarchy of the white-trash nutrition pyramid. The spirits. The green. The powder. The pills. I still hadn't had that long-overdue discussion with him, the one both Lee and Keith harangued me about, the same one they thought was imperative if we wanted Alex to remain above ground. I kept deferring, insisting that judgments, however well intended, seemed superfluous coming from me.

The phone rang. I picked it up. "Hello?"

"Hi, it's Val."

"Hey, what's up?"

"Is he there?"

"Uh, yeah."

"Put him on, whiz kid." She sounded bent. Very bent. One thing was certain. Valerie was no Velma.

"I should warn you, we've had a little…no, a lot of liquor, and…"

"Put him the fuck on, Daren."

I covered the mouthpiece with my hand. "Dude, it's Val."

"Oh, shit, we had a date."

"Whaddya mean, you had a date? We've been taking shots since we got out of school. You can't even stand, you fool."

"Tell her I'm on my way. Make something up."

"I already told her we were wasted."

"Oh well. It's not like she hasn't seen me wasted before."

"You can't drive," I protested. He was halfway down the stairs already. That excuse never worked with any of us. Especially me. I was an un-designated driver much of the time.

"Later, dude," Alex said.

"Later, Shag." I took my hand away from the receiver. "He's on his way, Val."

"Let me talk to him. I don't want him to come over."

"He left. I tried to tell him."

"What have you been drinking?"

"One-fifty-one."

"Great. Go catch him. I don't want to see him now."

"I can hear his van starting. Your house is only a couple of miles away. He'll make it."

She hung up.

I stared at the tube for an hour. I was drunk. It was hot, and my fan going full blast didn't help one iota. A sticky, grinding headache awaited me in the morning if I didn't down a boatload of water plus a few tabs of ibuprofen. The phone rang again. I decided to let someone else get it. Then I heard telltale steps approaching from below and hoped whoever it was wouldn't catch the scent of rum kerosene wafting down the stairwell.

"Daren? Phone. Answer it," Mom called up at me.

"Take a message."

"It's Lee."

I picked up the receiver, raising the earpiece to my throbbing head. I waited for Mom to hang up. There was a click and then a sigh from the caller. "Daren, I know you're there." Her voice was heaven, like a cold shower.

"I was waiting for the other line to hang up."

"You left the other night upset."

"Yeah. You were angry yourself."

"I want to fix it."

"Me too."

"So, how do we do that?" The call-waiting tone beeped. "Just a sec, babe. 'Nother call. " I clicked over. "Hello?"

"DAREN! Please come down, they're loading him now…WAIT FOR ME, OFFICER!"

"Val? What's going on?"

"Daren, get down here. I'm so scared, it's all my fault…"

"Val, where are you?"

"He crashed the van, Daren, he's bleeding…we had an awful fight, oh God, Daren—I'M COMING IN THE AMBULANCE, OK?"

"Go, Val. I'll meet you guys at the e-room. Maybe you should call his parents…"

"I already did. And I called Keith…"

Then the line went dead.

This'll be fun.

I clicked back over. "Lee?"

"Still here."

"That was Valerie. Alex was in an accident."

"Is he OK?"

"I don't know. Listen. I'm really sorry about the other night. We can talk about it. But right now I need you to come pick me up and take me to the e-room. I was drinking with Alex beforehand, and I'm too drunk to drive."

Silence.

Then: "I'll be there in ten minutes."

I went downstairs and splashed water on my face in the bathroom, looking in the mirror at my mother's eyes. Lee was there exactly ten minutes later, as promised. I slipped past Mom in the living room and got in the Buick. I took her hand, my head swimming.

"I know what you're thinking. I'm sorry."

She rolled her eyes.

"I party sometimes. OK, a lot. But it ends soon. I graduate in a couple of months."

She bristled, squirmed, frowned. She didn't believe me. I didn't blame her.

She drove through a cone path detour the police had set up for rerouting traffic around the accident, which had occurred a scant two blocks from Valerie's homestead. I glanced at the twisted wreck that once had been Alex's vehicle. The fiberglass body was crushed around the trunk of King's Avenue Oak, a fixture in DeeBee, deemed the largest oak tree in town. As far as the van...every inch had imploded upon the next. It looked like God had crumpled it up in his bare hands, except for the driver's side, which was perfectly intact, oval, as if a giant Faberge egg had been placed inside and then removed. I marveled at the precision.

Lee did not. "That could have been you, goddamn you." She held my hand tight. Five minutes later we swung into the hospital parking lot. "You'd better go see how he's doing."

I looked around the lot. Keith's Camaro was parked near the emergency room door, and Alex's parents' Cadillac. It was a surety I'd make a puerile appearance at best. Val ranting and raving, policemen,

Alex's holy-rolling parents, and me, wasted, a reminder of civilization's spiraling demise.

"Daren, I love you. Something's got to change."

"I know."

"You don't know as much as you should. Things *are* changing. I'm moving to Los Angeles at the end of the month. I have a roommate already. I answered her classified ad, she seemed nice, and she lives in Pasadena. I've got enough for a deposit and first month's rent, and my boss put in a good word for me at the firm's office in Glendale."

"Sweetheart, don't you think…ah, why didn't you tell me?"

"We've talked about it for a long time. I have to be closer to auditions."

We'd prepped for this inevitability, but hearing its actualization, the first thought that sprang to mind was it'd be the end of our romance and off she'd go into the real world, parades of city dudes with custom-made sex toys and deep pockets filing in and out of her apartment. The second thought, only a tad less frightening, was I'd have to immerse myself, at the very least on a part-time commuter basis, in the depths of the largest city in California.

"You're right, I know," I muttered.

"You're graduating soon, and starting college, and I was thinking it'd be a good time for a fresh start. Maybe down the line after community college you can transfer to USC or UCLA or somewhere in the city where we could live together."

"I didn't realize that was the plan."

"There *has* to be a plan. We can't wing it for the rest of our lives, can we?"

"I'm not winging it." *Am I?*

"Well, you haven't told me anything yet!"

"I don't *know* anything yet!"

"What I mean is that we're both at transition points in our lives. Maybe we can figure out how to meet in the middle."

"OK," I said, a little relieved. At least she wasn't dumping my sorry ass on the spot.

"How *was* England, anyway?"

"Great school. Horrid food. Cute guys with bad teeth."

"Cute guys, super."

"Not as cute as you. You realize you're relegating me to caretaker position. I wonder, did you always know you'd end up hankering a woman who can make you chicken soup as well as she can ride you, or is it a recent development?"

"Aw..."

"Go see him. I'll wait."

I stroked her cheek, my drunken Poor Bastard eyes withering under the light of her compassion. Yet Los Angeles loomed. I didn't want Lee cruising the Angel City solo. The traffic was ridiculous, bad enough to consider the eco-thing, which, for faux idealists like me, was a lofty aspiration. Sure, someday I'd own a self-sufficient organic farm in the deserts of Arizona or the forests of Canada, subsisting on solar panels and water power, where Lee and I, having reverted to a spacey yet brilliant Deadhead granola power couple, raised our three children named after astronomical oddities (Saturn the oldest, tending his hidden hydroponic weed systems in the attic, Wyrmwood the middle child, a withdrawn computer whiz possessing a genius-level IQ and a massive porn collection, and Sunbeam the youngest, born with nine toes and a heart-shaped birthmark). We'd have dozens of pets and horses and life-sustaining livestock like cattle and goats and sheep, and we'd drive hydrogen-powered vehicles, living in harmony with nature, tending our corner of the planet. Right, sure, totally plausible. I was convinced all the clichés were founded in reality, that LA was a city of apocalyptic portent, earthquake, fire, flood and mud, the rich and torrid, the plastic celebrity, west side and east side, the brown and browner, Watts and Brentwood, Encino and Malibu. I'd breathe its dirty sweet air and become a nameless drone. Couldn't wait.

I went into the hospital. Keith and Valerie stood at the doorway to Alex's room. Inside I heard Alex, who for some reason was cackling like a madman. Down the hall two sheriffs conferred with Alex's parents.

"How is he?" I asked.

Valerie snarled. She struck me across the face, splitting my lower lip.

"What the fuck!" I yelled, wiping blood from my mouth with the back of my hand.

Through a glass, darkly...

"When I tell you to do something, I mean it."

"Val, take it easy," Keith said.

"I don't see how that helped anything," I said.

"Fuck you, Daren," Val said.

"*What happened?*"

"I want a cigarette. I left mine at home. I had to run to get in the ambulance with him."

"They got in a fight. Evidently you and Alex tied a serious one on?" Keith asked. I nodded. "Yeah, you look peaked. Anyway, Alex tried to drive off. Val got in the van, they yelled some more. He kicked her out in her driveway, 'bout a quarter mile down the road he wrapped it around King's oak. You probably saw en route." He lowered his voice and whispered, "The cops think it wasn't just drunk driving. The EMTs told me he rambled something about wanting to die when they arrived on site."

"That's bullshit. He was delirious," Val said.

"They want to talk to you. He wasn't, you know, so gone he was talking weird stuff, was he? You know...like ending it, or something?" Keith asked.

"Shit, we were talking about Scooby-Doo, that's all. Nothing dreary."

I sucked my lower lip, tasting blood. Valerie looked like a whipped cur. One of the police officers came up, followed by Alex's parents. They were unhappy, to say the least. "You're the boy Alexander was drinking with?" the cop asked, taking out a notepad and pen. His parents had bounced me up a few notches on their shit list, which wasn't saying a lot; I already had top ranking.

"Can I see him first, officer?" I asked. He waved me in, grumbling. "Lee's out in the car, Keith. Keep her company." I tossed Val a pack of cigs.

"Oh, you prick, don't be nice," she said.

"Next time you slap me we're throwing down," I said, smirking. Keith took her out, and I walked into Alex's room. He was sprawled in a hospital bed, an IV dangling beside him. An ugly bruise marred his forehead, and his right eye was a crimson crescent of burst blood vessels, but other than cuts and minor abrasions, he seemed to be all right, more than all right. He was jovial. He saw me and put his hands behind his head, smiling, always cock-walking.

"Zoinks," he said.

"Jinkies," I agreed.

"This is gonna hurt in the morning."

"What were you thinking?"

"She was pissing me off. What happened to your lip?"

"Valerie happened to it. Answer me."

"I *wasn't* trying to kill myself."

"So what were you doing?"

"We were screaming at each other. I booted her out. I got the beast up to fifty in half a block…and I looked at Val in the rear view mirror, and I thought, fuck, man, I was so bent outta shape. I thought it'd be fun."

"What's fun about almost dying? I saw the van on the way. It looked like a grenade went off inside."

"She was screaming at me. I watched her flapping lips. She was spazzing out, and I just wanted her to stop. I could *still* hear her, man, a half mile away, over the engine and the radio. How's that possible, tell me? And then King's oak was there, and…blammo."

"You trashed yourself and your wheels. Just *because*?"

"Sometimes you have to cross the line."

"Why?"

"*Duh*, dude…to see what's on the other side. Sometimes the cast of thousands, it calls for sacrifice, or at least, no fear of sacrifice. Know what I mean?"

"Not even a little bit. You're full of shit."

"No. I'm all over this, relax."

"The fuck you are," I scoffed, no longer interested in his explanations. I went to the hall and talked to the cop for ten minutes, offering the standard *aw shucks* concessionary falsehoods (not the least of which was our whereabouts when we imbibed—the river was a classic go-to excuse for all of us, lest we bring authority down on our unsuspecting parents). I muttered meek apologies to his mother and father and shuffled outside. Valerie, Lee, and Keith leaned against the Buick, conversing.

"I think he's OK," I said.

"I was wrong about your girlfriend. We're having dinner tomorrow night. You'll be picking up the tab," Valerie said and kissed me on the cheek and went inside.

"Is she always that direct?" Lee asked.

"Absolutely," Keith replied.

"What'd she say?" I asked.

"She wanted to know how I fell in love with you," Lee said.

"And it was a sweet story, as always. Did Alex tell you anything interesting?" Keith asked.

"He says he wasn't trying to off himself. Says he was 'crossing the line.' Says he was tired of Val screaming at him. Wanted to see what was on the other side."

"That *is* interesting," Keith said.

"He didn't even care, dude."

"One-fifty-one will do that. Alex's father knows the cops who brought him in. They're gonna give him a pass. Still think he isn't cruising for a reality check?"

"For the last time, I'm not his mother. Let's go, Lee."

"Keith's right. If you don't do it, I will," Lee said.

"No, you won't."

"Then your friend is going to die," she replied.

I shook my head. "No. Alex is going to live forever."

My doppelganger, a twin contrary...

Zoinks indeed. Madcap high-jinkies afoot.

I2

I basked in the sun on a green, lush lawn at lunch, less than enthusiastic about attending classes. Two hundred-odd other classmates also
waited for our final exams days away. Ditching and leaving early had
increased exponentially. Small white butterflies and plump bees flew
between dandelions and tufts of crabgrass. It was a gorgeous day to be
young and free. Alex lounged beside me, rainbow Oakley sunglasses
covering a face still marred by Cordovan-shaded bruises from his
encounter with King's oak a few weeks before. He rumpled his hair and
spit Red Man tobacco juice in a paper cup. He'd been up with Keith all
night doing coke and smelled like rigor mortis warmed over.

"How are you and Valerie doing?"

"Not having sex. So, not great. You're going on the Hawaii grad
trip?"

"Keith and I are going to room together. I can't believe you're
not into it. Waikiki will be awesome. Eighteen-year-old drinking age,
white sand and blue bathwater, women in flimsy bikinis…what's not
to like?"

"Can't do it. I did it, Daren."

"Did what?"

"I signed up. Four years."

"You joined the army?"

"Not the army, nimrod. Air Force. Like my father."

Of all the people I had ever known, Alex was the most resistant to authority. I doubted he would deal well with a drill sergeant in his face, or daily calisthenics, or not being able to wear his Iron Maiden concert tee shirts and black leather motorcycle boots, or his three earrings. I could think of a hundred reasons why Alex wouldn't groove on the military.

"College wouldn't have happened for me. I'm not as *academic* as you are. I'll learn a trade and maybe get assigned to a base somewhere cool. Somewhere other than DeeBee, that's the important thing."

"Man. I don't know what to say."

"You can say good luck. Hell, I'll be done before you get your degree."

"Still...geez."

"It gets better. I ship out the day after grad, straight to boot camp in Texas."

"Your parents are OK with this?"

"Are you kidding? My dad's doing cartwheels because he thinks I'm finally getting my shit together."

"No drugs, no anti-culture, no more anti-government rants, no nothing?"

"I'm not giving it all up. You don't think military types drink?"

Keith walked up. "Hey, boys, we're still on for poker tonight, right?"

"I got little fundage," Alex said.

"It's just nickel-dime-quarter, like always. I have to hit my next class. One more absence and I'm toast. See you guys tonight." He trotted off.

"Gonna be a flyboy," I said.

"Nah, I've got shitty vision, they said. Somethin' else. They have lots of jobs."

"Maybe you'll be an MP at Area 51. If you *do* get classified, promise to tell me what the deal is with the UFO cover-up."

"Yeah, I'll do that, funny boy."

"You're running away from it."

"From what?"

"The red shift."

"What are you talking about?"

"Red shift. The black cherry cloud. Changing geography isn't gonna help."

"*Whatever*, Daren. I don't want to hear the wacky hipster shit today." He took out his chew, a gooey hunk of brown gook, and spit bitter mouthwash onto the lawn.

"That was nice," Valerie said from behind us. "I thought you were quitting."

"Relax. I'm giving myself my last free-for-all indulgences," Alex said.

"How's that?" Val asked.

"You haven't told her?"

"No time like the present."

"In that case, I'll let you get to it," I said. Valerie would take it hard, and she was known for excessive countermands. Alex nodded at me, shrugged, and started ripping her heart out. Mine wasn't feeling so hot either. I dreaded the coming changes of the guard. First Lee, now Alex, both headed out into the wide, wide world. My own immediate destiny, college—a.k.a. Extra Strength High School—seemed sterile in comparison.

Later that evening at the poker game, my mood hadn't improved.

Jim chewed on a cigar. He was near the end of his second six-pack of Corona, and his head nodded up and down. Alex was balmy wasted. Surfcat had fallen asleep hours before, twitching on my bed. For poker nights I dragged a creaky round table upstairs, at which we'd sit and drink and take one another's pocket change. The reason my parents never took issue with the raging going on in their house was simple: a touch of brandy here and there had hardly been unique in their youth, and as such, though they suspected we nipped at the bottle from time to time, they just didn't realize the extent. Red shift had evolved since their heyday, having mutated into something more scatological.

"This is when I take the rest of your money. I can feel it. I feel good," Jim said, gleeful.

"Five-card draw," I said and dealt. Alex's eyes lit up like a casino at twilight. He didn't have the best poker face. Probably why he had a grand total of three dollars and fifteen cents in front of him. I had about six bucks left, mostly in nickels. I glanced at my cards. Trash.

"I'll bet whatever you losers have left," Jim said, pushing out a stack of quarters.

"Alex bets first. And if you want to keep playing, try not to bankrupt us. Sportsmanship and all," I said.

"Screw that noise. I always lose twenty bucks to you boneheads, so if I want to storm out of this game in a blaze of glory, then so be it," Jim replied.

"I bet two bucks," Alex said, pushing out most of his remaining pile.

"Oooh, yeah, going for the gold. I'll see that," Jim said.

"Me too." I threw in three stacks of nickels. Alex asked for one card.

"Only one, Alex? Always a sucker for a straight. Two, Daren," Jim said. I flipped him two cards and dealt myself three, nonchalant when my flush draw busted.

"I bet the rest of it," Alex said, pushing out a dollar and change.

"I see it and raise. Two more bucks. You need a loan, Alex, you ask me," Jim said.

"I'm out," I said, mucking my cards.

"All right, Jim, if that's the way you want it, let me borrow eight bucks," Alex said.

"IOU, then?"

"Right. Whatever. See it and raise six."

"By the way, how did it go today with Valerie?" I asked.

A muffled voice from under a pile of blankets on my bed said, "Oh, she was on fire. The dean escorted her off campus after she broke several of the gym windows."

"I thought you were dead to the world," Alex grumbled.

"*Now* things are exciting. I call," Jim said.

"Kings over twos. Full boat," Alex said.

"Fuck!" Jim screeched. "Jacks over nines."

"Not enough!" Alex crowed, and Jim stumbled away from the table, disgusted. "Here's your eight bucks back, Jimbo." He pushed his debt of coins to Jim's corner.

"Don't have a coronary," Jim said.

"Party's over," Keith said, standing and stretching. He took off home, Jim crashed, and Alex and I drove around outlying suburbs of Durango Bay, drinking beer and shots of rum, trying to score weed from insomniac contacts awake at that hour. We stopped at several houses, attempting to rouse some of Alex's hooks, rapping on darkened windows, to no avail.

I rounded a bend near Alex's house, noting absently that I was weaving across the center yellow line of the road. I wondered if Alex noticed. I looked in the rearview mirror and assumed the black-and-white law enforcement vehicle behind me *did* notice. I counted seconds until the red lights turned on (four). Alex scrambled, trying to make a presentation of sobriety, lighting a smoke to cover the liquor odor. I pulled over as Alex frantically tossed empty cans and the near-empty bottle of rum under his seat.

"Don't bother," I said.

"Why not?"

"It was bound to happen sooner or later."

I opened my door and stumbled toward the cops to meet the approaching officer halfway. His partner called out from the passenger side of the cruiser, "Son, get back in your car." The oncoming officer grabbed the grip of his gun. Its leather holster creaked, sinister and promising.

"It's OK. No tests. I'm drunk as a skunk," I said.

The cop shrugged. "You don't mind if we determine that for ourselves, do you?"

I chattered the whole time they tested me, writing backward alphabets, following line-of-sight, standing on one foot and touching my nose, all the regular field tests. I'd been through them before. The cops mused on what kind of a half-ass dimwit would walk up to them announcing his guilt. They read me my rights, handcuffed me, then Alex, and stuffed us both into the back of their cruiser.

They dropped Alex off at his home on the way to juvie. They uncuffed him, and then he whispered to me, "Are you out of control or what?"

"Funny. That's what I was supposed to ask *you*."

"Whaddya mean?"

"You know, I should've looked. I should've looked at you, when we were in the desert, at the diner. Maybe then I'd know the real deal, and I wouldn't have to dance this stupid dance. Don't you get sick of walking on ice all the time? You're not me! I'm not you! The candle doesn't have two ends!"

"Dude, you're scaring me."

Dark and drunk, I replied: "Dude, you scare everybody! Are you dreaming me? Do you even know? Don Juan told Carlos his other astral self was dreaming *him*. Not the other way around, like Carlos thought. Wouldn't that be a hoot? I'm a figment. Better still, I'm *your* figment. How 'bout them apples, Alexandria?"

"Who the fuck is Carlos?"

"Someone better at this shit than I am."

"Fuckin' Daren, always got Pop Rocks and Coke on the brain."

"And yet here you go inside to your bed, and here I go off to lockup, and you're the unwashed soul on the road to death or worse, and I'm the upstanding citizen assigned to keep you in check. Go figure."

"Should I call Lee?"

"Don't even think about it."

He sulked in under the baleful glare of his parents waiting, scowling, condemning from afar. I sank down in my seat. If I hadn't yet taken the slot of Public Enemy Number One on their list by now, I had to be second only behind El Diablo his eternally damned self.

Durango Bay had no sanctioned holding facility for minors. They took me over the hill to Santa Crisca's juvenile hall. After a Breathalyzer test, which I failed at an impressive point-two-six rating (point-three-zero being the estimated crossing line for coma or acute alcohol poisoning), they tossed me in a cell, and I sat there, minutes dragging along like years. The confined space, coupled with my bleary state, was maddening. The cells were encased in chicken wired, double-thick, shatterproof glass. Three cops stood in the office. They filled out paperwork, drank coffee, and cracked jokes. I listened to the punch lines, disenchanted. They offered me my requisite phone call. I considered calling Lee and rang my parents instead. My mother yelled, then cried, then told me I needed the lesson and said she'd come for me in the morning, and perhaps I might use the downtime to consider my actions. I contemplated tossing out a vindictive retort like *I'm my mother's son.* She hung up on me before I got the chance.

Back in my cell, a distraught Latino kid in an adjacent chamber paced back and forth. Bloodstains dotted his gray sweatshirt. He stopped short and began to speak. His voice was muffled through the heavy glass, but his statements were, unfortunately, audible enough.

"I have these dreams. Not nice dreams. I wake up sweating and scared so bad sometimes I piss the bed. The dreams, they're about missiles bringing walls of fire and dirty rain. Little children burning, *ese*, their hair burned off. I watch it happen. My *madre* burns, my sister burns, they're all dying, and birds stop flying and flowers stop growing."

I was terrified. Not because it was my first time in kiddie jail or that I was going to be charged with a DUI, or that I was afraid of what Lee would say about my criminal activity, nor even that the delusory kid next door was on a bad mix of PCP and might come crashing through the cell glass to strangle me. No—of what he spoke, I was familiar.

"Do you dream?" he asked.

"In *my* dreams, I see the incoming warheads streaking across the sky," I admitted.

"Yes!"

"And the aftermath, the firestorm, the mushroom cloud."

"Yes! I am always alive to see the suffering."

Jesus, gimme a break, I was drunk driving, not heralding the end of the world.

"They're only dreams. In real life we wouldn't be watching. We'd be dead like everybody else."

That seemed to placate him. "Yes...that *is* a relief. Being with your family in heaven is one thing, *amigo*. Watching their faces melt is something else."

I'd like to go home now.

13

Tabitha fidgeted in her white graduation gown, flicking a dangling gold tassel out of her face. The class of '86 was sweltering. "It's too hot. I wish the dean would talk faster," Tabitha said. Our school administrator continued calling names and handing out diplomas.

"You look fine," I said. Alex and Keith passed a pint of Jack Daniels back and forth. Alex held out the pint; I shook my head. I had deferred any alcohol consumption until after the ceremony. I looked up into the stands full of flashing cameras and video cameras. Strutting fathers jockeyed for position, my parents included.

I'd been invited to UCLA and USC undergrad programs. Instead of accepting, I decided to attend community college in Santa Crisca instead, transfer into a Cal State or a UC after two years. I extolled the virtues of saving my parents a few bucks. Dad bit. Mom didn't. Nor did Lee, and she was not happy. She sat in the stands next to my family, Ray-Ban shades covering her deep browns and icy mood.

Alex whispered, "If he doesn't wind down soon, I'm going to pee right here in the stands."

"Alex, if you even think about whipping it out, I'll kill you," Tabby hissed.

A loud burp sounded across the crowd of graduates. Laughter disrupted the dean's oration. Alex and Keith got up to join the procession up to the podium, a bottle clinking on the tarred track beneath them. "*Alex!*" A familiar voice shouted from the crowd; it was Valerie, alongside Alex's parents, a bulky video camera perched on her shoulder. Most red-blooded fellas on the field had their eyes fastened on Valerie's chest, about to pop right out of an electric blue blouse. Alex twirled to the cheers of underclassmen as Valerie catcalled. She claimed she'd be joining Alex after finishing school, the next year, wherever he was stationed. I doubted they'd withstand the rigors of a long distance relationship.

Most everybody in our school's small stadium was elated. I was not. The DUI and the pending loss of licensure left me sedate and a little rancorous. I was due to be arraigned and sentenced on the same day in the middle of July, a month away. Perhaps I could appeal to the judge's sensibilities, an eloquent statement reminding the court I was shaping up to be a productive asset to society, an aspiring collegian with a high GPA en route to imminent graduate studies, and that giving me a pass would be helping the world at large. Cue laugh track.

When I took my diploma, I peeked at Lee. She was on her feet cheering with my parents. I knew her heart wasn't in it. A vision of Alex throwing himself on a military-issue saber flashed in my mind, followed by a distressing image of a beautiful ebony raven sitting on the shoulder of a battered scarecrow. The stuffed effigy was crucified on a large cross marking the life and times of one Scruffy, esquire. In one of its straw hands it held an elongated corncob bong, its bowl ever-burning like the flame at the Tomb of the Unknown Soldier. In its other hand was a ceramic jug of whiskey, a traditional XXX inscription etched into its side. I dismounted the dais and returned to my seat, shaking. My "diploma," a placebo piece of rolled-up paper in lieu of the real sheepskin, fluttered to the ground beneath me.

After the requisite tossing of caps, graduate chaos ensued. The football field became awash in chessboard splashes of black-and-white gowns, hodgepodges of families.

"I want to get a picture of the boys together," Dad said, circling us like a buzzard with his camera.

"You're not going to get wasted before Disneyland?" Jim muttered as we put our arms around each other for posterity.

"What do you think?"

"Rough week, eh?"

Lee stood behind a horde of parents dashing to and fro. Alex ran by with Val, rushing through the shutterbugging as fast as they could. Everybody had one hour to prep-rage before we would leave for Disneyland, our Grad Nite extravaganza.

"Smile, my darling boys," Mom said.

"OK, that's all I can do," I said.

"Lighten up, man. Today is the first day of the rest of the rest of your life," Jim said.

"Oh, shut up."

"Congratulations, Daren," Mom said, smiling and hugging me, and it felt good and safe.

I went to Lee and took her hand. She followed me to some tennis courts away from the crowds. I pushed open a gate, and we sat on a courtside bench.

"God, that was a clusterfuck," I said.

Lee was quiet, staring off toward the south. "You're absolutely sure about community college?" she asked.

"Listen, it's only a couple of years. It's better this way. Especially without a car."

"That's not the point. How long do you expect me to wait?"

"Wait for what?"

"For our life to start, dammit!"

"What have we been doing for the last two years?"

"I thought we'd move in together. Maybe someday get married, have kids, be professionals. All the American dream stuff, I guess."

"We *will* do those things, honey. After I'm done."

"After you're done doing what? Studying for a career? Or extending your adolescence? Which is it, Daren?" I said nothing. "Good answer," she snapped.

"We have to talk about this today?"

"It's life, Daren. Not just some obscure abstract for your keen analytical mind to ponder. You can't expect things to officially start when you're done with school. I can't wait that long. You are not the center of the universe."

"This is about the DUI, right?"

"You don't get it, do you?"

"I get you're thinking I'm a kid because I made a couple of mistakes."

"I have *never* seen you as a kid, and you know it. Sometimes, and I know you don't like to hear this, but we *are* at different phases in life. There *is* an age difference, under certain circumstances."

"That's all bullshit in our case. We've been over this."

"Yes, most of the time. But once in a while it creates hurdles. Face it. Hurdle them with me, for God's sake. You can't keep traveling both paths."

"Because I'm going to community college for a couple of years instead of shacking up with you in that pigsty of a city you're moving to, that's why all of a sudden there's an age difference?"

I knew what she was going to say before she said it. "Maybe we need a break."

"A break. All 'cause I drank too much last week."

"That's not the only part of it, but you *are* drinking too much. I know this isn't the best time, but I've tried to be there for you regardless. And I can't do that anymore. Not right now."

"Great. A DUI, then the love of my life bails out on graduation day. This gets better and better."

"Yes, and none of it's your fault, right?"

"I didn't say that."

"I'm not saying it's forever. I love you with all my heart. I've never understood why you need to drink as much as you do. You're so much better than that. And what with your mother and everything you know about alcohol…it's truly saddening."

"I guess this means, like, we date other people? Basically you want to rid yourself of excess baggage before you enter the Hollywood scene." Hot, twisted jealousy brewing, mixing with self-loathing, anger rushing to the forefront…

"Daren…"

"So you can be a whore, right? So you can make yourself available, right?"

"I'm leaving now," Lee said and walked toward the gate.

"Fucking whore."

I wanted to hurt her. I wanted her to feel what I was feeling. Her brimming wet eyes were heartbroken. Still she refused to cast stones.

"Not everything in life is self-gratification, you know. You could have killed someone. Getting arrested was a lot better than the worst-case scenario."

"Go. Don't worry about me. We're only soul mates."

"Do you know what hurts the most? My real fear is I've lost my true flesh-and-blood friend, the one who accepted me for what I am, and I'll never get him back because he can't reconcile our different places in life."

With tearful resolution the raven flew away, her words falling on me like a ton of bricks, more crushing than any lame insult I'd managed. I stood alone on the tennis court for a moment. My mind whirled. Her figure disappeared into the crowd, across the football field. My black gown fluttered in the breeze. I left it there. I needed no keepsakes for the day. I wandered, tending my lit fuse. I touched base with my parents, who wished me safe tidings on my journey that evening. I changed clothes in the stadium's bathroom and boarded my assigned bus.

On the ride down to Disneyland, Alex and Keith consumed a bag of 'shrooms. They'd also smuggled in a few flasks of aqua vitae. When the boys learned that Lee would be heading off to LA minus one boyfriend they were sympathetic, handing off two of the liquor tins to me. I took them and downed generous gulps of rum. By the time we reached Anaheim's city limits, I was snookered. I sat behind a couple of inebriated girls who babbled away, giddy with milestones. One of them, a shapely blonde named Kelly, used to have a crush on me a few years back. I flirted with her as the bus circled the giant Disney parking lot, and we talked of adventures awaiting us post-high school. We traded shots of rum, and I lamented the sad state of affairs under which I was operating, which, not so coincidentally, seemed to perk up

Kelly. Soon everyone stumbled out of the buses, high as kites, drunk as skunks, rolling stoned. Of course we were chaperoned by a few tired teachers working for overtime pay, who would park themselves on Main Street benches and let us wreak havoc unsupervised and wait for the early morning end of festivities. Our class joined thousands of other graduates lining up for the special all-night Disney gala.

I followed Alex and Keith as we weaved through the multitudes to get near the front gate, where, at the stroke of nine p.m., Disneyland would open its arms, and the mad dash for the rides, minus their usual lines, would be choice pickings for the fastest feet. They stared at the miasma of Disney neon. I didn't know how they were managing, there was so much theme park circus mass and movement and noise and stimuli. If I'd consumed any hallucinogens, considering the events of the last seven days, I'd have been a drooling zombie. Alex presented the plan—we'd bolt to Space Mountain and then head straight to Pirates of the Caribbean, the two flagship attractions. After that the park would be too full to hit any more rides without lines. He kept repeating over and over that we had to run as fast as we could to Tomorrowland before the throngs swarmed the popular area.

No big deal, aren't we always on the run to Tomorrowland?

Somebody from the mouse's kingdom rang a bell. The metal gates, adorned in wrought-iron caricatures of Disney icons, swung open. I was starting to follow the off-and-running charge when someone grabbed my hand. It was Kelly. She asked me where I was going. I explained to her we were headed straight to Space Mountain. She smiled a coy smile—*that* smile—and told me I'd have more fun at the Swiss Family Robinson attraction. Then she disappeared in the rushing surge of flesh. Instead of searching for my friends, whom I'd lost in the crowd, I walked to Adventureland, dodging sprinting teenagers along the way. Everyone in that part of the park scrambled for the Jungle Cruise ride and Pirates of the Caribbean. I stopped at the huge manmade tree house. No one seemed to be there other than a park employee monitoring the entrance. I nodded drunkenly at the girl, ascended a few flights of fake bamboo stairs, went through ropes and concrete and castaway exhibits, and reached a canopied platform area where Kelly stood alone smoking a bomber. We said nothing. She passed the joint, and I toked on it. I let the hit out slow, my head rushing as she stroked the side of my face and pulled me to her, kissing me, ravenous. I worried aloud that people would be coming up at any moment. She scoffed at the notion a "walkthrough" ride would have visitors soon. We stepped over a display's boundary ropes, and I hoisted her up onto a table, part of a contrived exhibit for dinnertime at the Robinson's island abode. I pushed up her short blue skirt. She wasn't wearing any underwear, already hot and slick. I dropped my jeans around my ankles and thrust into her. She cried out, running her hands under my shirt and digging her nails into me until I felt blood trickling down the small of my back. Chanel perfume and her more intimate scent wafted about us. I tried to imagine she was Lee as I looked out over Kelly's shoulder at the spires of Space Mountain and the Matterhorn. She twisted her hands in my hair as she came, and shortly I finished up as well. We heard the first few kids coming up the stairs. She pulled down her skirt, told me she had to meet her friends over in Fantasyland to catch Mr. Toad's Wild Ride, said it'd been great and she'd see me around the park later. Then she was gone. Just like that.

I struggled with my jeans as a group of kids reached the platform. One of them told me I wasn't supposed to be where I was (within the exhibit space, among other faraway places). I hopped the rope and made my way down.

That wasn't Lee. Who was that?

Who the hell are YOU?

Alex and Keith happened by as I walked through Fantasyland. They were tripping hard on Snow White's castle and didn't notice me one bit, which was good because I effused despair and stank of sex. I wandered over to Mr. Toad's Wild Ride. I considered enduring the long wait for the popular attraction. I looked for Kelly. One wasted girl passed by and asked me why I was crying. I told her I was lost. She asked me if I'd like her to help me find my mommy, taunting and catty. I almost took her up on the offer before she weaved away cackling. I didn't see Kelly there. Actually I never saw Kelly again. It was unnecessary for Mister Toad to emulate any wild rides for me at that point—I had it covered—so I didn't get in line.

Over at the Pirates of the Caribbean, I waited in line for a half hour and squeezed into a gondola with a group of hollering wastoids. Through the dark tunnels of everyone's favorite ride, I contemplated the tortured animatronic beings. Perhaps they had souls behind Disney software and plastics and they were screaming, trapped in an endless, repeating performance of mock swashbuckling revelry for drone-like millions, entombed in a subterranean gulag under the streets of Anaheim.

Tears spilled.

A pirate's life for me.

The rest of the night passed in a blur of cold, unfeeling nothingness as I drifted aimlessly, gazing at long lines and strung-out teens and tired park personnel until five in the morning, when all two hundred of us, give or take a few arrests, met back on Main Street and filed out. The bus ride home was more of the same, everyone in my graduating class crashed, snoring, spent, passed out…except me, staring ahead into a future unknown.

A few hours after the class of eighty-six had returned to Durango Bay, I asked my mother to chauffeur me to meet Alex at our local bus terminal. She waited outside in the parking lot as I shambled into the hub. He paced anxiously, smoking cigs, swaddled in the Air Force bomber jacket his father had given him. He too reeled from grad night festivities, each of us sharing what might be our last communal comedown.

"God, I need some sleep. Can't believe I have to go straight back to Los Angeles. I should've just stayed down there, took a cab. You look even worse than I feel."

"Long night," I said.

He was nervous, picking and preening. I grew amused at his attempts to improve his posture. "You think you can get rid of that slouch overnight?"

"Guess I'm going to learn how to stand at attention pretty quick, aren't I?"

"That and the other million things you don't have a clue about."

"You got that right." Other new recruits from north county Santa Crisca loaded up their gear, consoling family members, saying their good-byes. Alex had already bid adieu to his loved ones, including Valerie, who'd elected to stay in bed rather than see him off. He zipped up his bag and sighed. "OK then. Private Alex reports for duty. This should be a hootenanny. Oh, heck, we can hug. You're not going to try and grab my ass…I think."

"Only if you're lucky." We embraced each other awkwardly.

"I'll see you when my hair's buzzed between boot camp and deployment."

"Do me a favor and don't come back a freako militant."

"Deal."

He hopped the steps into the bus. The departing shuttle took the new recruits off to their futures. I stood in its dust wake for a moment, tasting dirt and exhaust and change.

Lost my love…my best friend…my wheels.

Onward and upward. Or not. Whatever.

14

I went to court for the DUI citation and lost my license as expected (one mandatory year, another jumping through hoops like tolerance classes and AA meetings). I attended the prescribed judicial remedies with the usual lack of investment, sleepwalking through them.

Keith and I went to Oahu about a month after graduating. We engaged in a flurry of raging, aloha style, bombarding the beachfront pubs on the Waikiki strip. My recent breakup was a compelling motivator, propelling me to new heights of hedonism, what with the Hawaiian eighteen-year-old drinking age and the scores of single young women. It was a liquored free-for-all. We did the tourist rounds, snorkeling in Hanauma Bay, sailing catamarans, riding mopeds out to Diamondhead, taking a rented Suzuki jeep to north shore, where we ignored native *haole* jabs as we watched famous surfcats shred the infamous waves. Certain altercations in rapid succession proved it was indeed possible to be sleazier than the Disney tryst with Kelly, the details of which, at the end of the week, were vague: dancing at a pulsing nightclub, a New York brunette with pear-shaped hips snapping gum and drawling in a slutty Jersey accent, her long legs rising out of the rental convertible's back seat; two nights later, an innocuous flirtation at Oahu's international market with a redhead Southern belle on vacation from Atlanta resulting in a coke-fueled fuckfest in a stinking, wet, humid bathroom stall. On nights I didn't hook up, I was equally depraved, whether I was bobbing for apples in tubs of gin and tonic at a predominantly Polynesian party, hacking on green seaweed Keith had "scored" from a local rip-off artist, or popping cheap speed and hybrid ecstasy, all to an endless soundtrack of thumping bass and blinking strobes in club after club, one hundred-proof sweat rolling off me twenty-four seven.

When we returned, Alex was waiting for us, back home, his parents having taken him back in with his solemn vow that he'd clean up and attend both AA and NA meetings. Valerie was already putting aside funds for her own place to get Alex out of there, though she had another year of high school to complete. He'd lasted short of three weeks. He punched a drill sergeant square in the nose, claiming he was bent as a three-dollar bill, and ran naked across a runway loaded on cheap Canadian whiskey, just missing the oncoming landing gear of an approaching C-130 transport. For those infractions, along with his frequent insubordination, the Air Force had added a dishonorable discharge to his permanent record. His armed forces career arc had petered out faster than its inception. Walking out the base gates, he decided to sample the pickled hell of central Texas before coming home, mourning his failed enterprise, hitting on married immigrant senoritas at seedy roadhouses, staying up with the barflies long after the witching hour, polishing off any drugs he'd managed to beg, borrow, or steal, sleeping in alleys. He hitchhiked down to El Paso, took a gander at Pancho Villa's blackened trigger finger under glass at a pawn shop, slipped across the border to Juarez dodging aspiring kidnappers and Border Patrol agents. Under the influence of several watery Tecate beer bongs, he inadvertently stumbled upon a red-light traveling carnival, a Tex-Mex ghetto troupe part titty show, part cockfight, its centerpiece attraction a macabre collection of mummified, decapitated human heads. Retracting his bravado, Alex scrambled back to El Paso and promptly purchased a one-way bus ticket home with his last C-note.

His cheeks were bleary and gaunt, his gait was that of a long-imprisoned derelict, his eyes greener than ever, radioactive. *I'm a done deal, Daren. What do I do now? I got nothing. My blacklisted ass will be cleaning pools and shoveling shit for the rest of my life.* I reassured him it would all work out, give it time, simpleton idioms everybody used in end-of-the-line quandaries. I lacked an appropriate response.

With our trio now whole again, we returned to familiar ground, his slaphappy vow to his progenitors never having been written in blood. Rum and vodka and gin no longer got the job done. Only Jose Cuervo and Jack Daniels passed muster. We went through eightballs in a few hours. It was getting bad one hot Sunday morning, as most Durango Bay folk were huddled in houses of the Lord, when my second waking thought was doing a line before drinking my coffee. My first waking thought, as had been the case all summer, day after interminable day, was of a raven flying free, unshackled from tethers.

During our long odyssey through childhood, Alex and I had developed a mutual love for all things Van Halen. We used to thrash around our rooms to tracks from *Women and Children First* or *Diver Down*, playing air guitar, emulating David Lee Roth-style swagger. Eddie's wailing solos had converted us into diehard Halen groupies. One of the first cassette tapes I ever bought was *Fair Warning* (still Van Halen's best album). It didn't matter what I was doing, whether it was raging with the boys, making love to Lee, doing homework or sitting with a thumb in my ass, Van Halen was my personal background soundtrack.

As a result, a black limousine hauled us in style down the 405 to Inglewood in the heart of Angel City. We headed for the Great Western Forum, where our favorite band was playing the hometown leg of the current *5150* tour with the new lead singer Sammy Hagar. Like most Van Halen fans, we'd been aghast at Roth's departure. Yet the new album wasn't bad, more pop than usual, but we reserved judgment. We respected Hagar's solo and Montrose stuff well enough. The politics of Van Halen didn't concern us much. Eddie was still Eddie, and we wanted to rock. As Alex was destitute, Keith and I had chipped in to cover all of it. With the limo, two eightballs, four bottles of Jack Daniels, and third-row center seats, our evening was amounting to somewhere around sixteen hundred bucks. It was my last hurrah, in a manner of speaking. I'd quit the grocery job, ready to transition to Santa Crisca and undergraduate student status, riding my parents' coattails for another four years.

Fair Warning blasted from the limo's speakers as Alex cut up a gram on a black mirror in his lap. Keith gulped Jack Daniels, higher than he'd ever been (me too—I was gizzard-coked). Flying that high, even hard whiskey was wasn't taking the edge off. Alex stole the bottle of hooch from Keith and took a swig, grimacing. Keith grinned, his dark brown tan reminiscent of our Hawaiian decadence.

"I don't want it cut that thick. Make it fine. Thinner, man, thinner," Keith said.

"Why don't you just grab a rock and swallow it, if you're in such a hurry," Alex said. He was skittish. Before the limo picked us up at my house, Keith and I ran a covert mission and retrieved Alex at a field near his home. His parents had forbidden him to go to the concert, reminding him of his oath, the one he'd already broken a hundred times over, and he'd had to sneak out, embarrassing as it was for a legal adult to do so, if he wanted to continue living under their roof before Valerie got the funds together for an apartment.

That familiar emerald gloom set around Alex inside the limo's cab. I'd come to recognize it as a cohort sibling of red shift's cherry wine cloak. It would have been stupid to ask the others if they saw it; of course they didn't, just as at the diner Alex and Keith hadn't experienced the otherness. Perhaps it was a kind of synesthesia, my senses fritzing, crossed wires reassembled and jury-rigged into my neurological makeup from too many days of hallucinogenic sojourn, but no…I remembered Alex's initial red shift, long before I'd begun experimenting with chemicals. If it was an internal problem, it'd been mired since birth. I doubted it was explained by a quirk in meddlesome biochemistry.

I massaged the bridge of my nose. My sinus cavities were sizzling. I lit a cocoa puff. The coke-flavored tobacco tasted like mint and hickory.

"Trade ya a shot for some of that smoke," Keith said. He tossed the bottle to me, and I handed him my cigarette.

Alex turned to the driver, a poor mid-twenties fella who desperately tried to ignore our illegal underage activities. He wanted the big tip, and he figured he'd get one from the small-town, upper-middle-class brats in the back seat. "Hey, turn down the music for a sec, OK?" Alex asked through tinted separation glass.

"No way," Keith protested, but the music cut out. We watched Alex's racing hands carve three long lines down the center of the black glass. He passed the mirror around until we had all skied our slope. They sat back, eyes bulging, eyes black as onyx. Alex dipped his fingers in a glass of water and sniffed drops up in his nose. He picked at remnants of powder on the mirror. "Finger-lickin' good," he said, and dumped out more rocks from a bindle fashioned from a quarter-page of a *Playboy* spread.

"I'm cool right now. Put that shit away. Christ-aching vacuum," Keith said. Alex paid him no heed and began cutting anew. His T-shirt was drenched in body sweat, and I felt the considerable wetness underneath my own clothing. None of us had noticed that we were over-moist and that we were shivering because of the air-conditioning going full blast.

"Roll a window for me, Keith," I gasped. I felt sick. Too cold-amped. Too speedy. He pushed a button on the door, and the automatic window retracted down. Winds bringing gasoline and freeway tar whipped through the car, hot and oily.

"What are you doing?" Alex snapped, covering the mirror with his arms.

"Sorry. Toss a rag over it or something. I need air for a minute," I said, taking deep breaths. I leaned my head out the open window, gauging people in passing cars. Billboards and black telephone wire lined the side of the southbound 405 as far as the eye could see. I looked northwest, toward Santa Monica and Malibu, past the highways, over suburban tracts, out to the ocean and its raked sands. I did not see or feel any ravens. I panned to the east and tried to vibe her presence, looking at the mountains beyond Pasadena and Glendale where she had moved. Somewhere over that way she lived. I could not feel her. Even a guru-lama bloke would have had a hard time sorting through the junky airwaves and Angeleno millions. I tried to use the magic of occasional access. Nothing. Figured. Vacated of light, only a husk, the amphetamine handicap striking once again, the black juju had never been under my control; why would I presume I could call upon it at will? Answer: hubris, and nothing more.

I struggled back to reality, pulling my head back inside to find Alex pondering me. He paid too little attention to his cutting; the pile of coke on the mirror looked much larger than the last one, and it was full of uncut nuggets. I nodded at Keith, and he rolled the window back up.

"All the angels," Alex said.

"What?" I asked.

"There's no fucking choirs."

"Don't start. You're not freaking on us. It's just the snow. Chill," Keith said.

Alex stared at us. Green-black glow emanated from his hooded eyes. His teeth were gritting so hard I heard them grinding from across the cab. Sunken cheekbones made him look like a boneyard mascot.

"Yeah, give it a rest. There's no need for the cloak-and-dagger mumbo jumbo," I said.

"He's yanking our chain," Keith said.

"Whipping of the soul," Alex murmured. He cut faster, chuckling to himself, hands aflutter, sweeping the pile into three large rows.

"*Great Western Forum, next stop.*" The driver's voice from the speaker interrupted our conversation. The limo slowed on the off ramp, falling in line with a thousand other vehicles en route to the concert. The driver maneuvered through traffic backing up on Manchester Boulevard. Through the tinted windows, we saw dozens of scalpers, guys selling bootleg Van Halen tee shirts, and small-time drug dealers hawking at concert-going carloads. The blue-and-white oval structure of the Forum rose up before us like a white trash cathedral promising fleeting, empty glories. A neon marquee sign by the entrance to the huge circular parking lot flashed: *Tonight! Avalon Enterprises bring you Van Halen at the Great Western Forum. Peter Gabriel and Kate Bush, September 2.*

We looked for police barricades, a checkpoint Charlie, roadblocks, any signs of certain doom. Alex had spun a jinx. He watched the Forum marquee blink on and off, muttering. I wasn't sure, but I thought he'd mouthed *Abandon All Hope All Ye Who Enter Here*. I was sure he'd never read any Dante. But I'd been wrong about Alex before.

The lot was massive, endless rows of Cabriolets and Novas and Z-28s alongside BMWs, white and black limousines, policemen everywhere in paddy wagons, on horseback, on foot. Yellow-jacketed security guards with walkie-talkies patrolled in golf carts. We rolled down the windows and listened to thousands of car stereos playing various Van Halen songs. Alex told the driver to keep cruising in a circle around the event center. For a half hour we drove in silence, smoking cocoa puffs, drinking more whiskey. Tailgate parties were in full swing, aromas of BBQ sauce and beer and marijuana drifted in the limo. One young lady wearing a shirt with stenciled red 'VH' letters ran up and bared her breasts for us. We hooted. Debates about the validity of the new lead singer, "Van Hagar" slags and the like, flew about. A huge four-wheel drive, banana yellow with chrome-plated bumpers, blared out *Hot for Teacher* as we passed by. I wanted to be joyful, wanted to revel in the elation of seeing Eddie Van Halen, in the third row to boot, within guitar pick-catching distance even, but Alex's damned green cloud cast a downer.

"People are listening to the old stuff a lot more than the new album," Keith mused.

The limo stopped suddenly. We looked to see why the driver had braked. A security guy monitoring the limo parking area poked his head in and spoke to our driver.

"Shit," Alex said.

"It's nothing," Keith said, not very convincing.

The driver shook his head, throwing his hands up.

"It's not nothing," Alex said, resigned, and leaned down and plunged his nose into the pile of coke, snuffling in a huge amount, coming up with frosted nostrils and a powdered milk moustache. The hit was huge. His eyes bugged out of his head. He clenched his fists. I thought he was going to have a coronary on the spot.

Alex's voodoo bullshit was manifesting, of that there was little doubt now.

The yellow-jacket walked back to our rear windows.

"Dump it, dude! Hide the shit!" I said. Keith scrambled to conceal the bottles of JD.

"Ah, God…" Alex gargled. "What do I do with it?"

"Dump it, on the floor. Now!" I said.

The security guy knocked on the window as Alex dusted off the mirror. The coke spilled to the carpet between his feet, and he slid the mirror behind a crevice by the wet bar. We froze like deer in headlights. Keith managed to work the auto window on his side and clicked the button to roll it down.

"Hello, boys," The guy was a cocky fuck. He glanced around the cab. "Smells like trouble in here, yup, yessiree."

"Is there a problem?" Keith asked. I had to bite my tongue not to laugh. Our eyes were evidence enough there was a problem.

"Is one of your names Alex, perhaps?" he asked.

"Nope," I said. "You got the wrong car maybe?"

The yellow-jacket smirked at Alex. "Let's see some ID, kid."

"Forgot my wallet," Alex said. "Besides, you're no cop."

"But I am," said a blue-shirted officer behind the security guard. "Produce it, son. And if you're not Alex, you two are next," He rapped on the window glass at me and Keith. "Heck, you two are next anyway, ain'tcha."

Alex pulled out his wallet, hands shaking, green eyes vibrating, and gave his driver's license to the cop, who perused it and nodded. "Yeah, that's you, Alex. Gosh, the description we were given fits you like a glove, don't it. Some parties concerned about your well being alerted Forum security staff, as well as our local boys on patrol for the show tonight to keep an eye out for your limo. Even had the limo company give us the license plate, isn't that nice n' easy. They seemed to think you might be breaking laws of some sort."

"Is that so," Alex grunted.

"It is. These people really went to great lengths, wouldn't you say."

"I would." Alex said, seething now.

"I imagine you can guess who."

"I can."

"You look very much under the influence of narcotics, son. By the by, you forgot to wipe your nose. Dead giveaway. Jesus Christ, kids these days. Out of the car."

Alex stepped out, defeated. The cop searched him, then handcuffed Alex and handed him off to a fellow blue-shirt, who started reading Alex his rights. The limo driver whined and stammered from the front seat, explaining to the cop he had no idea what had been transpiring. I frantically motioned to Alex to wipe the end of his nose, completely covered in white, futile as it was. I didn't know what else to do. He saw my terrified pantomime and shrugged. *Sonofabitch.* The second cop led him to a paddy wagon and off it went, presumably to a holding area until the wheeled lockbox was full of concert lawbreakers and they'd take the day's haul of outlaws to one of LA's county pens.

The first cop leaned back in the limo cab. "I just can't imagine poor old Alex there doing all that cocaine all by himself, can you boys?"

Well, fuck, here we go...

The yellow-jacket spoke into his walkie-talkie and became agitated. He issued a few irritated commands to someone on the other end. He tapped the cop on the shoulder and hurriedly whispered in the guy's ear. "You gotta be kiddin' me," the cop said. The yellow-jacket shook his head, and ran off into the sea of cars surrounding the Forum. "I guess it's your lucky night. As much as I'd like to give your friend there some familiar company where he's going, there are more far more pressing matters on the east side of the lot than a couple more druggie kids ." He waved to our driver and motioned for him to move on. "But hey, who knows, maybe I'll catch up with you two later," he sniped, and then he was gone.

Our driver muttered vicious threats though the window as he parked. "I need to call my boss and cover my ass, you little pricks."

"Shut up or you're not getting any tip," Keith said, the first to recoup.

It had all happened in less than five minutes.

"Damn," I said.

"What do we do now?" Keith asked.

"Gimme a shot," I said.

Keith passed a bottle, and I guzzled a couple of swallows. We breathed for a few minutes, letting our hearts recover from their mad racing as our driver rushed off to a phone booth. People began entering the Forum. Sound began to erupt from the opening act, some LA metal cover band. I knew what Alex would have wanted us to do. It was a distressing conclusion. That didn't make it less true.

"We're going in," Keith said, beating me to the punch.

"What?"

"You heard me. Fill the bullets. Take your last shots. We're going to see Halen in our third row seats, and that is fucking that. It's what he'd want and you know it."

"I know," I said.

"Ah, just tell me, Voice O' Reason, are we gonna burn in hell for this?" Keith asked.

"This and all the rest of it," I replied.

We guzzled a few more draughts of whiskey, stuffed our coke bullets down our underwear, and left for the show without notifying the driver. I wondered if the limo would still be waiting for us later, or if the cop would make good on his threat.

"He knew. He fucking knew," I said as we walked.

"Maybe his parents said something to him about intercepting him," Keith said.

"Clearly something of that nature,"

"If he did know his parents would go to this much effort, if they said something to that effect and warned him or whatever, why didn't he give us a heads-up?"

"Maybe he thought there'd be enough people here that we'd get lost in the crowd even if his parents had five-oh on the lookout," I mused.

We passed pat-downs at the door, bullets unheeded. On the way to our seats, I bought a T-shirt, the official, sanctioned kind. It was emblazoned with tour dates and a green-and-black VH logo. The colors reminded me of Alex's fog, and I felt sick and sad. I considered buying him a shirt, but figured he'd probably pass on a keepsake for the occasion given the change in plan. We made it to our seats and took in the huge mass, twenty thousand people behind us, chanting for Van

Halen, the crowd a living, breathing thing. When the band came out, we stood up on our folding chairs and roared. The set was pounding, a clean execution of musical prowess and big, bad fuck-you attitude typical of Van Halen. A bump from our bullets, every few songs or so, kept us going straight through. During the encore I looked back at the throbbing auditorium. Thousands of tiny flames from upheld lighters lit the sweaty darkness of the arena. Two forces vying for dominance warred within me, one digging the concert, the other focused on Alex's empty seat. It was impossible not to think of Alex in a pasteurized jail cell, coming down from the giant hit he'd sucked down, in deep shit.

And I wondered if the raven felt me here in her new land of urban decay, my presence stirring her from the drudgery of her now pointless, empty life, and maybe, just maybe, she might sense my vibe, hopefully not doing so while naked under some guy, but rather, staring at a portrait of me surrounded by candles, worshipping her Daren shrine with utter devotion.

Walking out after the gig, my ears rang incessantly. They had incurred definitive hearing damage. I was somewhat surprised to see the limousine still waiting, albeit with an irked driver, and relieved the cop was nowhere in sight. Keith lunged for what remained of the drugs and the booze, and I stretched out on the bench seat, spent.

A week later, Alex went to rehab at a plush facility in San Francisco. He called and informed me of the overdue intervention. I saw him once before he left. I was hoofing it home from the grocery store and he drove by me. He waved and kept going. I understood.

15

Three months passed. Alex returned from rehab. He parked himself in Valerie's new studio and started waiting tables at an upscale dude ranch. We saw little of him. He wasn't supposed to surround himself with users. Valerie, pro inebriate that she was, received a free pass, though I found it difficult to understand how he was countering her dipsomaniacal forces with his newfound, untested defenses.

Lee called to tell me where she'd settled, somewhere in Pasadena, and about her new day job in the architectural firm's Glendale office. She'd managed to acquire a low-ranking agent, no small feat, but was disappointed in the agency's support, as the woman seemed half-assed about landing her auditions. The idiot broad said brunettes were out and larger-than-life blondes were in and suggested a platinum dye job and augmented breast surgery, at which point Lee informed her she'd sooner turn tricks at the muscle gym-pits of Venice Beach. She'd gotten involved in Glendale's local theater groups and taken a few vocal classes. Then we started arguing about the semantics of our breakup, which quickly ended the call in curt fashion.

Keith and I rented an apartment a few miles from the community college. We moved to Santa Crisca with the shirts on our backs, a ten-speed bicycle for me (my sole means of independent conveyance for the foreseeable future), and parentally paid tuition. The new pad was cramped: a small kitchen area, a bathroom, and a medium-sized living space, which served as our shared bedroom and entertaining area in one. We furnished it with calendars of supermodels; purple milk crates stuffed with textbooks, dirty laundry, and bongs; and the mandated tapestry of dogs playing poker.

Lo and behold, college wasn't that different from high school. It was still whitewashed, star-spangled education. The reins of the world dangled before us. With a typical post-baby-boom dearth of interest, we entered the rat race headfirst, its final destination outlined not by well-meaning instructors nor by personal inspiration, but by television, pop culture, and the fact there was little else to choose from. To resist was heresy. We were children of the West. Its facades fell into place as had been deigned: imagination gave way to logistics, colorful harmony faded to glum order, and almost all of our remaining magic was lost in the transition, our hegemonies of wonder struggling to stay afloat in the soup of media blitzkrieg.

One Monday afternoon, bored and out of cigarettes, I ditched my last class, an inorganic chemistry course that ran ragged over my right-brained tendencies. I wandered around campus drinking strong coffee from a Styrofoam cup. Young collegiate men and women skittered about, backpacks and handbags rustling. Skateboarders broke up listless packs of grumpy counterculture and aspiring Greeks. I admired a massive banyan tree in front of the student center. Its canopy spread out like a gigantic umbrella, and a bed of trampled, brittle leaves surrounded its trunk base. It smelled like stale cardamom. I shuffled through the aromatic waste and perused assorted flyers stapled to the tree. Numerous pictures of missing children blanketed the north face, their sweet visages canceling one another out in a jumble of pain and unknowing. One little girl's eyes, pristine as fresh snow, were heartbreaking. A yellow poster advertised seminars on new age meditation. A handwritten three-by-five card offered crystals and incense, its slogan the venerable image of a Gray extraterrestrial. Several posters called for wanted roommates, bottoms slivered into tear-off flaps. There were petitions and announcements for legalizing hemp, prayer meetings, and demo CD parties for local bands. I stepped back and saw the green behemoth truly. The efforts to sell mysticism and relief-in-a-bottle were gaudy. The weight of despondent parents was miserable in the mix of commercial offerings. I looked *behind* the advertisements; the tree was sagging, bent by the confused duress of human beings. The staples made its bark bleed. Paper-sheathed in horrors, glitz and money, cries for help, and demands for compliance, the tree had surrendered. It had been imposed upon. My head began to ache. This time I was able to whisk the curtain back with a concerted effort of will. The tree shed its victimized pageantry and became just a tree again. I collected my thoughts as I rubbed my pulsing temples.

I rode my bike home. It was a beautiful day, ice plant and pollen in the air. I clicked into high gear and glided down the sloped road leading to my apartment building. Inside, I tossed my backpack down on an easy chair and flicked the TV on. Psych books tumbled out of the pack's opening, like a hint, and I ignored them. I flipped past talk shows and afternoon cartoons. The blinking light on the answering machine caught my eye, and I hit the play button.

"Hi, it's me. Keith, save this message for him if it's you. I know last time we talked a couple of months ago, it wasn't good. I miss you. I want to see you. Um, if you're not seeing anybody, of course…strike that, I don't care if you are. Call me at work, OK?"

My heart jumped at the sound of her voice. I dug in my pack for my address book and found her work number and called her on the spot. The phone rang only once.

"Good afternoon, Samson and Associates, how may I direct your call?"

"You can direct me to the nearest auburn beauty in the office."

"Excuse me?" She didn't quite recognize my voice.

"You heard me, darlin'."

She laughed, and my soul rejoiced in the ravensong. "Hi."

"Got your message."

"How's school going?"

"All right, I guess. General ed crap. Sorta boring."

"I'm sure you're acing them all."

"'Course."

"Of course." She paused for a few seconds. I heard her typing on a keyboard, her fingers tapping in unison. "I miss you."

"Ditto," I said.

Angels do *sing, Alex. Suck it.*

"You seeing anyone?" My voice cracked as I asked her the question that had consumed me, nay, eaten me alive, for the last four months.

"Not really. I mean, no. Not for a while."

"Really."

"And you?"

"Nah."

"You're lying. I can feel it."

"Seriously. I saw some people this summer…well, that's not accurate. I, uh, dated a little."

"You slept with some bimbos, you mean."

"Yeah, I guess you didn't hop in bed with anyone since we split?" She paused. As a confirming diamond rod pierced my heart, I managed to stutter, "W-well, then."

"I didn't call to compare our dating habits."

"I want to see you too."

"Good. I miss seeing your face. Hearing your voice. Hey, I have to go. Can I come and see your new place this weekend?"

"You bet." I gave her directions. "Friday night then?"

"Thanks for getting back to me."

"I'm glad you called."

"I still love you, Daren."

"And I you."

I danced around the apartment. As easy as pie, she had made my world more topsy than turvy. Millennia passed until Friday came. I asked Keith to find something to do until late, or maybe all night. Seven p.m. ticked off, and there came a knockin', and there she was, calico-porcelain beauty as virile as ever. We said nothing. She jumped in my arms, ripped off my clothes, and threw me on my bed. What followed was shattering, ending in tears and calm, cool safety. We scrunched together in my tiny twin bed. I breathed in blackberry-cinnamon, savagely, relishing the long-absent musk.

"I don't like it," Lee said, stroking twelve-day stubble on my cheeks. I'd been toying with the idea of a beard and had been less than successful in growing a full patch of facial hair. "It's scratchy. It makes my upper lip tender."

"Tenderness is next to godliness, they say."

"Coarse. Very coarse."

"Roses. Lips. Velvet."

"It itches when I kiss you."

"In a manly way."

"No, in an 'it-sucks' way. Shave it."

"It's not even grown in yet. You have to give it a chance. It'll be soft and cuddly once it's filled in right."

"And how long will that take?" She reached over and sipped a glass of ice water. Drops of condensation fell on my skin. The cold wetness roused me from post-coital dreamstate.

"I dunno. Three months?"

"Is that all?" she posed, giggling.

"Well, I'm not a real man quite yet, you know."

"Could've fooled me. Actually, you've been fooling me all the while."

"Tell me about LA."

She sighed. "Lots of maybe auditions coming to naught, some gigs in Glendale singing at a piano bar, a couple supporting roles in dinner playhouses. I hate the nightlife. Loud and bright in the dark, you know?"

"I think I do."

"It's harder not having a SAG card. The dues are expensive. It's not about talent."

She was sad. Her idealism was suffering in the real world of acting. She didn't pace herself with the rush of the almighty buck, and so far it had served her—until the city. True enough she'd only been there six months or so, but a little dab'll do ya.

"Maybe I shouldn't have left, Daren. Maybe I'm not cut out for it."

"That's ridiculous. You know that isn't true."

"Do I?"

"Yes, you do. An Indian summer is not enough time, Lee. You have to run the circles. Takes years."

"Maybe."

"Maybe nothing. Stick to it."

"I guess that means you don't miss me very much."

"That'd be a poor guess. Speaking of which…so how about those LA boys?"

"Losers. All with *fuck me* or *serve me* expectations."

"Tell me about the lucky souls you gave a shot."

"*A* boy. Singular. I'm no whore, you know."

"You know I didn't mean that at graduation. I was being a prick. I'm sorry."

"OK." Simple forgiveness. I was unworthy. I gazed at her. She was spent and content. During our lovemaking she had been unreserved, venting. "God, I haven't felt like that in a long time. That was the first time since…"

"Since the last guy?"

"Ha. No, I was going to foolishly float your ego some."

"Please continue then."

"I miss this, Daren."

"Likewise."

"Was it, you know…good with somebody else?"

Comparisons with affairs and former partners are a dangerous gamble. One toss of the dice and *poof*, a heart blows in the wind. If one's lucky enough to hear the right answer, even if it's a lie, one should count one's blessings and move on…quickly. Certain presumptions ought not to be questioned. Those kinds of bets only pay off if one remains the other person's best lay, which sometimes isn't the case. I was confident Lee and I had little to worry about. We had awakened each other sexually. We'd mapped every part of our bodies and their delicate responses. The soul mate factor didn't hurt either.

"It sucked with other women," I said.

"Women. Plural. Oh, great."

"Seriously. Squirt and roll kind of stuff."

"That's nice. Treating women like objects. Thought you'd be the romantic."

"Ah, no, that was the last thing on their minds."

She laughed, and ravensong soothed me once more. Greedy, I consumed every note. I had not heard her *muzak* for too long. I was so happy she was back in my bed, in my mind, in my heart. She made all the clutter fade away. Clear of red shift, she and I *were*.

"How many?" she asked.

"Details on Guido the Pimp first."

"He took me sailing. He had a yacht anchored in Marina Del Rey. We went to Catalina a couple of times."

I cracked up. "You must be joking." Lee was a Victorian angel best suited in lace, with chardonnay and English tea. An actual London fog would fit perfectly on her and damned formfitting as well. The idea of the raven sunning herself on a schooner, coconut lotion in one hand, Diet Pepsi in the other, that pearl skin burning under the sun, was absurd.

"Hey. I love the ocean as much as you do, sport."

"And this guy...lemme guess. Fat, balding, promising meetings with producers?"

"No, an architect at the firm, crew-cut black hair, nice build, Air Force background."

"Ah. The Tom Cruise in *Top Gun* thing."

"Well, sort of."

"Mm-hm. And the sex?"

"You know, I swore I wasn't going to tell you."

"Oh, goody, I love stuff like that."

"His bedroom had ceiling mirrors."

"Good god. That's right out of seventies porn."

"Maybe. I can think of kinkier things I've done."

"I suppose you can."

"Sometimes I'd be looking over his shoulder, looking at myself in the mirrors..."

"Are you *sure* I want to hear this?"

"And the only way I got through the whole thing, *every time,* was by thinking of you."

"You're right. My ego *is* grateful. How long did you see him?"

"About three months."

"What happened?"

"He wanted to go to Death Valley, I said no, he called me stupid, I said good-bye."

"That's it? You broke up with the poor guy 'cause he wanted to take you to the desert?"

"He called me stupid."

"I've said much worse to you."

"That's different. You didn't mean it. He meant it. He'd obviously said that to women before. A lot. It was easy after that. So back to you…how many?"

"I sure didn't have any *relationships*."

"You just got laid."

"As simple as that."

"Details."

No way was I going to mention Disneyland. It wouldn't go over well, telling her I screwed some girl on the night of our break-up. I gritted my teeth, swallowing a lie of omission.

"In Hawaii I was pretty sleazy. Had some one-nighters."

"How many one-nighters?"

"Um…two. I barely remember them."

"That doesn't help your case."

"Are we on trial here? We were broken up, right?"

"Right," she said darkly.

"We're not jealous at all, are we?"

She swung on top of me, the moist, hot part of her blazing between us. "Maybe a little," she rasped. Her dark hair shrouded her smoldering eyes as she moved on me. "Maybe a lot." She rocked back and forth, moaning, and I moved up to meet her, and we joined again. Arching her back, riding her wave, she drew herself up and down. The talk of others had infuriated us into a state of rawness, an urgent pressing desire, and we were synchronous, rolling sensations of vulnerability drawing and creating us.

We slept late the next day. After a midday breakfast, we parted as an official couple again. It was the best kind of reconciliation, life-changing, momentous unbridled destiny, fresh baked, out of the oven, ready to eat. Yum.

Weeks passed, and autumn set in Santa Crisca. October flashed by in a jumble of academic obligations, sandwiched in between bright-blue visits from Lee, splendorous and decadent and wonderful. On Hallow's Eve, Keith and I decided against our better judgment to attend the annual university blowout; we'd gone several times in years past, and getting out there was a chore unto itself, what with the DUI checkpoints and small armies of police and tens of thousands of students, both homegrown and visiting, descending upon the college slums of Santa Crisca. We parked at a lot a few miles away and made the long trek in, past the cordoned-off roads and immersed ourselves in the mob.

Ghouls, apparitions, and demons howled. Their bulbous eyes and drooling fangs took on black-light hues under fluorescent streetlights. Dancing heathen jigs, the gremlins and ghosts and technofreaks paraded, predatory, marching in ritualistic processions of X-rated depravity. The lack of fluid reality troubled my blunted senses. Packed clusters of frat houses, burrito shacks, and expensive slumlord apartment buildings crammed curb to curb with ragers. Drunken Halloweenies consumed everything in reach, mostly one another. The main drag of Santa Crisca's UC student district was submerged in mounds of trash, plastic cups, party favors. Burning dumpsters and mattresses added brimstone to the stench of tapped keg and vomit. Costumed revelers followed the road's north and southbound trajectories. As far as soirees went in Santa Crisca, Halloween at the university couldn't be topped. All trembled before the black-and-orange bash at the seaside steppes of the university's flop-town. We bypassed several police checkpoints—the law enforcement presence was formidable. Sheriffs and local PD from all over the county had been called in for crowd control, stationed on every corner, many on horseback, outfitted with riot gear, helmets and visors, extra-length nightsticks. It was not unwarranted. If the masses rose up (and they did, on occasion, over the years), it was not safe for anyone to be there, especially a cop.

A huge body swathed in a giant condom costume dove through us, throwing condom packs every which way. The delighted crowd parted for him, scoffing at his antics, scrambling for the prophylactics.

"Safe sex! Safe sex! Have lots and lots of great safe sex!" the condom-man urged.

"Okaaaay," Keith said, bewildered.

"Like anyone here is gonna slap on a raincoat tonight," I said.

"Someone's going to slap that dude on if he stays up late enough," Keith cracked.

I tried to pick up individual conversations. "Have another piece of pie, you fat motherfucker." I winced at the gross condemnation, issued from a huge football frat lunkhead to a poor obese gal dressed up as the Kool-Aid guy. I prayed she hadn't heard the insult, picked up an empty brown beer bottle, and heaved it at the bozo from behind him. It crashed into his head and shattered nicely, a showering of glass tinkling to the pavement. A little blood and a lot of swearing and death threats followed. I wasn't worried; there was little chance the moron would determine who had tossed the bottle in the plentiful hordes, but a couple of cops on horseback had seen my anonymous revenge. They rode in. With Keith whooping and cackling, we bolted through the nearest fraternity house, over a few fences and hedges to the next block, where we lost ourselves in the crowds. It hardly seemed possible for more people to fit on the few square blocks of streets already brimming with bustling, burping thousands.

"You're so goddamned chivalrous, Lancelot," Keith said.

"Dumb bag of rocks deserved it and then some," I replied.

The shindig eventually got dicey enough for us to leave, and as it was a rare sober outing, we felt no need to see it to its bitter end. We hiked back to the car and went home, made mac and cheese, brewed coffee, and watched late-night seventies kung fu movies.

The doorbell rang. It was three-thirty in the morning.

Lee, bleary-eyed and craven.

"I'm pregnant."

"Um," I replied.

"Trick or treat," she said.

16

The makeshift performance hall, the bingo room of a church nestled between a Jack in the Box restaurant and a dog park in west Glendale, is chock-full of folk-band types, community college drama majors, and film student dropouts. We wait, anxious, joining the house in idle talk. A black piano and a mike sit onstage.

Two numbers, one jazz singer, one poet, do their thing. They're pretty good. The poet orates in a free-verse style easy on the ears. I don't pay much attention. Everything I am is with Lee. She runs a hand through her hair, and I reassure her about her appearance. She beams but keeps fidgeting. As the emcee announces her turn in the program, she gives me a kiss for luck. She doesn't need it. Her selection for the evening is Memory, from the musical Cats. We've attended the psychedelic kitty stage romp at the Pantages Theater several times. It's her favorite song, and she's rehearsed it for months (when she first chose it as her number, I suppressed an imperious biblio-dork opinion about Webber's hatchet job on Eliot's poetry. Still, there's no denying it's a haunting melody).

She prances up to the platform, pure form and grace, a Jellicle lynx undiscovered. The pianist begins playing. Dangling tassels on Lee's black leather boots sashay with the rhythm. Her voice is soft and reverent, *vital, angelic harmonies in pitch and tone. She never looks more beautiful than when she performs. Her eyes fasten upon mine, she manages a wink, and I understand, as her essence bores into my dumbfounded heart, she is singing…to me.*

She finishes, lips quivering with the resonance of her last note, and bows her head. The audience, small as it is, gives a standing ovation, led by yours truly. She bounces back to me, aglow. I want to take her out of there and do unspeakable things. Courtesy demands we stay until the remaining fellow artisans present their respective offerings of craft.

On the way home we are quiet. Words are cumbersome after that display of white presage. I don't know where she gets this kind of juju, but it's more potent than anything I've got, its trenchancy far greater than my chintzy fortune telling. I presume raven magicks are an elite power. That night, after accountings to friends and family over the phone, Lee the proud peacock she deserves to be, after cocoa and fudge-covered Oreos and hot showers, we share each other. I take in her blackberry-cinnamon as she falls asleep. I am happy. As I watch her slumber, while she dreams of Carnegie and Broadway, I fight the part of me that wants to warn her off, the innocent schoolboy always drowned out by the disharmony of the cast of thousands. He pleads with me to tell her to run as fast and as far away as she can, before I can downright ruin her, as mold corrodes a fine cheese, as vinegar spoils a magnificent wine. I do not listen to him. He is young and fearful. It is not I who will corrupt her. It is she who will redeem me.

17

Sundowner winds blew bits of Los Angeles crest mountain seed into my hair. I sprawled in a chaise lounge on the deck adjacent to Lee's apartment, the dirty air of LA spread across the city, downtown high-rises impaling the rusted gloaming.

"Another Sunday evening in the San Fernando valley," Rachel said, handing me a cup of French vanilla roast.

"Why don't the winds blow away that shit?" I asked, pointing at the glazy brownness.

"That stuff's a permanent fixture. Did you know LA's east basin has the highest per capita rate of respiratory ailments in the country?"

"And here you are living in its midst."

"Life's a beach."

Lee's coquettish roommate was charming and earnest. Her cerulean eyes contrasted with her olive complexion and golden brown locks, a small woman with an angular chin and a pert chest. It worked for her, like a robin or a nightingale. Most astounding, Rachel surpassed Lee's previous record in the arena of red shift—she had never touched a drink or taken a drug in her entire life. Ever. I'd never met anyone having that distinction. There was something unwavering, enviable, about a person whose consciousness hadn't once been altered by toxins. She was outspoken, having little qualms in correcting inadequacies. Mine were a sad lot to speak for anyway, and she loved to remind me of it. We had established a comeuppance rapport with each other. Her bipolar friendship with Lee, pals one day, adversaries the next, resulted in endless barbs concerning our age disparity. Rachel teased Lee, Lee's hackles rose, and I remained impassive. Been there, done that. But all that had changed now. Rachel was about to eat one huge pile of crow. I smirked and sipped some more coffee. Catfights. *Meow.*

Inside their apartment was the wreckage of the wingding they had thrown the night before. Glossy paper hats, confetti, and wine glasses littered each nook and corner. The party carnage inside wasn't like the usual aftermath of gatherings I normally attended. It looked *festive*, not orgiastic. What a yupster scene it'd been. A few dozen young LA neophytes drinking red vino and smoking brown cigarettes, complaining about traffic and commercialism and every other sore spot about Los Angeles they seemed to put up with anyway.

I'd finished the first year of college with the usual GPA average. My parents were pleased enough. Instead of taking a summer job, I'd signed up for a summer semester of school. I was far too comfortable taking checks from Mom and Dad, hot on the trail of white-collar professionalism, rationalizing it by presuming it'd balance out in their old age when I'd care for them, uh huh, sure, okey dokey. My summer classes burned a mere three days a week, so I spent the rest of my time with Lee at her Pasadena pad, taking Greyhound mass transit down or bumming rides from southbound associates, or sometimes she'd come pick me up.

As I'd predicted I came to know Angel City through hell and high water. We teased the street clowns at Balboa Island in Newport and hung out Saturday nights at the Hard Rock Café in Beverly Hills, where we'd ogle Keifer Sutherland or Charlie Sheen holding court with their entourages. We drove to Gladstone's in Malibu for seafood, taking Sunset Boulevard in from east basin. We caught moonrock Laserium shows at Griffith Park, stalked movie stars' homes in old town Pasadena and Bel Air. Mann's Chinese theater, Westwood, hole-in-the-wall diners in Reseda and Torrance, Third Street Promenade in Santa Monica, Venice, Manhattan Beach, Redondo, Palm Springs, Big Bear, the whole gummy shebang. The Angeleno scene was everything I'd thought it'd be. Not boring, big enough to both entertain and provoke, yet bereft of soul. It didn't matter. Bottom line, it was where Lee lived, and that was enough to endure whatever the place threw at me.

Rachel's orange pajamas were wrinkled and looked slept in. That is to say, *slept in*. She rolled her head side to side, rubbing the back of her neck.

"Oh, I must have tweaked my back, or something."

"Or *something*," I said, the corners of my mouth turning up.

"Shut up. What can I say?"

"You can say, 'Sorry, Daren, was wrong about the younger man-older woman thing. Pish-posh, do forgive me. Accept my deepest apologies.' And so on."

"OK, OK, Lee was right and I was wrong."

"She's going to rip you, and you deserve it."

"What *is* it with you Durango country boys?"

"Living a hundred miles north of LA makes us country?"

"Close enough. What is it, really?"

"Well, it's the big cocks, obviously."

She giggled as her face turned red. "She *is* going to gloat about this, isn't she?"

"You'll live. By the way...I never thanked you...um, for taking her. Thanks."

"Taking her? What are you...oh. Sure. No problem."

"No, I want you to know I appreciate what you did."

"Don't worry about it. She didn't want you there, you know. It's a girl thing. I know a lot of women who were the same way about it even with their husbands. You shouldn't take it so personally. That was ages ago."

"Yeah...but thanks anyway."

Eight months previous, Lee decided to get an abortion. It was an aberrant conclusion, an action far out of her spiritual bounds. Ending the synthesis of our powerful aggregate was tempting fate. I'd told her I would support whatever decision she made, even though I was terrified of being a father at eighteen. I'm sure the only thing that frightened her more than being a mother was, again, my being a father at eighteen. Rationales easily sprang to mind: her acting career, my collegiate progress, and no real finances to raise a child. The convenience of abortion is its ultimate grievance. Above and beyond the sanctity of life, it was more about whether we wanted a child together yet, whether we were ready for that. Tearful, morose, she'd made the appointment. She was adamant about going alone. I insisted on accompanying her, but she refused. She scheduled the procedure midweek, when I was in school, and Rachel took her. On that fateful day, shame gave me an excruciating headache to enjoy, a whopper of a migraine, every time-numbing second. Degrading, illicit imagery flooded my mind, her legs straddled in clinical blue stirrups, her intimacy splayed wide as our child was sucked out of her. Afterward Rachel called me and said there had been no complications; Lee had crashed and would call me the next day. I cried and hoped I'd be forgiven someday. I caught a ride with Alex the following weekend—he was going to San Diego to see *sober* friends—and when he dropped me off, she was standing at the top of her apartment's stairs, distraught as I'd ever seen her. We watched videos and ordered pizza. I held her as she cried, on and off, through the night.

Now, Rachel said, "She's still sleeping? That's not like her."

"She had too much wine. Most of us did. Not many people could drive. I called a lot of cabs for the old folks. We were pretty lit, except you of course. But you slept all day today too, didn't you?"

"None of your business."

"Right. I'm sure your morning exercise didn't have anything to do with your late rising."

"Do you always have to be so crude?"

"In time you'll come to appreciate it."

"That's what Lee always tells me."

"You're not going to tell me how it happened?"

"Well, hello, sleepykins," Rachel said.

Lee came out to the deck, puffy-eyed in a white terry robe. "What are you doing up?" she asked, sitting on my lap and hugging me.

"It's four-thirty in the afternoon, babe."

"But we didn't go to bed until ten a.m. And I know how much you need your beauty sleep after an all-nighter."

"I was restless."

She took my coffee for herself and blew on it. "Miracles do happen. Well, the party wasn't too bad, hmm?"

"A complete success, I'd say," Rachel said.

I smirked beneath Lee's calico mane, sucking in hot sundowner air. She drained the last of my java. "Um. More coffee. Where's Keith? He better not have driven back to Santa Crisca. I told you he could crash on the couch."

"Indeed. I gave him the option," I said, suppressing a shit-eating grin. "I think he found somewhere to stay. Somewhere better than the couch."

"No! Really? One of our friends? Who?"

"Yes, Rachel, who was it?" I posed.

Then Keith appeared, clad in a short silk robe that only just covered his nether regions, borrowed from Rachel's closet. "Good morning, boys and girls. Um, good evening, I mean. Sheesh. Daren, gimme a smoke. Hey, I got an idea. Girls, tell me where the cooking stuff is, and I'll make us breakfast for dinner, OK?"

He was stoked. He got a lot more than he bargained for when he'd accepted my last-minute invitation to their yuppie get-together. I reckoned he ran out of absolutions, after the party ended and everybody had gone home, about the time I lay in bed early that morning trying to ignore the noisy going-at-it in the next room.

"Oh, you bitch. After all the crap you've given me, Keith was the guy in the inner sanctum last night?"

"Whoa. Whaddya mean by 'inner sanctum?'" Keith asked.

"Well, damn, I was wrong, you were right. OK? We're done. Eggs and cheese in the fridge, Keith," Rachel said, embarrassed.

"There's months to go before we're done," Lee said, giggling.

"Screw breakfast, let's hit the drive-thru at In n' Out, get us four double-doubles, animal style," I said. A rousing chorus of agreement followed.

Lee and I were different than before. We'd crawled from our self-made muck and evolved into something else, seasoned and stronger.

Today, Los Angeles was a good place.

Perhaps I had underestimated Angel City.

18

No, this can't be right. There was a deer, and now the car is turning too slow; it should be going much faster, all this. Yes, the car is rolling.

I'm flying?

I land hard on soft, wet earth. The impact knocks the wind out of me. I am flat on my back. I gasp for breath. I open my eyes. I see the underside of the Camaro careening straight down at me. It makes a monstrous metallic grunt, somehow not flattening me to pulp. The metal undercarriage hops up and down from the spinning drop, just missing the bridge of my nose. I feel the breeze from the bouncing chassis. The Camaro has landed on top of me. Its hydraulic suspension has saved my life.

I look to the left, wondering why the automatic drive hasn't kicked in and the Camaro hasn't rolled over me. Lying right beside me is Keith. He looks unconscious. Or dead. Beyond him, between the two front tires, I see the serrated cylinder of a drainage pipe. I realize we have rolled off the road into the culvert by the golf course. It is sheer luck the car's front end has wedged against the angled road embankment, for the drive is still engaged; on a flat stretch of road, the back wheels would have kept rolling and popped Keith and me open like zits. The engine roars in protest.

Something pours on my trench coat, soaking me in a chemical shower. Gasoline. I try to turn and crawl, and now I know something is damaged as a sharp, grinding pain erupts in my left shoulder. My left arm itself is dangling, limp and useless. I cry out in pain over the din of the engine. I wonder where Alex is. He isn't under the car with us. "We gotta get outta here, Keith," I gasp. He doesn't respond. The pain in my shoulder goes nova. I bite my lip and use the right side of my body to crawl out from under the Camaro. I stumble to my feet, lurching in my sopping coat, gas burning my eyes and nostrils. My shoulder is dislocated. The only thing I can think to do is to jerk my arm back into the socket somehow. The pain is exquisite and incapacitating. I grasp my wrist with my right hand and pull my limp left arm up over my shoulder. Pangs of agony almost put me down. I jerk the flopping limb upward. It slides back into the socket, tearing ligaments. I scream. Rat-bastard, it hurts.

Gas still gushes over Keith. I don't know what to do. I look for Alex. The deer's head lies on the road, grisly, and its decapitated body is flattened against a hill above the drainage ditch. Keith's Camaro is a white, misshapen thing in the blinding light of the full moon, splattered with bloodied venison. There will be no repairs. It has joined Alex's van into the depths of history. I hobble over to the wreck. Its driver-side door, crumpled like tin foil, is wide open. A torn seatbelt hangs out. I reach in and turn off the ignition, hoping that no sparks will fly. The Camaro sputters and ends its death whine.

No sound at all for ten seconds, other than the splashing of gas. I am lost.

*I speak to Keith, shaky. "Dude, are you OK? Can you h-hear me? Keith?" He doesn't answer. All the accident clichés are running hilly-nilly through my chaotic mind—*don't *move victims, gasoline spillage, fuck, what do I do?* I cry as I decide to decide, and suddenly Alex's voice comes from over behind the Camaro: "Daren? Aggh..." He has been thrown somewhere in the golf course next to the road. I blunder over to him. He's lying behind a bush. It looks as if he's been thrown *through *the bush. There's not much left of it.*

"You OK?"

"Uh...no, I don't think so. But I'm not dead. Fuck, we rolled, didn't we."

"Keith won't answer me." We stumble back to the wreck.

"Keith! Can you hear me?" Alex yells, panicked.

We hear a groan.

"Keith, there's gas spilling all over you. Can you get out of there?" I ask.

"Ah...um. Oh. Fuck. I can't move my legs," Keith says.

"But your legs are right here, man," Alex says, and then shakes his head, cursing himself. I catch his eye. We are fucking A afraid. We are not dealing.

Alex picks at his forehead and his back. He is picking out bits and slivers of glass, I realize. He is bleeding everywhere from razed cuts. I look at the Camaro's back window, which is of course broken out. He must have been thrown through it and flew straight into the life-saving bush instead of the hard, skull-crushing pavement. More luck. Luck abounded. Luck was one son of a bitch.

"Keith, can you move at all?" Alex asks.

"Can't feel my legs. What's happening?"

"Take it easy, man. Everything's going to be OK," Alex says. The gas stops pouring out on Keith. The tank has run dry. "Can't move him if he can't feel his legs."

"Keith. There was a deer. We hit it. We rolled the car. We're in a ditch by the golf course." I pronounce these statements like an idiot tour guide. I don't know what to say or what to do. My liquored peppermint glamour melts away into the moonblaze around us. It's as if we're caught in a celestial spotlight, on trial, our improvidence the charge, a kangaroo court.

All rise.

Keith...rise, goddamn it, please rise.

"The Camaro is...totaled?" he grunts.

"It's trashed, dude. We gotta get some help. Now," Alex says, pulling out an inch-long glass sliver from his elbow.

"I'll go. Nearest house is a quarter mile," I say. My shoulder throbs. I strip the fuel-sodden trench coat and throw it to one side with my good arm, then crawl up the road bank and half-bumble, half-run down the street. Two cars pass me on the way and don't stop. I try to wave them down, even daring to step out in front of one cruising at sixty plus. They *honk and veer away. I swear at them yet don't blame them. I make it to a residential cul-de-sac and knock on the nearest condo's door. It's four a.m. A lady in curlers answers the door and screams when she sees me. Turns out I have a healthy gash over my forehead, and it's coated my face in a red sheen, and I smell like a filling station, and my baby browns can't be looking very sane. I reassure her I'm not the devil and tell her there's been an accident and to call 911.*

After dressing my head wound with a peroxide-dipped bandanna and giving me an old flannel shirt to wear, the nice lady is driving me back to the accident site to meet the police and emergency teams. We arrive just as paramedics load Keith into an ambulance. Alex is enduring the questioning of two sheriffs. I thank my benefactor as I get out of her car. Alex runs over. The sheriffs bluster, chasing after him. He reaches me and says under his breath, "Story is, you guys only had a few. Only a few. OK? Three, maybe four brews between the two of you. I tried to tell them I was driving, since I'm sober, but they know. They're taking into consideration the deer, but...well, fuck, they know there's booze involved, the cab reeks to high heaven of it, even with all the gasoline."

"How's Keith?"

"He can't move his legs, man. That's it."

They take us to one of Santa Crisca's e-rooms. Alex and I are stripped down, put in white gowns, and loaded onto gurneys as most of the staff scramble and run about attending to Keith. They wrap him into a coil-reinforced rubber torso-brace, which I know is for patients with spinal cord injuries. Keith begins yelling, demanding the doctors let him know what is going on. A sleepy nurse extracts pieces of glass out of Alex with tweezers while the cops question us. Pretty straightforward, the most amateurish Columbo could figure this one out—yes, it's classic drunk driving on Keith's part, though the "deer ran in front of us" alibi, true as it was, might work, at least until they see the results of Keith's blood work. They take our statements and leave, adding that they'll talk to our friend as soon as he's able. Alex tells them to fuck off.

Paramedics take Keith out, transporting him to a better-equipped rehab facility across town. He says nothing to us. They have heavily sedated him. They give us codeine for our pains. Alex refuses at first, not wanting to break his sobriety code, but relents soon enough. Later we are laughing in the hospital hall, unreserved, wailing hysterics. The nurses tell us it's the codeine. We know better. As my parents wait in the call room, as another nurse binds my shoulder and bandages Alex's lacerations one by one, we laugh.

I phase out. The next thing I'm aware of is waking to the sight of my parents' house. They have taken us from the hospital in Santa Crisca back to Durango Bay. Alex's parents are out of town and are speeding home from a business meeting in San Francisco after receiving the call from my parents. Alex and I trudge upstairs to my old room and take long deep breaths. Every bone and muscle in my body screams. The post-accident comedown from the shock and the codeine is extreme. Alex flops in my old bed and in an instant goes nite-nite. I take a small pipe and a nugget of stale hashish out from a closet crevice, stashed emergency swag hidden long ago. The cast of thousands applauds my preparation for the unexpected. It's an empty accolade; they're a nasty, sarcastic lot, I've learned. I smoke the hash. It helps some.

Soon, downstairs, I hear voices...Lee, my mother and father, Jim, Valerie. How much time has passed if Lee is already here from Angel City? I wonder how my mother is conducting our tale of woe and decide I don't care. I debate going downstairs to ask if Keith's parents or Rachel are at the hospital with him, yet I'm too tired to move. So I watch early morning game shows, stoned on hashish and codeine, bruised and battered. God, I am exhausted. I am done. Except there are nagging oddities floating in my concussed chaos, pervasive impressions of a stunning woman with a platinum mane and startling orange-sienna eyes, a room of light, a sense of peace. There's a strange taste in my mouth, a sweet citrus acidity that the earthy hash doesn't burn away. I can't put my finger on any of it. Probably just shock. My brain's rattled, buzzing and reeling with both legal and illegal intoxicants, spitting out random nonsense.

Alex's eyelids flutter, eyeballs underneath rolling in REM's reckless abandon. He's dreaming. The way his face is scrunched up, as if he's swallowed the sourest of gobstoppers, it looks like a bad dream. I don't wake him. He may be dreaming me, and at the moment I'm in full Don Juan mode, less secure with the notion I will continue to exist if he stirs.

19

City nightglow was incandescent, shimmering through the glass elevator's smoked windows. The translucent towers of the Westin Hotel reflected a cascade of corporate headquarters and affluent high-rises as our lift ascended over thirty stories of concrete and steel. Countless pairs of white headlights and red taillights crisscrossed the maze of the LA freeway system far below. Untold happenings upon happenings transpired as Lost Angelenos began their nighttime tango. The elevator shuddered as it came to a stop, swaying in a draft. It was an uneasy sensation. I held Lee's hand tighter. She looked ravishing, black, low-cut cocktail dress, burnt umber hair lustrous, red lips pursed and moist.

"Oh. This is high up," Lee noted.

"I make myself look out the windows to be cool, but really, heights scare the hell out of me," I said.

"I know, Lamb Chop. I could feel it."

"Feel what?"

"The fear, of course. You're different when your adrenalin gets rolling."

"Maybe so."

"You ass," she muttered. Then she kissed me, hard. Tender rebukes like these had been frequent since the accident. Keith incurred temporary paralysis, tweaking the nerves of his eleventh vertebrae. With several weeks of physical therapy, supervised by the stern care of Rachel, he had fully recovered. Thanks to the arresting officers' oversight of failing to read Keith his Miranda rights, Keith had avoided any criminal charges and had rebounded as if nothing had happened, typically *whatever* of the Surfcat. The irony of both my buddies avoiding DUI charges while I had not, irked me. Three drunken excursions among many, three near misses. Even Alex was advocating renewed efforts of caution behind the wheel. What was next was evident. Lee and Valerie had formed a pact to chaperone us whenever possible if transport was required. They were tired of roadway shenanigans and refused to wait for one of us to die before taking action.

As such, Lee insisted she be the designated driver for the concert at hand. Another Van Halen tour had come around, supporting their sophomore effort with Sammy titled *OU812*. Alex had landed three choice eighth-row seats on the floor at the Los Angeles Coliseum, two hundred bones apiece. The gig was a huge traveling metal-gala titled *Monsters of Rock*, an American sequel to the European Monsters festival. The lead bill featured Van Halen, prefaced by six hours of warm-up from the likes of Kingdom Come, Metallica, Dokken, and the Scorpions. Our girlfriends were ticked that Alex hadn't chosen to acquire six tickets. He'd touted the need for a boys' night out after Keith's recovery. Knowing firsthand the endurance required of daylong rock festivals, we reserved a two-bedroom suite at the downtown Westin Bonaventure Hotel rather than drive home late that night.

The elevator door opened, revealing a group of Japanese businessmen wearing black ties and suits, waiting to go down. We passed through them and walked down a hall laden in plush carpet, its walls decorated in simulated opulence, potted palms, brass statues, and replicas of modern art. I slid a card key in the code slot and opened our room door. The view was breathtaking. Nearby high-rises cast glossy, illuminated shadows across a darkening sky. The city breathed and heaved. In the adjacent room, Keith waited. "Finally. We're already missing Kingdom Come."

"They suck anyway," I replied.

"We were riding the glass elevators," Lee said.

"Where's Alex?" I asked.

"Um…in the john."

Alex popped his head out. "You tell them yet?"

"Uh…no."

"Good. Daren, get in here."

I was puzzled. Lee looked suspicious. Then it hit me. I stared into Keith's eyes. He dropped his gaze downward. "Let's just get on with the night," he said.

"Look at me when you say that."

He raised his head and winked. Eyes dilated and black.

Railed.

They'd been skiing.

Oh, fuck.

I charged into the bathroom. On a marble sink counter were two long lines of coke and a large bindle of rocks.

"I'm off the wagon," Alex said. "I'm gonna do Halen right this time. You need to deal with it. And tell Lee to chill if she freaks. That's how it is."

"Is it now."

"Nothing you can say or do will change that." He worked one of the lines with a razor blade. His eyes were coal-black, green brimstone behind them once again.

"Dude…but *why*?"

"Because I was lonely. I was outside you guys. I was off limits. It sucked."

"No, Alex. *We* were outside *you*. Jesus, why am I the last one to know?"

"You've been with Lee all day…"

"No, that's not it."

"All right. It's the same reason why you just gave me the third degree. You're the ethics barometer. I didn't want the moral majority vote."

"I am *not* the 'ethics barometer.' Have you taken a good look at my life recently?"

"Yeah, well, you're the closest thing we have."

"And Keith agreed I wouldn't approve?"

"Sort of."

"Who cares if *I* approve? It's your life."

"For better or worse, cap'n."

"But it's always worse! Keith almost died, remember?"

"And yet you two have hit the sauce since, no?"

Got me there.

"Yeah, but…"

"But nothing. What, I'm the only one who has to stay in the ivory tower? Fuck that. Ashes to ashes, dust to dust."

"Spare me the drama."

"So don't preach to me, and let's make sure we enjoy this thousand dollar party."

"I don't want any coke or booze. I'm straight tonight. I promised Lee."

"Fine."

I went back out, where Lee, having determined for herself what was going on, continued to assail Keith with a serious tongue-lashing. "Don't you have any idea where this all ends? What's the matter with you? Do you not remember the iron head brace? Did you forget the sensation of *no* sensation in your spindly little legs? You idiot!"

"Lee…you don't get it," Alex said.

"What don't I get?"

"This is what I am. This is all I've got."

"No, Alex, this is not all you've got. You have Valerie. You have the world in front of you. You have a heartbeat and all of your fingers and toes. You virtually exist on disposable income. You have a lot more than most third-world citizens could ever dream of."

"You don't know what it's like," Alex said.

"No? I've been in love with an addict for some time now. I believe that entitles me to an opinion."

"OK, Lee, that's enough," I said.

"Can we postpone the lecture for tomorrow? That way Rachel and Valerie can join in, and we won't have to hear this three separate times," Keith said.

We sulked in unison. I cleared my throat. "Babe...we can take a cab to the Coliseum. I'm not going to partake tonight, I promised. You can stay here at the room."

"Oh, no. I too made a promise. I'm taking you whether you like it or not."

"Then you're just going to have ignore what's about to follow," Alex said. "I told you and Val this was a boys' night out. You've already managed to commandeer Daren; leave us the fuck alone."

"It's not enough to get booted from the Air Force, or to wreck any vehicle you climb into, or risk disfigurement and death. It's always more with you!"

Alex grinned. "Too much is never enough."

"There's no God-genie in the lamp, Alex," she said softly.

His face darkened. "Don't do that."

"Alex, do what you're going to do. We need to get going," I said. With that he retired to the bathroom, defiant, like a spanked child. Keith followed him in. Lee was furious. I tried to console her, and she pushed me away.

After a while she let me take her into my arms.

"I'm sorry," I said.

"Why did he have to do it? All that work. For what?"

"He didn't leave our world as was necessary. He avoided Keith and me, in the beginning, but I don't think Valerie saw the need."

"Val's been drinking this whole time they've been living together?"

"I'm not versed in their home life, but no, Valerie never stopped drinking."

"For fuck's sake."

"Neither did I, babe."

"Yes, but you're not responsible for Alex."

"Nor is Valerie, and on that light, you are not responsible for me either."

"Sometimes I wonder," Lee said.

"As you should," I replied, and that made her laugh...only a little.

Later we drove on Wilshire Boulevard through the USC district to the Coliseum. The boys in the back seat peaked on pre-show buzz. She pulled up to an arena entrance lined with orange cones and security guards and porta-potties. We had missed the first two acts. We didn't care. We were there to see Van Halen. The boys piled out the back, scrambling for the concessionaire.

"Thanks for driving," I said.

"Oh, sure. Anything for a lonely night by myself in a glamorous hotel."

"Lee…"

"I'm just kidding! Go on, have fun, *try* to be more safe than usual. And do me a favor. Take me next time. I'd like to see that side of you that cheers for Van Halen. I know how much they mean to you—it's all you ever listen to. It sucks you never asked me to go."

"I'm sorry. It didn't occur to me you'd be into it."

"You're mistaken."

"Fuck it, let's find a scalper right now."

"No, no, not this time. Another time, just you and me."

"You got it."

"Promise me."

"I promise, the next Van Halen gig is all about you."

"Call me after the show, and I'll be here in thirty, OK?"

"I love you."

"You sure do," she said, and drove off.

We bought the requisite crappy T-shirts. Alex and Keith chained-smoked menthol cigarettes. They checked their coke bullets taped to the insides of their legs under their boxers. Keith had a bag of weed stashed down his butt crack. The Coliseum gates beckoned, bracketed by policemen on horseback. Yellow-jacketed event staff manned metal detectors.

We reached the front of the line and I passed through, then Alex. A svelte black woman patted down Keith. "OK, sir, whaddya got? Whatever it is, put it in this bag and move on. There are thousands of people waiting behind you."

"I don't have anything!"

"You can either be arrested and miss the show or lose the contraband. Take your pick." She motioned to the blue-shirted lawmen behind us. Keith slipped his hand down the back of his pants, took out the baggie of weed, and put it in a large plastic sack she had extended.

Inside I saw a plethora of pills, joints, tooters, and flasks…an interesting approach, amnesty for non-protest, under the threat of the hovering constables nearby. Their coke bullets went undetected.

"Oh, man, that wasn't an omen; don't tell me that was an omen," Keith panted as we reconvened inside the venue. "That's all our dope for the night. Felt me up good."

"It's not an omen. You didn't stuff the bag down your ass far enough. What are we going to toke now, when we're coming down from the coke?" Alex asked, chewing the insides of his cheeks. He was *too* on, the kind of relieved buzz that hits an addict after being on the wagon for an extended period of time, all new yet so familiar.

"Someone will pass a joint. Someone always does," I said.

We formed a single-file procession through the congestion, Alex, me, then Keith, trying to reach our premium floor seats. There were about one hundred thousand people there. It was already vibing me, threatening overdose. We heard Metallica winding down their set, and a roar from the capacity-level crowd.

"She was angry," Alex said.

"Yep. She gets like that when we're pulling the kid-stuff around her."

"I'm sorry I mouthed off."

"You may want to tell her that."

"I will. Pop quiz. Are you ready?"

"Whatever you say."

"You know how all the great and terrible prophets preach an end time, right? See, what a lot of people don't get is that mostly they're talking about an end time to the *current* age, not necessarily the true end of the world. A lot of them pretty much say the same thing, that after the great big kick in the ass, then and only then will humans be blessed with a thousand years of peace and prosperity."

"So?"

"What do *you* think about that?"

I pondered his query as I followed him, reaching into my Levi jacket pocket, taking out my smokes and lighting one. "Well, what sucks about that is the generation of humans who get to bite the bullet and pay destiny's piper, so to speak. I guess."

"Such a smart boy you are, Daren. Yes, it's unfair that the few who pay for the historical many are Es. Oh. El."

I looked down the stairs. No sign of Keith. I assumed he was somewhere in line.

"We lost Keith."

"He's got his ticket. We'll meet him at the seats. But back to the point. Shit goes down all the time, right? All part of life and the universe."

"Yeah. Planets rock and roll, duh."

"Nothing gets by you, Huck. Thass why I loves ya."

We ascended the last flight of stairs and walked into the arena upper loge. We stopped cold, flabbergasted. The entire half of the football field in front of the stage was covered in flesh. Metallica cranked out the end of their encore, to which a gigantic mosh pit swelled and palpitated. A long line of yellow-jackets and blue-shirts stood at the field's halfway point, bracketing the soundboards, having given up on enforcement of assigned seating. We did not pay two hundred dollars a ticket for general admission. It dawned on me at least twenty thousand nosebleed seat-holders had rushed the stage at some point during the earlier acts.

"Fuck," Alex said.

"Oh, *great*," I added.

In despair, jaws dropped, we watched the mob revel, trampling the area where our precious seats should have been, now worthless. We either had to fight the crowd to get near the stage or kick it back in the vacated sections.

"I'm going to kill our ticket broker," Alex said, pale-faced.

We waited for Keith to come though the line. About a quarter of the way through the Scorpions' set we gave up, figuring we'd cross paths with him sooner or later. We reached the floor and made our way toward the center.

"Damned if going up front's going to happen. Do you want to brave that?" Alex asked.

"I'm too irritated to mosh, man."

"Me too. Let's try to find some seats farther back."

We moved through the stinky packs of hard rockers.

"You believe in karma. What does this mean, I wonder?" Alex posed. He was crushed by another Van Halen concert gone awry. He was coming down off the coke. He wasn't looking good. We found a couple of unoccupied chairs behind the soundboard command post and sat there for the Scorpions' set. Alex swore repeatedly, chiding himself for letting Keith have the bulk of the stash. His bullet had run dry. Soon he stood up and told me he was going to find Keith if he had to risk life and limb. I wished him well. He didn't want to include me in the mission anyway. Van Halen's roadie crew took a long time setting up their stage. The crowd became restless. I was sure a riot was in store, as the folks in the upper loge of the stadium began throwing anything they could get their hands on, which in turn aggravated floor patrons into a series of fistfights and restless arguing. Food wrappers, beer cups, toilet paper rolls, and articles of clothing rained down on the field. By the time Van Halen came onstage, I was disenchanted. The bad vibes and the day's events had tainted the whole experience.

The fucking audacity of arena rock.

The show ended. I waited as the multitudes filed out. I made my way to the Seven-Eleven across from the Coliseum where we were supposed to meet if we'd been separated. Alex was there, burned-out and enraged. He'd never found Keith and had walked around the arena frazzled during Halen's entire set. We waited for Keith to show. After an hour we grew impatient. I suggested we call Lee to come and get us, that it was probable Keith had hailed a cab back to the hotel.

"Look, the hotel's just right over there," Alex said, pointing at the spires of the Westin Hotel and the downtown skyline. "We can walk. Twenty minutes. It'll take Lee that long to get here. Besides, she's probably already picking Keith up, wherever the fuck he is. I need the fresh air. That show was lame."

"Why not," I agreed.

We walked east. For a while the streets were packed with departing concert attendees. It thinned out once we got near the 110 Freeway, and we started realizing it was a much longer hike than we'd anticipated. The city closed in on us, shepherding us to who-knew-what, unknowing of what possible barrios or turfs we were treading. Occasional low-rider cars cruised like sharks, glittery and painted in metallic, pastel shades, Cadillac Coupes, Chevy Impalas, tricked-up Fleetlines and El Caminos. University strip malls gave way to barred liquor stores, pawnshops, deserted auto yards, and warehouses. Way, way out of our element. *Country bumpkins, ayup.* We might as well have had signs on our backs that said Fresh Meat.

A black '57 Chevy pickup, slammed down to non-legal street levels, rumbled behind us and came to a stop. The double barrel of a sawed-off shotgun protruded out a tinted window.

"You don't belong here." A young husky voice, gravelly and sneering, came from within the darkened cab.

"Excuse m-me?" Alex said, stammering.

"Run, motherfuckers, run."

The shotgun cocked.

We ran.

The laughter of children followed.

Blocks upon blocks of concrete passed by, empty streets of secrets and broken deals and blood, echoing with the clatter of our running footsteps. We took a few breaks to catch our breath, wheezing, hacking with smokers' coughs. At last we reached the brightly lit steps of the Westin. A valet appraised our disheveled appearances with disdain. It had taken us close to two hours to get there. We rode up a glass elevator, as ghosts.

"Whoa," Alex said.

"Yeah," I replied.

We agreed not to say anything about shotguns and lowriders. Neither of us wanted Lee or Valerie to think we'd tempted fate a second time so soon after the accident.

We entered our room, where Keith resided on the bed watching late-night tube and Lee paced back and forth in front of the floor-to-ceiling windows.

"Where the hell have you been? I was worried sick!" Lee demanded.

"We walked," I replied.

"You walked back through Watts," Keith said, aghast.

"It wasn't Watts and you know it," I muttered.

"What happened to *you*?" Alex asked.

It turned out he'd never made it through the second venue checkpoint. He'd stood near a group of bikers who started brawling. Keith had watched from what he thought was afar, and when the police barreled in, they did not think he was *afar* enough. He was expelled from the arena, unrighteously ejected. He too had hit the Seven-Eleven, earlier than expected, until Lee returned to the hotel to take his call. She came straight back to retrieve him, and they'd had virgin daiquiris in the revolving bar at the top of the hotel while they waited for us.

"How was the show?" Keith asked.

Alex and I grumbled.

"That good, eh?"

I relayed our own discords, omitting the unexpected sprint of terror.

"You're kidding. Think we can get our money back?"

"Not likely," Alex said.

"The entire night was a dismal failure, then," Lee said.

"Apparently that's par, for me, when it comes to the King of Six Strings," Alex said.

"We still have a luxury hotel bed waiting, milady," I said.

"There is that. Let's go. We'll leave you two to stew. And for the record, it was a stupid idea, walking."

"Yes, yes," Alex groused.

"We wanted some air," I said. I flashed on racing through a freeway underpass where a homeless commune had been established. Its alley walls had been painted with garish gang graffiti tags. Makeshift mini shantytowns of cardboard and sheets and discarded construction supplies had been assembled in the long tunnel by dozing bag ladies, mental hospital escapees, and other casualties of the Los Angeles underworld. Nobody had killed us, though to be fair, we'd passed through at top speed.

"Whose bright idea was it?" Lee asked.

"It was a mutual decision," I insisted.

"Listen, I'm sorry about before," Alex said.

"Save it. Try again when you're clearer in mind. You were doing well, Alex. I was so proud of you," Lee said.

"I'll be OK, mummy. I'm a big boy," Alex said.

"You know, I could always handle the drunken cow tipping and the occasional bong hit. I just don't get the suicidal bents. Can these lost boys really be the little drama geeks I met once upon a time?"

"You could've avoided all this heartache simply by boinking an age-appropriate drama dude instead of seducing our resident jailbait philosopher," Alex replied.

"Point taken," Lee admitted.

"Nah, it was meant to be," I said.

"Counterpoint trumps the former," Lee said, pecking me on the cheek. She went and readied herself for bed.

Alex took me aside and we smoked sour cigarettes, sweaty and drained from our unsolicited marathon, studying a picture-perfect urban view out the window. Keith succumbed to a delirious beer stupor watching pay-per-view porno. I scanned the distant cityscape near USC and tried to determine the area where we'd encountered the black pickup.

"I'm sorry she's ticked, man."

"She'll get past it. Does Valerie know?"

"She will tomorrow."

"You've got to stop letting Val be the last to discover your major life decisions."

"Well, she hits when she's mad."

"I'm aware."

"We're missing something, aren't we."

"For some time now."

"What do we need to know?"

I stubbed out my smoke. "A lot more than we do."

"Is there some specific reason why I can't pull off a solid Van Halen gig?"

"Probably." I left for my room.

I slipped under the covers with Lee.

Perhaps I had overestimated Angel City.

20

The Pacific Ocean thundered beneath us as Santa Monica sparkled, its electric palm glitz beginning to fire up. Keith mixed margaritas at the terrace bar while Lee, Rachel, and I wallowed in the bubbling Jacuzzi. I sucked on a Marlboro, thinking of a half-dozen unfinished papers due on Monday. I was burnt. The constant commuting to LA had resulted in my classes becoming more tedious than ever. Our immediate surroundings were an unexpected boon brought to us by Keith's generous uncle, a specialist in facelifts and boob jobs. His Malibu condominium rented for five thousand a month—four bedrooms, big-screen TV, redwood tub mounted on a monster deck extending above the tide line, all the continental trimmings. Plastic surgery in Westwood was a good living.

"When are they supposed to get here?" Rachel asked.

"Alex called from a taco stand in Zuma. Said PCH was crazy backed-up. They'll arrive soon," I replied. Alex and Valerie had accepted our offer for a couple-fest beach house weekend. I persuaded Alex to leave any brain candy at home, limiting us to wine and seafood and nightlife, Angel City's sport of kings, the rules of which Keith and I had largely mastered during our tandem journeys to see the girls. Our fake IDs fooled most bouncers. We marched around the flat metropolis as if we owned it, Lee and Rachel in tow. We passably quoted quality vintages of local wines. Super metro. And the beat went on.

"One virgin for you." Keith handed Rachel an alcohol-free margarita. "Nasty ones for the rest of us." He slipped into the tub. "Ahh… it's nice in here."

"So is that how she really is?" Rachel asked, sipping her drink.

"She's the wicked witch of the east," Lee said. She plucked my smoke from my fingers and took a drag. She never inhaled. I smiled and wondered whether she did so purposefully or if she just didn't know how to inhale. In truth I thought it was the latter. After all the years of bullshit she still kept her innocence, ever immune to red shift. Amazing.

"You're not talking about Valerie again, are you? You're going to give my woman a complex, Lee," Keith said.

"I already have a complex, thank you very much," Rachel said, covering her small bikini top with her hands.

"Trust me, when she gets in we'll both be ignored," Lee said.

"Wait until later when we take it *all* off," I said.

"What?" Rachel gasped, horror-struck.

"He's kidding," Keith said, slurping his margarita.

"Or am I?"

"Valerie is a shining star in the eyes of the Y chromosomes," Lee said.

"Fiddlesticks," I said.

"Hey, Val's my friend. I can say it to her face. I *have* said it to her face. She knows it. She likes swinging 'em around. I would too, if I had 'em," Lee said.

"Exactly. Valerie's boobs are our team mascots," Keith said. He raised his glass to me. I responded in kind.

"That doesn't make me too happy," Rachel pined.

I tuned out, swirling the clumps of ice in my glass around in a clockwise direction. I spilled some in the bubbling tub water. The margarita slush melted in an instant, leaving a tiny swish of red. I debated options. The decision of transferring to a Cal State or a University of

California was upon Keith and me. Our tenure at the community college was complete. Under the impression that I would soon be attending UCLA, Lee was scouting apartments in west Los Angeles. She had it all figured out. We'd move into a one-bedroom Westwood apartment, complete with hipster urban deco and fluffy Eddie Bauer linens. I'd get a cheap commuter car after I got my license back. She'd continue the secretary-by-day, actress-by-night bit. I'd finish up the undergrad routine and continue on in a graduate program. The problem was, despite repeated exposure during the last few years, I was certain I couldn't live full time in Angel City, and I hadn't been able to tell Lee. I *did* want us to live together. We'd been together for four-plus years, give or take a few months, and we had yet to cohabitate.

I'd talked to my mother about my concerns one morning, and she suggested I look into the curriculum at Chico, a Cal State campus north of Sacramento. We had family there, some cousins on my dad's side. I'd heard of Chico. It was a revered collegiate destination after *Playboy*'s 1987 poll of party campuses. Chico had been number one, what with its riots, rural location, and records for binge drinking. When I mentioned the prospect to Keith, he jumped at it. Moving from a small collegiate town to another small collegiate town was appealing on a number of levels for us.

I gazed at Lee, who was at the climax of an audition story I'd heard twice before. She puckered a kiss at me. I winked at her. I had to ask her soon, had to get her input on it, though it wasn't difficult to predict how it would go down. *What do you think, sweetheart? How do you feel about spending another two years apart? Instead of two hours of driving distance, how about eight? How does that sound? When I get my degree, we can settle down, and we'll start a family; no sweat, it's only two more years, and we'll have summers and Christmases together, and it'll work; we can handle it no problem, OK?*

"…enough blankets. Did you check?"

She was speaking to me. I shook off my daze. "Whazzat?"

"I'm not sure if there are enough blankets for everyone. Off you go to check the linen supply. Chop, chop."

"Um, right now?"

"Yes, now."

"It's *your* uncle's place," I said to Keith.

"Sorry, bartender duty."

"All right, all right." I lumbered up out of the water, shivering. "By what criteria am I supposed to check our inventory of blankets anyway?"

"Oh, it's a conundrum. You'll have to open a closet and look. Wow, college is really sharpening your adult living skills," Lee said.

"Ha, ha, cupcake, you're quite the razor wit."

"Did I ever tell you how much I adore you?"

"Yeah, whatever."

"They're in love, Rachel. Isn't it sweet?" Keith said.

"They do the older gal-boy toy thing quite well," Rachel said.

"Rachel, there are only three things to remember when you're committing statutory rape," I said as I dried myself with a towel.

"OK, that's not funny. You've been of legal age for some time now, sport," Lee said, frowning.

"She doesn't like it when I remind her of her cradle-robbing past."

"Those were the days," Keith agreed.

"No, I want to hear from the sage. Share that magic wisdom," Rachel said.

I wrapped the towel around my waist. "Number one. The best part is meeting each other at your sexual peaks."

"Let's try to keep it decent," Lee said.

"It's not true?" I asked.

"OK, he's right, the sex is outstanding," Lee conceded with a sigh.

"Well. I agree with that. So far," Rachel said.

"Hoo-ra, chalk up a gold star for me," Keith said.

"Number two. We *do* want you older babes to take care of us like our mommies did."

"That's for sure," Lee said.

"Number three. When your flesh turns ancient and mummified, you'll understand when we take a mistress." I made my way indoors as Keith and Rachel laughed.

"Don't you mean *mommy-fied*?" Lee bellowed from outside amidst another bout of laughter. My wet feet slid across the marble-tiled kitchen floor. I went to the hall closet. Inside, piles of blue cotton blankets and fluffy comforters were folded on the top shelf.

The doorbell rang. I went to answer it. They stood there in full regalia, Valerie swathed in a shimmering gold strapless gown and matching purse, Alex in a dark Armani jacket and slacks, a bottle of Dom Perrignon in his hand and a rumpled pair of bathing trunks in the other.

"We're here, man. The fun can commence," Alex said.

"It's already commenced," I said as I kissed Valerie on the cheek. "You guys look official."

"I thought you said we were hitting Sunset," Valerie said.

"Later, Val. LA doesn't start happening 'til later."

"You're *so* cosmo, you douchebag. Lead me to the ocean-side tub I've heard so much about," Alex said, ruffling my wet hair.

"On the deck. Bar's on the end. I have to check the bedrooms for readiness per the request of the queen of ceremonies." He headed out as Valerie followed me into the first room, where I noted a made-up bed, and the next room was also immaculate, ready for strange people to have strange sex. *Like the place isn't fully stocked? Five thousand a month better include a maid service at the very least.*

"So who is this Roxanne?" Valerie asked.

"Rachel."

"Roxanne. Rachel. Whatever."

"Lee's roommate."

"Yes, Einstein, but who is she?"

"An LA woman, Val. Much like yourself."

"An old hag like yours, I hear?"

"That's right."

"What is it with you two?"

"We're hot for teachers."

"I'm the young hussy tonight, then."

"Something like that. 'Course, you're *always* the hussy." I closed the drapes behind the bed and we went to the kitchen. "Rachel's cool. She doesn't rage, at all. Don't bug out when she's sober and we're not. Not everyone is like us."

"I've been hanging out with Lee for years. I think I can handle it."

"No, you don't get it. She's really square. Makes Lee look like the whore of Babylon."

"Hey, she can drive, then. I won't rag."

"And don't swing those things in her face." I motioned to her breasts. "She's still in honeymoon phase with Keith, and she's a little sensitive."

"Haven't they been seeing each other for over a year now?"

"Yes, but she's still enamored."

"In a Jacuzzi with my three favorite men? And I haven't been out for months? And you want me to tone down? Dream on." She cackled and went in the bathroom to change into tub-appropriate gear. I leaned against the kitchen counter and looked out to the Pacific through a window. Alex popped the champagne bottle on the balcony. The cork flew high in the air, arced over the rail and down to the sand below.

Then the curtain flew wide open, as if some apathetic force, fed up with my caution, yanked the drawstrings back in a fit of impetuosity. Angel City joined with me. Undaunted by my fears it showed me itself—sights, sounds, smells, feelings, a flurry of extrasensory sensations. The cigarette butts in the drains, the billboards and the drive-through liquor stores, the scrap yards, the jewelry and garment districts, endless malls and fast food outlets and car after car after car. Horrific sexual abuse, panhandling, murderous beatings and drug deals, chemicals and unregulated factories, a Venice juggler's twisted homicidal dreams, a Newport housewife's aching loneliness, a surfer under a wave at Redondo Beach, his lungs full of water. Squealing tires during a drive-by shooting in Reseda, bell-ringing cash registers of ten thousand department stores, bloodstains on the synthetic putting green of an abandoned miniature golf course in Palm Springs, dirty sex with tattooed bald men and Cuban transvestites in a dilapidated motel, a pedophile walking over Bob Hope's star on the Walk of Fame in Hollywood. And too, there was wonder, joy, newborns clean and untainted, cresting into the world, the purity of first loves, straddling the line between lust and heart. A cop in Costa Mesa taking a frazzled junkie to a shelter instead of the pen, a middle-aged woman with fifteen hundred smackeroos in her purse, cash, on a whim deciding to give it all to charity. A thousand birthday parties and children a thousand times more, party hats and wrapping paper and streamers and balloons and laughter, so much laughter. A beet-red kidney slotted for donation, resting within a plastic bag inside an iced Igloo cooler, a doctor smiling, telling a patient chemotherapy had resulted in total remission, a realtor in Encino pulling an elderly man back from the path of an oncoming bus.

So much light, and so much dark...

All is one.

Then I remembered. A detour, a *major* detour.

In a jolting spasm, a sudden, detailed recollection heavy with déjà vu surged onto my psychic shores like a churning tsunami.

21

I see it, right before Keith nails it. A flash of brown fur and craggy ant-
ler, big doughy eyes, a horrid wet crunch. A patch of gravel, crunching
stone, the Camaro slides, and here is this deer in the wrong place at the
wrong time to boot. Alex bellows something, Keith is overcorrecting, he
is too wasted to compensate. It is quiet, which is bizarre because the car
is starting to roll, and I expect the three of us to start tumbling around
the cabin like dice on a craps table, accompanied by a spectacular movie-
caliber ejaculation of a crashing motor vehicle.

In the next moment I stand on the road.

What gives?

The Camaro is frozen in time, immutable. Legs connected to Keith
are cocked at an odd angle from underneath the car. Another pair of legs
lies parallel to his, oddly familiar.

The whole world is weird and still.

A deer's head rests nearby. A milky sheen grows across its eyeballs.

Then a soft buzzing sound fills my ears, irritating, like a swarm of
bees at first, increasing in volume, becoming rapid ticks and tocks of a
huge clock. It repeats, faster and faster, until the heavy drone encom-
passes all.

Something silver and thin, like a rope, floats in front of me. I try to grasp it. It is out of reach. It looks fleshy, pliable.

The buzzing ceases.

The world is tranquil. I do not know how this can be; we just totaled Keith's car, and my friends could be dead.

Oh. Boy.

I stare dumbly at the decapitated deer head. It looks neither sad nor horrified. It just looks dead. To my right the deer's broken, headless body is splayed up against a shale road bank. Then I notice my hands. They are crystalline, golden, and luminous. I am clad in some kind of white robe, silky and airy. It feels as if I am breathing, yet my chest is not rising and falling. I peer into the depths of the robe. I am naked underneath, all equipment intact. I am fit and trim. No more of that small beer-belly. Six-pack lines along my abs instead. Nice. Damn, I look good. My skin emanates a slight glow, like candle-lit yellow glass.

Time seems funny. The last few moments are as five seconds, five years, and five thousand years all at once. Before I reflect deeper on the phenomenon, as is my custom, I am drawn into a dark tunnel, which seems infinitely wide yet slender enough to fit only my passing. My limited knowledge of physics is inadequate to address the contradictions. I look back and see the car, the road, and Keith's crooked legs receding into oblivion.

I am moving at unimaginable speed. There is none of the breeze or wind that usually accompanies open-air travel. I reach outward. The sides of the cylindrical passage seem to be concave. My fingers pass through something. Something nice. It feels spongy, dry warm foam, comforting. It is dark, darker than any night, blacker than any heart. At first the abyss has no points of reference except the near-yet-far concavity of the tunnel. The abnormality becomes less interesting when another facet of the shaft presents itself. It is so peaceful. Like a breath of frosty dawn air or the split-second before the sun drops below a red horizon, like a mother's embrace or a father's approval, all these things and more. Like coming home. And I know that is exactly what I am doing. I am returning. I know not where, why, or how. I sense others in the shaft with me...many, many others. It is not my personal passage, it seems. I peer around the tunnel and perceive other forms speeding through the cavernous surroundings. Some of them are human. Some of them seem to be animals. Others do not appear to be human, animal, or earthly at all, or at least, not of any species of which I was familiar. Yet the oddities continue to pale next to the incomparable feeling of peace in this place. Dark and strange as it is, I know I can remain here indefinite if need be.

Something draws me on.

I experience difficulties with the wonky time thing. My tunnel ride might be taking an eon or a second. A dot of white comes into view, far away. It is just like all those quacks' claims on what transpires during near-death experiences: light at the end of the tunnel, first a sharp pinhole, then a white dwarf sun, then it rushes over me and I am thrust into it, and beautiful gold-alabaster rainbow fills my mind, my heart, my everything.

Peace.

Wonderful.

The light permeates my very being. My "body" drizzles into the serene lambency, like a drop of mercury drawn to a larger pool of the same. It isn't really light, not simple electrons and positrons streaming from an energy source, not quantifiable stimuli for my optic nerves to process. Somehow I know this light is a force, a foundation for a great many things. Energy. Matter. Space. Dimension. Thought.

Love.

All.

And the peace I felt in the tunnel seems mere illusion now because the peace within this light is incontrovertible.

I want to stay there forever.

And yet thoughts of Lee come to bear.

The Catholic Kid inside me, one of the few members of the cast of thousands not agape at the circumstances, is glad to discover that so far I am myself, not having transformed into a mindless, harp-plucking angel singing adoring choruses, nor a luckless condemned castaway toiling in flaming mines.

I'm still me.

The light coalesces. Shapes and edges begin to form. A wide space around me becomes a rectangle, a room, and then an incandescent chair appears, then a transparent table, a pitcher of liquid and a tall crystal glass on the tabletop. The room is emanating the same tawny glow I myself am giving off. I am compelled to sit, so I do. The chair is hard but comfortable. I feel a presence behind me. A virtual slideshow starts to appear, of perfect quality and detail, every sound and sight and scent intact, perhaps only in my mind, perhaps on the glowing wall in front of me. I cannot tell the difference.

I'm a baby. My parents look down upon me. I am huddled in a crib. A mobile dangles above, fluttering to and fro, plastic brown horses and cowboys with lariats.

I'm four years old. I stub my toe on a blue agave cactus. The barb runs through the nail. My father curses as he drives me to the emergency room.

I'm ten years old, throwing a fit as I discover my kid brother Jimmy has torn up my set of rare baseball trading cards.

Twelve years old. Kissing a girl. Her name is Karen. I feel the tender moistness of her trembling lips. The image is so real it's scary. I understand the nature of the universe in this tiny slice of my tiny life, as real and important as proteins, white dwarf star matter, Mayan pyramids, and the resolution of martyrs. All is one.

Countless roundabout arguments with Mom, brotherly bouts of sibling rivalry with Jim, Alex, Keith, the schooling, the red-shifting, the drugs, the booze, the decadence, Lee, grade school-high school-college, right up to the Camaro sliding on gravel and slamming into the deer. It is all there, each and every moment, no matter how trivial or innocuous. It's funny realizing, assuming this event is uniform across the board, that the billions of human lives having graced the earth throughout history have been recorded for posterity. Helluva video cam, that is. I feel a modicum of embarrassment. The slideshow lingers, if the term can be applied in this timeless place, on significant events entailing conflict or dissatisfaction on my part. Every time I'd bitched or wanked or complained, and the mundane too, every sexual encounter, each time I'd scratched my ass or blew snot out of my nose and all the other acts of human grunge, the sacrosanct privacy, my innermost thoughts revealed…to whom?

"Every time I jerked off? Was that really necessary?" *I say aloud.*

"If I had a nickel for every time I'm asked that," *the presence replies. The voice is soothing, deep, and amused.*

"I don't want to be dead."

"Again, if I had a nickel…"

The liquid in the pitcher looks very drinkable. I pour myself a glass and raise it to my lips. It is some kind of fruit concoction, cinnamon, exhilarating piquant citrus. I still have a tongue? Taste buds? A stomach? It is better than my mother's homemade sun tea. Incredible.

"You're really often put out, aren't you?" *the presence notes.*

"Seems that way, doesn't it."

"No matter. What did you think?"

"Think of what?"

"Life."

"Brief, obviously. And if that was life, what is this? And where are you?"

"I'm sorry. Just a moment."

Another chair appears on the other side of the table. A form is sitting in it, amorphous, then it materializes and solidifies, first only rounded edges and a blank androgynous face, then dainty lips protrude outward, a small button nose, stormy orange-brown eyes. Long, golden hair cascades down from an oval-shaped head, and a body becomes manifest, draped in a white robe the same as mine. A stunning woman sits across from me, putting the finest crafted silicate creatures of Beverly Hills to shame.

"Is this more satisfactory?" *the woman asks. She is stupefying. Beyond human beauty.*

"Sure. But this is ridiculous. I shouldn't be dead. My mother will circle the drain. And Lee…things were going…well, they were going better. Why did I have to die?"

"Why does anybody have to die when they do? Why do children get leukemia? Why are thousands of women raped and butchered by mercenary blood armies? Earth has no shortage of frailty and cruelty, as you well know. The Jews at Aushwitz, the Christians in Rome, the displaced tribes of the African Ivory Coast, the homeless of New York's Skid Row, the oncology wards at Cedar-Sinai, any patient in your third-world psychiatric asylums."

"Why indeed. Here's why. It's not fair so many people suffer."

"Fairness is a human desire, not reality. When so many of you despair over the imbalances, what you are really feeling is anger. Your desire to vindicate, your deep lust to punish that which puts the undeserving at a disadvantage, it is noble in one sense and unnecessary in another. Pain is circumstance. Most suffering is base corporeal primal ooze, survival impulses of fear and greed, and in every case I've ever known—and I've known more than you can imagine—these factors have contributed in a positive manner to the essence having experienced them. Eternal journey and all that, don'tcha know."

"Yeah, but there are degrees, aren't there?"

"Some beings experience the extremes of corporeality. All of them learn from their trials. Although given your species' potential, I'd have expected more enlightenment at this point. Retribution is for the close-minded. Rehabilitation requires strength."

"I don't go for that relativity crap."

I'm lying, and I know she knows it. I don't know why I'm being oppositional. Something about her is provocative.

"Bullshit."

"Angels can swear?"

"I am no angel."

"Are you…God?"

"Earth beings utter that word during carnal activity more than in any other situation, least of all spiritual."

"Then who are you?"

"Myself. And you. And everything that was and everything that is and everything that will be and everything that might have been, should have been."

"Oh, well, as long as we're being clear, Malibu Barbie."

"Watch it, youngster. Sarcasm turns me on. Call me a concerned citizen."

"My guardian spirit?"

"Spirits are their own guardians. You're currently journeying in the lower dimensions, and we'll leave it at that. Unlike most others in this situation, you're going back. You're not dead. Short visits happen from time to time. Byproducts of free will, the hazards of physical reality, dimensional overlap, often a combination thereof. It's complicated to explain. Order, chaos, balance…all that shit you already know, big guy. In your case it was deemed we let the 'system' bring you to this point, if only to remind you being a living contradiction need not be such a proud ambition. Wishing and shitting in both hands is tiresome, don't you think?"

"I didn't know my mother had spoken to you."

"Ha! Anyway, those 'peeks beyond the curtain,' the ones you're always stressed about? They're real. You have a certain predisposition. I cannot elaborate further. Rest assured you're not mentally ill."

"You had Keith roll the car just to get me here?"

"Of course not. We simply took advantage of an opportunity that posed itself."

"OK, if I'm not wacko, then what is it, that stuff?"

"Perhaps a sort of hyper-empathy, if you will."

"I already knew that, kinda."

"As you say."

"And that black-cherry cloud thingy? That's real?"

"You have a unique perception, and you see it as only you will see it, but the construct you identify as 'red shift' is absolutely real."

"That's the best explanation you've got?"

She smiles. She is magnificent and pure. Beams of light reverberate from her. Her orange eyes swirl with spiraling strands of silver in their corneas. It is a dazzling effect, like tiny, fiery galaxies.

"You will recall few if any of the details of your visit here when you return, at the precise moment of exit. Time's a-wasting. You need to skedaddle."

"This sucks. I'm not going to remember any of this? What was the point?"

"There will be a part of you that knows. It won't be easy to access. Down the line you may recollect this interchange with appropriate provocation or motivation. Perhaps sooner than you think. We thought a quick palaver, albeit buried in your *overmind*, would serve the interests of all concerned."

"And who might be concerned, pray tell?"

"The universe, of course. Don't be so provincial."

"If you're going to wipe my slate clean, then you might as well spill the beans on the great mystery."

"Ever pushing the envelope. Silly rabbit."

"Kids are for tricks, yes indeed, Barbie. What's the meaning of it all?"

"Sorry, that's off-limits. However, here's a hint a quick stud-muffin like you doesn't even need—it's specific to each and every individual."

"What a lame copout."

"You *are* a little hump, aren't you? Off you go. Live your life, and while you're at it, add some lovin' spoonfuls to that world. It needs all the help it can get."

The room fades away, as does the orange-eyed blonde.

Then I am falling.

There is no calm reassuring tunnel this time, just breakneck speed, terror, confusion, vertigo, a hard painful thump, and then the Camaro veers out of control.

22

I remembered.

I knew the meta-web now, composed of ley lines of energy, trans-dimensional rather than geomantic, sterling at their genesis within a center of All. At this outer segment in which I resided, this southwest-ern portion of North America, their ends coagulated together, cauter-ized to a red-black clot sullied with loam. Anguished fountainheads of sorrow, the despair of acceptance, bloomed in a mad, weed-strewn garden, pinnacles of modernism, the breaking and making points of stagnation, where celluloid heroes and greenbacks combined to define humanity, where it was writ how life would unfold on jeweled scrolls and in fine print, where penalties far worse than death, the gulag of exile, the freedom of lunacy, the masquerade of liberty, were meted out at the whims of the elite. All dark light, coexisting with true light, one begetting the other, scales balanced, circles completed.

In the condo's kitchen, drenched in cold sweat, I shut my eyes, clapped my hands over my ears, and collapsed, my knees whacking the linoleum floor. I curled up in a fetal position and hugged my legs.

It was just a city (*so much more than a city*), a personification, and I'd known it all along. Red shift had its greatest puissance there in the land of make-believe. I knew the raven felt it too, albeit not quite on my terms. Perhaps her ravensong protected her from its full effects, or maybe I was more an adopted child of dark light and thus more vulnerable to its influence.

I could not live there. I would lose what remaining luminescence I had left, dwindling minute by minute as it was, enough to hold dear.

Valerie came out of the bathroom as the onslaught of omni-imagery ended, her curves bulging in an ultra-revealing red bikini. I tried to stand. My teeth chattered. Stinging sweat slipped into my eyes.

"What are you doing?" Valerie asked.

"Nothing." I gasped, hobbling, then falling again, tripping over my clumsy legs and dropping to the floor. This time it hurt a lot more. My knees were badly bruised. Valerie bent down and tried to help me up. Crazy as it was, she resembled an uncanny amalgam of the warrior waitress in the desert diner and the blonde cherub with the pumpkin-colored eyes. Then again maybe it wasn't so crazy.

"Daren? Are you all right?" I shrugged her off. I crept up to the counter, shaking. "I'm getting Lee right now."

"No, don't, I'm fine."

"I can't believe you already drank too much. The sun hasn't gone down yet."

"It's not that, Val. I'm not wasted."

She ignored me and trotted out the door to the balcony. Nausea overcame me. I swallowed bile. My knees throbbed as I limped back to the bedroom, where I'd put my bag. I fell down on the bed. The plaster ceiling above, pockmarked and rippled with cottage-cheese stucco, looked like the surface of a far away foreign moon.

Lee came in, a black towel wrapped around her dripping body. "What's wrong? Are you OK?"

"I think so."

"Val said you passed out in the kitchen."

"Did no such thing…ugh." I fought another dry retch, clenching my fists.

"Daren, don't play around. You only had one drink."

"It's not that."

"What is it?"

I reached my hand up to her face, tangled my fingers in her chlorine-scented hair. "Do you remember when I told you about the time we went to the show in Laughlin?"

"With Alex and Keith."

"Right."

"The diner, and your vision. I remember."

"Well, that wasn't the only time. It's happened other times too. It happened again a few minutes ago…and maybe a big one when we crashed the Camaro."

"Really?" She walked into the bathroom and stripped. She put on a terry robe and wrapped a new towel around her wet hair, rubbing her mane vigorously.

"I don't think I'm going to UCLA."

"What do you mean?"

"I don't think I'm finishing up in LA. It's a bad vibe for me here, Lee. You know that."

"For me too, and *you* know *that*."

"Yeah, but you have to be here."

"Don't you?"

"With you, yes. With the rest of it…I don't know."

"I thought you wanted to live with me."

"I do."

"I thought we were going to spend our lives together."

"We are."

"*When?* What the hell did you see in your stupid vision?"

"Bad things…and good things, too. All things, actually."

"All things," she repeated, skeptical.

"I don't think I'm the kind of guy who's supposed to dwell in this place."

"You're not some Merlin-wizard destined to live his days hermit-like in a cave. Quit being stubborn."

"It happens, Lee!"

"I don't doubt you have visions. I doubt your interpretations of them. Los Angeles is not Hell itself. You're so obstinate about it. You always have been. There are plenty of ordinary people living ordinary lives right here in this so-called pit of despair."

"I know, it's stupid, you're right."

"Where do you plan on going instead?"

"Well…I was thinking about Chico. I got family up there."

"That's the school with the riots? The party school, right?" She burst into tears, stormed to a roll-top desk littered with bills and folders and scraps of paper and started flinging files and pens and whatever else she could grab at me.

"It's a small place, and I like small places, and…"

"No, you're an alcoholic drug addict, and you want to be in high school forever. As if the long distance thing isn't hard enough, you bastard!" She picked up a heavy ceramic vase on a nearby nightstand and threw it; I ducked, and it crashed through the bedroom window behind me out past the balcony rail.

"Hey, hey, everything copacetic in there?" Alex called out.

I walked to the shattered window and peered out. The tub folk looked back at me, cowed from the uneasy aura now cast over the house.

"Sorry about that," I said.

"*Oh, he's sorry! He's real fucking sorry! A sorry selfish little prick!*" Lee howled.

"Daren, you're not being an ass, are you?" Val demanded.

"He's a little boy. *A scared little boy!* Rachel, did you know Keith's looking to move five hundred miles north?" Lee wailed.

"No, actually, I didn't," Rachel said.

"We're mulling over possibilities. Nothing's carved in stone yet," Keith insisted, shooting a few eye daggers my way.

Lee huffed and rolled her eyes and fled out the front door of the condo.

"Ah…sorry about that. My fault. We were talking about college, and she got upset."

"Why did she get upset?" Val asked.

"Val, zip it," Alex said.

"Sit tight. We'll work it out. Enjoy the bar. See ya in a bit."

I paused long enough to grab her jacket and ran after her, sprinting past the condos' security kiosk. When I reached the main road I saw her about a hundred yards away, walking south toward Santa

Monica down the Pacific Coast Highway. She wandered off the road, jumping over granite seawall boulders down to a beach. She stood silhouetted against silver beach break, a Kilroy half-sun peering at us over the ocean horizon.

I came up behind her, dropped her jacket on the sand, and encircled my arms around her waist. She stiffened. "Don't," she said, but took my hands in hers nonetheless.

"Please try to understand," I said.

"Do you want to be with me forever?"

"You know I do."

"Then why are you doing this?"

"There is nothing in the world I wouldn't do for you. If this has to be the way, then I'll go to UCLA. Fuck it."

"You'll be miserable."

"I can handle it."

"I'll be miserable knowing you're miserable."

"You're already miserable. The only reason you're here is because of necessity."

"The only thing I've ever wanted is to be an actress."

"And I'd never ask you to give that up. I just need you to be patient a while longer."

"It's that bad? Those visions?"

I shivered. "Like mini heart attacks, almost."

"How often has it happened to you?"

"I guess about half a dozen times. The first...when that homeless guy blinded himself at Rubio's...no, wait, when Alex and I were kids. This red-black boogey thing-a-ma-bob...it's hard to describe."

"You really think you see *beyond*."

"When we rolled the Camaro...I may have...I dunno, stepped out for a bit."

"*Stepped out?*"

"I don't know. What I do know is it's more than I can take if it continues."

"The drugs and booze can't help."

"That's very true. I'm going to work on that. After I finish undergrad, we'll move to San Diego, or San Francisco. You can act in prestigious regional theaters in either one of those places. We've talked about it. And I can go to grad school up north or down south. I know you don't want to stay in LA."

"I know. I have to be here, and I can't be here. Damn it all. Well, San Diego is an hour away from LA auditions, I suppose. And there's the Old Globe Theater. I'm so tired of good-byes. I hate those words. I loathe them. You and I say them so much."

"I know. We're almost there, baby."

"Do you believe in fairy tales?"

I swallowed a cynical retort. "Some."

"Do you know the only thing that has kept me from going nuts down here in this hellhole is I knew each weekend I'd be seeing you and holding and kissing you? Is it possible for two people to keep falling in love over and over?"

"I think we know the answer to that."

She wept in my arms. I held her for a long time. Night fell.

"I hope they were smart enough to go without us," Lee said.

"Rachel knows where the club is. I bet she didn't want to go without you."

"Aren't you cold?" Lee asked as I picked up her jacket and draped it over her shoulders. I was in my bathing trunks, shirtless and barefoot, shivering like mad.

"Nope," I lied. We went to the seawall and started back. Malibu had hit the streets, Beamers and Mercedes and Euro-imports whizzing by.

"When we fall asleep together, you know what it's like?" Lee asked.

"Tell me."

"It's like eating banana cream pie while watching a nineteen-forties Gene Kelly musical, wearing my favorite terry robe and fuzzy slippers, nude underneath, and you bestowing hugs and kisses on me, especially kisses, and whisking me away to our private Lear jet waiting to take us to a semi-deserted island where we're greeted by friendly natives who take us to the innermost part of the island, where we run naked through fields of green grass and swim in warm ponds shaded by trees bearing fruit sweeter than we've ever tasted, and we make passionate love under moonlight, and that's where we spend the rest of our days."

We stopped on the side of the busy highways, and I brushed a tear away from her cheek.

"That's the most splendid thing anyone's ever said to me. I don't deserve you."

"You just figured it out?" she said, eyes twinkling.

Maybe we can make this work after all.

"I'll owe you, I swear. We'll have kids, a big fancy wedding, anything you want."

"You got *that* right."

When we arrived at the condo, our cohorts were gone. A scrawled note from Alex stated, *At the Whiskey. Come join us.* A footnote in Val's handwriting: *Lee—leave the asshole home, and we'll find you a real man.* Lee smirked, I grunted, and we brewed some coffee. They returned about four a.m. Lee slept, and I was wide-awake. I didn't join their post-clubbing chatter. I was busy plumbing the depths of my mindscape, cavorting on desert islands with Gene Kelly while flocks of ravens circled overhead.

Later that month Keith and I scheduled a pre-enrollment trip to Chico to tour the university grounds and gather reconnaissance on living arrangements. We met Tim there, a long-lost cousin of mine, stopped by his trailer, a yellow, rusted hulk plopped in the back of a junkyard. I knocked, timid, expecting some hick Sonoma-Jersey hybrid to come out with a scattergun, barking at us to *git off his prop'ty.* A grizzly, black-bearded young hipster greeted us with a lengthy bong and a sack of Chico green. We'd come to the right place.

Chico was no Santa Crisca. It was *slower* there, people cruising mountain bikes, eucalyptus trees and brick coffeehouses lining the streets, rock gardens and PUD tracts and secret crack houses and hidden dope fields, the populace an eclectic mix of Bay Area refugees, retro hippies, alternative dropouts, granola fanatics, wayward outlaws, and Green Party members. The surrounding areas consisted of almond tree orchards and strawberry fields, cleaved down the middle by the Sacramento River. Tim mentioned the local staple, and I discovered folks there pronounced "almonds" as "am-munz" where I'd always heard it as "all-munz." I razzed him about it, but he was well versed in the code of ball breaking and dished it as well as he got it. It was reassuring to find the relativity of *dude-ness* was a constant throughout California. We clicked with Tim so much so that he asked us if we were looking for a third roomie, and we invited him to join us on the spot. In a few days we put down deposits on a three-bedroom townhouse. After clearing it with Rachel (who had taken the move with a bit less hostility than Lee), Keith dug in, claiming he'd stay until school rang in if I'd pack up our apartment's meager belongings back home. I agreed and hopped a train downstate.

After finalizing preparations, Lee and I took a vacation to Mazatlan. It was grand: tequila, dancing, parasailing, horseback riding on the beach, the tropical works. Her alabaster skin sunburned as expected, and sadly I was unable to locate banana cream pies anywhere about town. And yes, on the third day, as we sunned in a rented cabana, a vendor idled by. He had hats for sale, of course. I didn't mention the *deja-vu* to Lee. I never told her about my intuitive reverie, that she'd appeared behind dark wings in my dreamtime before I met her. It seemed silly to think I would repeat verbatim the same things that I (he) said the first time around. I bought a hat and did indeed fumble with the bargaining, yet unlike the first "me," I remained firm on price and he acquiesced, perhaps because I was wise enough not to use a Scarface accent. So it wasn't exactly like before. As in the dream she balked at donning the hat initially, then agreed after I mentioned—*again*—the prior night's calisthenics. I tried to vibe the incorporeal me from the past. No dice. The whole experience was far too non-linear for my feeble bag o' marbles. I bit into the soggy lime topping my cold beer as I (he) had done once upon a time. It was tart, memorable two times over. Freaky-deaky. We ran out into warm Pacific surf and splashed and caroused, and I soon forgot him (me). Whatever.

After the trip we were melancholy in the face of my impending departure. I reassured her about The Plan over dinner one night in DeeBee just before leaving. When she dropped me off at my parents' place, she was tight-lipped and brooding.

"Don't you say the words. Don't you dare. I'll be flying to North Cal inside of thirty days. No need. I don't want to hear them, ever," Lee said.

"You got it. I'll pick you up at SF International in a month."

"Call me tonight when you get there."

She wasn't going to say it. No good-byes.

I avoided closure with Alex and Valerie. I left a short message on their answering machine detailing our imminent move to Chico. Neither Keith nor I had seen them since the condo in Malibu. No immediate callbacks had been forthcoming. It was safe to assume they weren't thrilled about our decision to hike upstate, or maybe they were raging away, hiding from the usual realities. Likely both. I decided to pass on finding out. My transition was occupying too much time to have a go-round with my shadow twin.

One long-awaited development in the nick of time for the move—I had satisfied all of the Department of Motor Vehicles' standards for reinstating my driver's license. The VW squareback had long since been rendered obsolete by California emission standards, so my parents gave me an ample going-away gift to facilitate my journey, a used Nissan pickup with low miles and good maintenance. After two years of hitching rides, mooching, and paying Greyhound fares, the little truck might as well have been a chariot of Zeus.

My exit from the homestead was a little less daunting than my departure from Lee.

"Remember, grass doesn't grow on a busy highway," Dad said.

"Thanks, Pop, I'll keep that in mind."

"Stay away from any student organization that requires members to wear red berets," Jim said. He'd gotten a seedy one-bedroom in Dee-Bee and was now doggedly following a blue-collar construction trail.

"Will do, Jimmy," I said.

Mom was quiet. "You're not going to bid me a fond farewell, Mother dearest?" She shook her head, hugged me tight. "The cat's already packed in the truck," I whispered in her ear. A tear rolled down her face. Excruciating. She went inside, no words, probably to a bottle. I was becoming accustomed to the women in my life shunning rituals of parting etiquette.

I hopped in my newfound wheels and rolled out. The pickup's bed sank low with the combined goods of my roomie and me, even with the extra U-Haul trailer hitched to the tow ball in back. Up the barren stretches of Interstate 5, through California's Central Valley agriculture and cattle country, I passed dozens of semis loaded with farm goods and harvested crops, sucking in the odiferous stench of compacted vegetables. Five hours later I reached the Golden State capitol and took an off ramp to stop for fuel. At the nearest gas station, a group of homeless scalawags congregated on the corner. One of them came up to me while I was pumping gas and asked for a buck. I gave him a five. I wanted to ask if he was Jehovah or Joshua incognito.

"Thanks, sonny, you don't know how much this means," he rasped, smelling of thunderbird wine.

"No problem."

"Really. You don't *know*."

I thought he was giving me a hard time. Then I gathered his drift.

"You're right. I don't know. My apologies."

"That's better," he said and walked back to his cronies.

I headed out of Sacramento northbound on Highway 99, toward what would prove to be the cessation of a great moribund age and after years of effete posturing, coming upon insanity at long last.

23

Flashing strobes bordered on inducing seizure inside the dungeon-like club. Dense sundries of smoke, clove, bong, hashish, tobacco, lay thick above us, a kaleidoscope of vaporous woolpack. Death-defying drinks titled Block and Tackles sat before Keith and me, equal parts tequila, rum, vodka, gin, triple sec, Kentucky whiskey, grenadine, melon liqueur, lemon wedge, shit-brown in color, thoroughly disgusting.

The speakeasy-cum-Roman-orgy served as the second leg of my twenty-first birthday celebration. I was the last in our crew to reach the coveted age of ascension. Alex had flown into Reno to meet Keith and me for a weekend in Lake Tahoe, then San Francisco. The first day in Tahoe was blurry: evergreens and Vikingsholm at Emerald Bay, blackjack at Bill's Casino, flashing slot machine lights, tinkling coins, a suite overlooking the lake on the top floor at Harvey's. The free drinks had flowed until we stumbled out of Harrah's at dawn. After coffee and biscuits and gravy at Denny's and a couple of joints, we set off on our next mission, finding a certain underground club in San Francisco. My cousin Tim had given us directions and the password to a place in the Castro district "we'd never forget." The fact that we needed a password to get in was reason enough to interest us; moreover, the password was *fuckadilly*. At the door we paid fifty-dollar cover charges per person. Tim had insisted the price was worth it just to see the sights. We weren't sure what he'd meant.

We were now finding out what he meant. Upon recovering from our initial shock, Alex retired to the restroom for extracurricular skiing activity. Keith and I snagged a table after its previous occupants vacated to join a bout of vicious group sex occurring nearby. Slender neon tubing snaked across the walls and ceiling, glass slogans spelling out indulgent rhetoric like *Yesterday Is Now* and *Stuff Is All You Need*. The "club" was a dank stone basement tricked up with futuristic deco, its sleek mezzanine hosting scattered cocktail tables, floor-to-ceiling mirrors, and plastic blue wrestling mats wet with bodily fluids. A chrome railing lined the balcony circling the second story, and there was a dance floor with a chalky-black deejay stage. A monstrous sound system had the place pulsing as several hundred people crammed the roadhouse. No matter where we looked, San Franciscan counterculture engaged in unreserved debauchery, almost every patron fucking, dancing, or ingesting some intoxicant. Many were using condoms, just as many were not. Spent rubbers of all shapes, sizes, and colors littered the saturated floor. In front of our table three young women strapped on dildo apparatuses, oiling them up with lubricant, moaning, high on designer drugs, eyes dilated and bottomless. To our left a giant black man pumped in and out of a middle-aged brunette, her buttocks, worn with stretch marks, rippling under his thrusts.

"That's somebody's little girl," Keith said, referring to a blonde not a day over nineteen receiving extensive oral attention from not one but two leather-garbed men. The duo of mustachioed-Goth jocks ceased their strange, double cunnilingus and began taking the blonde from above and below. We looked away, our hayseed tolerances at maximum, but there was nowhere to rest our eyes, every direction illustrating a shocking form of lecherous sexuality. For a city rife with AIDS awareness, it was unbelievable, paradoxical. Corners packed with groups taking hits of nitrous oxide, bar tables surrounded by loadies sucking on multi-stemmed hookahs crammed with potent variations of northern green, coke bullets passing back and forth between gropes and orgasms. Couples both hetero and homo screwed and came on the mats, on the stage, on the railings. Most attendees were naked, and the few who weren't sported fetish-type gear, lace teddies and heels, schoolgirl skirts and pigtails, black biker leather and vinyl and S&M costuming, studded masks and spiked collars. The San Franciscan underground sex club made Halloween in Santa Crisca look like white-gloved proper high tea and scones at Windsor.

Egad, these nomads of gonads. Check, please.

"Dude, we are outclassed here," I said.

"No shit. No way can I tell Rachel about this."

I'd never felt a place so void. The reckless chaos, the purity of the dark light, was seductive. The despairing cave and its Neanderthal inhabitants fascinated me. The majority of folk present weren't all demons or incubi or pagan devil worshippers or strung-out anarchist bikers or mindless black tar heroin junkies. No, they were mostly regular joes, comprising the club's bulk stock trade not of the happenstance spectator variety such as us, but rather stemming from the wide spectrum of Bay area color. Union Square squires, North Beach nine-to-fivers, haggard sirens of the night from the Tenderloin, UCSF med students, Berkeley upper grads, Stanford jocks fresh in from sushi-karaoke joints off Embarcadero, skinheads, and gangbangers highlighting their bouts of barhopping between Haight and Van Ness, East Bay middle-classers enjoying a forbidden fruit bang-a-rama, suburbanites from Oakland, Vallejo, Livermore, and Walnut Creek, assorted gimps, pimps, dominatrices and their sadomasochistic slaves, post-duty cops, pre-duty dishwashers and waitresses prepping for graveyard shifts with biological speedballs of adrenalin-enhanced orgasm. The allure wasn't born simply from primal evolutionary urge to spread seed nor the luster of the spicy menu offerings. I was as red-blooded as the next tomcat and the temptation of easy access blowjobs, rim jobs, threesomes, and multiple fillings of any and all crevices with a veritable harem of skanks was, to say the least, heady. I didn't want to cheat on Lee and never had unless I counted the Disney Swiss Family Robinson fiasco after the graduation breakup. The real draw was the mindset, the moral—or amoral—freedom required to release inhibition across such a broad scale. What a rush it must have been for them, a sensory bacchanalia, especially the first time, the choice to enter that domain and return to their daily normal lives forever changed. Did they really not anticipate unknown lasting effects on psyche, or did they just not care? Either way the place was proof positive that black magick voodoo wacka-wacka 'tweren't for the squeamish.

The stench of cum and marijuana became putrid. I puked and what felt like gallons of brackish liquid gushed out of me. I sputtered and coughed. Keith gaped. After a few rounds of dry heaves, I looked around, and not a single person had noticed my fit of nausea.

"You OK?" Keith asked.

"Not really. Let's bail."

"About time. We just got drunk at Alex and Val's on my twenty-first, watched Letterman and crashed, you know?"

We deserted our drinks, trying to edge by the black giant without touching any flailing body appendages, of which there were many. The brunette cried out, spent and whimpering. My clothes had accumulated a sodden texture, and I shuddered at the implications. Too much aqueous human sludge was squirting and dripping and oozing, in the air, on the floor, by land and by sea. At the next table a man dressed in a black blazer and nothing else sipped a martini while masturbating. There was a pile of cocktail napkins at the edge of his table, and I took them and toweled off as best as I could. Then it was Keith's turn to yak, splashing his own brown mess near the man's feet. The Block and Tackles had overwhelmed our compromised systems. Blazer Guy swore at Keith yet kept stroking away. We ignored him as best as we could. *Our best* was not cutting it.

A tall woman approached, albino skin glowing in the dark, a Celtic white corpse-whore straight out of Yeats. Deep crimson hair dangled over surgically enhanced breasts, and she wore red eye shadow that glowed like hellfire under the strobes. She had emerged from a group of seething twenty-somethings engaged in an enthusiastic marathon of mass fellatio. The only piece of clothing she was wearing was a plastic transparent bra. Her nipples were blue and puckered because the hollowed brassiere was filled with a marine-colored gel, like the liquid in one of those desktop novelty wave machine gizmos. She smiled at me, then at Keith. "You seem to be the only men in here unoccupied. Wanna fuck?"

"Ah...no. Thanks anyway. I'm just sort of..." I looked over at Keith for help. He was pale and distant. "We're just sort of tourists." My eyes wandered her body, lingering on the blue fluid, its buoyancy jiggling her silicon double D's. A fishy slick sheen coated her thighs. I wondered how many guys she'd had so far that night. She was a *Red Sonja* version of Deborah Harry, enhanced to the Nth degree, an eighties Amazon in unchaste rapture.

"Tourists! You're even cuter when you say that. Are you sure you don't want to fuck?"

"I'm sure."

"Your loss." She grabbed my crotch as she passed, giving it a painful squeeze.

"Ow. OK, places like this shouldn't exist," I muttered.

"Let's go. To hell with Alex. I'll wait in the car if I have to," Keith said. But Alex appeared from the bathroom as we reached a row of linebacker bouncers near the exit. Two blondes followed him, black-eyed, frosty-nosed, naked as jaybirds. Alex's jaw was grit so hard tiny varicose veins throbbed in his cheek.

"Dudes! This place is out of hand!"

"We're out of here," I said.

"I have not yet begun to rage!"

"Fine. We'll see you at the car."

"What the hell, dude? It's your birthday!"

"Don't be a dick," I said.

"Lighten up! I'm just having a good time! Like you two bozos should be doing."

"Alex, let's go," I said. Keith nodded in agreement.

"There's that barometer again. What would we do without you, Daren?"

He took his two anonymous babes into the crowd.

"Idiot," Keith said.

We left. The cold, foggy air of San Francisco was evergreen compared to the basement, no sex or smoke or liquor in it, only normal urban discord, diesel fuel, pigeon shit, spoiled garbage bin produce, industry, and asphalt. Castro District regulars swarmed the streets in burlesque transgender regalia, robust and unapologetic. More than once we were approached and propositioned. We smoked a joint right out in the open. I reminded myself to reprimand my cousin for what was now an obvious joke on us SoCal boys. A few hours passed, and Alex stumbled out to the car, where inside Keith and I dozed. He dove inside, clearly at his limit, strung out and dehydrated. We hit a twenty-four-hour coffeehouse and sobered up. Afterward we said little as we dropped Alex off at SF International. I refused to inquire about his doings inside the club. Didn't want to know. He shuffled away toward his gate. The red-light district mecca had taken one of us and banished the others. I was thankful I'd been one of the exiles. I'd have given even odds I could've been the sacrificial lamb instead.

Oh, Dusty.

24

Time in Chico was a roller coaster. A year passed in alternating inter-
vals of dawdling and cursory eras. I double majored in social psychology and general philosophy. I was disillusioned. My suspicions
had been confirmed. The Western study of mind was biased, blasé in
exploring metaphysic aspects of existence. More whitebreads teaching lil' whitebreads, same as it ever was. My philosophy teachers
smoked cigarettes during class, wore dark sunglasses, and were well
on their way to coronary arrest brought on from too much scotch
and not enough sunshine. Early curricula focused on classical Greek
disciplines, Plato, Aristotle, and Socrates, then Descartes, Spinoza,
Kant and Kierkegaard, Hume and Locke, Heidegger, Sartre, prag-
matism, utilitarianism, nihilism, theism, all the assorted *isms* of the
White Way. I took a liking to phenomenology and existentialism, the
anarchic German romantics' works, Nietzsche and Schopenhauer.
They were mostly sexist narcissists. Yet their method of embracing
knowledge through ignorance of the known was a tenet I appreciated.
Nietzsche was a sister-lusting, opiate-addled *ubermensch*; nonetheless, an *ubermensch* he remained.

Several of my professors hailed from across the pond (two Brits, a Spaniard, an Austrian, and a Swede, each owning doctorates in existentialist pomposity), and they fulfilled their stereotypes like the good soldiers they were. Merlot-soaked outlooks on life, check. Thin cigarettes, check. Disgust for us doomed-to-fail waves of the future, check. Even the bygone, six-feet-under masters I was studying were dark-lit crackpots, much the same as their modern brethren I loved to loathe, their apotheosis of mental wetworks passed down through generations, tweaked by black plagues, white tyranny, red scares, and the toil and rubble of war upon war. Though my mentors' scathing impressions of the immigrant upstart empire in which they were now marooned, mired in imperialist Mc-Wackery, were spot-on for the most part, their conclusions were impotent. It wasn't that I disagreed with them, I did by and large in regard to the weathered American ship of state, but condemning a two-hundred-year-old child for adhering to longstanding colonialist tradition inherited from a two-thousand-year-old hodgepodge of Anglican and Mediterranean lineage seemed superfluous. I challenged them frequently, both via pen and paper and with in-class raised hand, tired of their Life Is A Brief Joke With No Punch Line redundancies—*novel approach, never heard that take before, double fucking yawn.*

One exasperating Briton, a scarecrow of a fellow complete with tweed jacket and elbow patches, spectacles, and ivory-bowled pipe—the entire shtick ensemble—led a baker's dozen of us rare philosophy students (berets encouraged, not required) through a semester of English think-tank glitterati including Hobbes, both Bacons, Russell, and Locke. His most annoying habit was interrupting his prepared lecture and taking tangents into seething anti-American sentiment, scoffing at our lowbrow culture. During one afternoon class after parrying a number of queries from me regarding fallacies of the subject matter, he grew angry (in truth, I found Locke's anti-authoritarianism views intriguing; I was just screwing with the teacher because I was bored, because he was roused with ease and deserved a little ulcer-in-the-making). He asked me if I might dip into my well of wit and determine if I believed there was anything of significant value the Isles had brought to world record. I thought about it for a moment and conceded Pax Britannia had earned its middleman historical status when it carried the torch of conquest and racial decimation between the eras of Pax Romana and Pax Americana, and that apart from Elvis Presley, Chuck Berry, the Doors, and Van Halen, true classic rock and roll was born, bred, and perfected in England, no doubt about it. Other than those accolades, the former dubious and the latter well earned, I failed to see how shepherd's pie and the insufferable Limey trait of Constant-Stick-Up-The-Ass were noteworthy contributions to global social cartography, at which point he threw up his hands in disgust and dismissed us for the day. Anarchy in the UK indeed. Pots had to be careful about insulting kettles. I'd finally figured that out, which is why I'd begun to cease passing judgment on my mother, or Alex, or any other soggy fool in the soup bowl of Terra Firma, within the confines of my meager abilities to do so.

The psychology forums were more frustrating. I stopped paying much attention when it became clear the major's emphasis was based on hard science of the brain, biopsychology and behaviorism, Freud, Piaget, Maslow, and Skinner. None of their teachings contained anything I felt imperative to incorporate for future use. Still I made the grades. As usual, classes and grad school prep weren't difficult to master. When I wasn't bonging with Keith and Tim, watching *Star Trek: The Next Generation,* playing Nintendo, or mountain biking, I was ascertaining how and when I would see Lee next.

The last time I'd seen her was at her father's funeral. The bone cancer had won in the end. Cancers tend to do that. It devastated Lee. I took two weeks off school and helped her move from Angel City back in with her mother in DeeBee, putting her acting career on hold as she mourned her father. We'd been meeting maybe once or twice over two-month spans. Six hundred miles was farther than I'd thought. The long-distance gig was shaky ground. I failed to see how people did it for years and years.

She kept me apprised of news on the home front. Alex and Valerie weren't doing well. Their common-law bliss became problematic when Alex's in-and-out-of-rehab woes had increased in intensity and frequency. He'd visited several facilities across California with no long-term success and was feeling it, prone to volatile mood swings and wicked gluttonous binges. When Lee suggested Valerie hop on the wagon as a token of good faith support, depriving Alex of temptation at home, Val told her she'd sooner hump the entire junior varsity team. She had it under control, "unlike the three stooges."

I picked Lee up at the airport in Sacramento a few months after the funeral. We took the necessary time to reacquaint. It wasn't becoming easier. I biked to a campus sandwich shop and brought back lunch. We ate the fixings on a tattered couch stinking of bicycle grease and bong water. She asked me how I was grooving on my secondary major.

"Pretty boring," I said, munching a ham and Swiss on rye.

"Come on. You and philosophy are like chocolate and peanut butter."

"Some of it's OK."

"Well, it's good to know you're not the *Bodhidharma* you think you are and that the world may yet have some archived information of use to you," she teased.

"Ah, when you utter the names of Zen masters outta that luscious mouth of yours, it makes me wanna bend you over hot and heavy."

"I'll remember that later, when I remind you to be as selfless as possible, at peace with your inner self, no earthly desires motivating your actions as you unhook my bra."

"Heh. Actually it's funny you mention that. Do you know there is only one semester's worth of offerings on Eastern dogma here at Chico State, and it's taught by a University of Nebraska good old boy? I mean, not to be racist or anything, but…"

"But you figured that course ought to have a Tibetan cave monk at its helm."

"Well, yeah, duh."

"Too many cartoons, kid."

"Maybe. I figure I'll read the curriculum's books rather than sign up for six months of Okie-sponsored Buddhism. That said, I never took to the idea of reincarnation."

"Gee, that's a shocker."

"How so?"

"First off, schoolboy, Buddhism rejects the idea of a soul. It's Hinduism that promotes the idea of reincarnation. Secondly, the idea of spending eternity being anyone other than Super Daren must be downright incomprehensible."

210

"Maybe," I groused.

"Megalomaaaaaaaaniac. Well, which of the fellows who won the West are you most relating to, if any?"

"Aristotle was a smart guy. And Plato. A few of those Greek guys were millennia ahead of their time. And I do like Nietzsche, though he was a twisted sideshow freak in his personal life. Descartes had a point or two."

"I think, therefore I am."

"Yeah. It's all good to know, I guess."

"Can it be that someone has actually learned something?"

"Perish the thought."

We finished our lunch and went to my room. She was tired. We slept through the afternoon. That evening I fixed her a collegiate dinner (Kraft macaroni and cheese, sliced hot dogs thrown into the mix). I taught her how to play chess, which she took to like a duck in water, beating me the second and third games. I'd never bested my father, who'd taught me how to play, and I didn't have the luxury of thinking I'd thrown the games. She really *did* beat me, quick as the slip between cup and lip. Keith and Tim had friends over and engaged in a number of arcane drinking games, whereupon the white noise level became boisterous. We decided to head over to campus for a brisk walk.

Red maple leaves swirled about, and thunderhead clouds with moonlit linings rolled in. A few frat boys sped by in a white Chrysler convertible, bawling out testosterone-laden comments to Lee, who ignored them. At the school, a clock tower sheathed in black shingle and ocher brick reared above the student common.

"I miss my father," Lee said.

"I know."

"I miss singing."

"You'll be singing again soon."

"I miss *you*."

"I miss you too. I'm sorry."

"Why are you sorry?"

"I'm sorry I came. I'm sorry I didn't go to UCLA. It was a huge mistake."

We meandered through campus toward the sport fields, passing through student groups leaving late night library sessions. I led her out to one of the college's baseball diamonds. "Keith and I wanted to get out of Santa Crisca, right? And you knew how I felt about LA. But this place…it isn't right either. I'm not myself here."

It was true. Chico, while pleasant enough, was rural and isolated and not the best place for my mind to wander. It was too far from the raven. The addendum had failed.

"Let me guess. That bad vibe followed you all the way up here to Bumfuck County."

"I guess it did."

"Oh, don't tell me this. You were supposed to be happy if we made all these sacrifices for our future."

"You made the sacrifices. Not us. Not me. You. I was wrong, Lee. I was just…*wrong*."

"Well, well. Daren's not the wunderkind he's appeared to be after all this time. There's hope yet for us mortals."

She giggled and took off running. Deafening thunderclaps reverberated through the stadium. Lightning sizzled, illuminating the horizon, white coruscations catching her in mid-leap, freezing her in time. I chased her around the diamond, rust-colored gravel crunching under my feet, as I smelled the outfield's limed turf. I tackled her at second base, and we went down laughing. I knelt on one knee. Thunderheads rumbled louder, ominous, like the rolling of a sky-wide billiards rack, an epic electric pause in the air as if God was chalking his stick for a high-stakes game of Nine Ball with his fallen angel nemesis, "Cool-Hand Luke" Morning Star. No time like the present. I held her hand, looking into her eyes. I took a deep breath.

"Lee…will you marry me?"

Tears came forth. "Yes, Daren. I'll marry you. I would have married you six years ago and damn the consequences."

"I don't have a ring. It was spontaneous, and I'm a poor, starving student."

"That's OK. We've never been slaves to tradition."

She was ecstatic, but there too was overwrought weariness. Her grief for her father had turned her inside out like a tossed salad, a sidetracked woman spinning a roulette wheel.

25

The holiday season arrived. I went home for Christmas break, four weeks off before my final semester of undergraduate education.

"When Christmas day is here, the most wunnerful time of the year..." Valerie sang as she draped tinsel around a windowsill.

I was grumpy, nursing a Heineken. "Cut the caroling."

"It's my house, and I'll sing if I want to while I'm decorating." She looped a long strand of wooden cranberries laced with pine boughs on the fireplace mantle. Her tree, a tall evergreen giant, glittered with gold balls and silver bells, a white ceramic angel at its peak. A miniature toy train ran in endless circles around the tree's base. The locomotive had a tiny plastic engineer decked out in railroad stripes hanging out its side, dangling precarious from his perch to nowhere, following the nonstop track around and around.

Hmm.

"All right, do you want shrimp or steak on your skewer?" Alex asked. He slapped on a sauce-smeared apron.

"Steak, onions, baby tomatoes, peppers," I said.

"Anything else, *mawster?*"

"Lee going to stop by?" Valerie asked.

"She's working late."

"She's mad at me, isn't she?"

"I don't know."

But I did know. Lee had reached the end of her rope with Alex and Valerie's devil-may-care immodesty and the lack of commitment to their mutual health. She refused to see them.

"Bullshit, Daren. You and your girlfriend have always been the aristocrats. She thinks I make his decisions for him, doesn't she?"

"If you want to drink with Alex, that's your deal. I've done the same; I'm nobody to judge."

"And Lee is?"

"She's not like us, Val. You know that."

"Oh yes, she's Lady fucking Madonna, we've been through the drill. And the great infallible bachelor and all-powerful Oz—how is he handling the engagement?"

"It's cool."

"Alex shit his pants. I can't believe you didn't tell him."

"Didn't come up."

"Have you two talked about *anything* worthwhile?"

"Only about you. And Chico."

"Try harder. We don't see you as much, and it affects him. Believe me."

I grunted and went outside, where Alex turned over kabobs, brushing juicy bits of meat with a garlic-parmesan glaze.

"So," I mustered.

"Yup."

"Anyway…"

"Daren, what the fuck." He ladled globs of the garlicky sauce on a few more skewers and dropped them on the grill.

"Valerie's not happy about Lee."

"Neither am I. She's put on big britches that don't fit her. You oughta tell her to back off. We're not all super-nuns like her bad-ass self."

"Hostile much?"

"I'm sick of the evil eye. It's that simple."

"And the up-and-down rehab, how's that going for you?"

214

"I don't appreciate the condescending tone."

"I'm not condescending, I'm worried."

"You're worried. And yet you're still who you are. Keith is still the pot-smoking beach bum. Val drinks us all under the table, Lee's better than the rest of us. You and I drink whiskey together. But I'm the one who must change, or else." He put down his barbecue tools and poured a couple of shots of Jack. We downed them.

"You're the one who's most at risk."

"Really. Are you absolutely positive about that?"

I shrugged.

"I didn't think so."

"What happened, Alex?"

"I realized most of the world is not Durango Bay."

"Like we don't know that already?"

"No, we really don't, Daren," he said.

"I gotta go. I have to see Lee tonight."

"Come on, dude, we're just drinkin' and talkin'. Have some eats."

"Nope. See you guys."

I drove to Lee's house, where somebody was waiting, always waiting.

I pulled open the sliding door to her old room. She started in before I finished sliding it shut. "I can't do it. I thought I could. I can't. It's too much," she said, ranting.

My heart raced. She'd been crying for a while. Her eyes were torpid and sallow.

"No, don't say that, sweetheart, we can do this…I only have *six* more months to go."

"Yes, six more months until we start our life together. We get married. We have children. All that's bullshit and you know it!"

"Shh…your mother will hear."

"*I don't care!*" She was at wit's end. It had caught up to her. Everything. It was evident. I wondered why it had taken as long as it had. "I have been waiting for you…God, *forever*! I'm thirty years old! You have your whole life ahead of you."

"Aw, don't start that shit. I'm only eight years younger."

"It's NOT shit! It's my life! *When* are you going to wake up? It'll happen again. First it was high school, then college. In June it'll be some other damn thing."

"No, we're getting married. We're getting our own place. We're moving to San Francisco or San Diego. That's *The Plan*."

"You'll make some other stupid decision that only involves yourself, like going to grad school in fucking Montana. I can't do it again. I can't wait anymore. *I have to have a life!*"

"Or maybe when all this is finally about to happen, you're getting cold feet."

She gasped. "Oh, yes, that's EXACTLY it, Daren. You see right through me."

"*Is* that it?"

"You went to Chico. You kept smoking your dope. You kept drinking your booze. I call you, which is *all* we have for two months at a time, and you blow me off and tell me to call you later, or I ask you to come down for a wedding or some damned thing I need my *boyfriend* at, and you tell me it's too far a drive."

"This isn't easy for me either."

"Doesn't look so bad to me. You fuck me when I fly in. You don't have to work, and your parents are giving you a free ride. What's not to like?"

"I'm getting an education." *Are you for real, dude?*

"You hate it. You think you know everything already."

"You were OK with this before I left."

"I *had* to be OK with it. I was in love with you."

"*Was?*"

"It's harder now. I never see you."

"That's great. You preach, but you don't practice."

"Look who's talking! You tell everyone how things should be, and you don't live up to your own standards."

I slid open the door again and stepped out, hyperventilating. Her swimming pool's surface was glassy, reflecting the man in the moon, whose countenance had a ruddy shade. Watery ripples contorted his knowing face. *Red moon rising. Bad omen.*

"We've been fighting a lot this year, you know," she added.

She was right. The distance was killing us.

(I was killing us).

We were losing each other.

(I was losing her).

I knew where she was going, where she wanted me to go. Where she needed me to go.

"One of us gets mad, usually about something mundane, and the other reacts, and we cut each other to ribbons or make meaningless comments about our faults and weaknesses. It's sadistic, don't you think?"

"I suppose so," I admitted.

"I see pain and mist in those eyes I love so much. I know you better than you know yourself. I wish that you didn't have to hide it from me. Is it really so precious that you have to have it all to yourself?"

"I…it's not precious."

"You are my life, Daren. I have given it all to you. But dreams aren't enough for this life. I want more."

"Lee, don't do this. Don't fucking do this! I can't believe you're gonna bow out at the finish line. Goddamn you."

"Damn *you*, Daren."

"I'm sorry. I didn't mean that."

"It's a poor excuse to say you didn't mean it. You always try to right your very obvious wrongs. You have little consideration for other people's feelings when you're in God-mode. Which, incidentally, is far too much."

"You want me to go?"

"Yes."

"We're breaking up?"

"For now."

"What does that mean?"

"I don't know."

"You're breaking off the engagement?"

"I don't know. Right now…it might be a good idea if we cooled off, took a break…see what happens in the spring, or maybe when you get home from college."

I fumed. "You want to fuck someone else, that right?"

"You need to go now."

"How can we work it out if we're dating other people, for Chrissakes?"

"I never said it was about dating other people. If that happens, it happens. You have to *see* some things. I've tried to tell you. You have to figure it out yourself. You and your friends are waging a dying campaign."

"How poetic."

"Daren…it's too much to endure any longer."

"Whatever."

"Only one man has stolen my heart in my life." I opened my mouth to respond. "No, don't say anything. Just know that you are that man."

She slid the door shut and drew the blinds. I stood there until I heard weeping. Then I left, cursing the man in the moon as he spun grim tales and blighted legends.

26

Atop a small canyon in the hills of Chico, lingering rays of sunbeam imposed on my thoughts a brief complacency. I wondered what she was doing right then, and if I really wanted to know the answer.

I talked to Rachel on the phone a lot. She had accepted a mole position only because she was convinced my situation with Lee was temporary. Two months had dragged by since we broke up, not unlike crawling through a field of barbed wire wrapped in a shag rug. Lee had started seeing some DeeBee dude with whom I was not acquainted. Rachel wisely omitted gory details during our conversations. I posed insipid queries to her of whether it mattered that I cared. Rachel, insistent Lee was rebounding, kept my spirits up as I attempted to finish my senior seminars before graduation.

It's OK, the boys said. *Taking space is good. It'll come around. Don't sweat it.*

I swallowed bile, the bitter tang leaving a salty taste on my lips. I straddled my bike and rode back down the trail.

If you love somebody set them free.
If they come back...
What a crock.

The trail led along a ravine next to the Sacramento River. I rode hard, pedaling angry, stewing. Twilight set in as the sun and the moon peeked at each other across the sky, like gamblers' poker faces, ready to bluff. When I got home, Keith and Tim were watching *Jeopardy!* I sat next to them and stared blankly at Alex Trebek. The phone rang, and Keith answered it. "Hello? Uh, hi. How's it going? Sure, he's right here." He covered the mouthpiece. "Dude, it's Lee."

"I'll take it in my room." I ran upstairs and picked up the receiver. "Hello?"

"Hi," she said, timid.

An awkward pause ensued. "Ah, if this gets any more high school, it won't be pretty."

"I wanted to hear your voice. I'm sorry. Maybe I shouldn't have called."

"No, no, I'm glad you called. I was thinking about you today. I was riding in a canyon outside of town, and the sun was setting, and it reminded me of you. What's up?"

"The usual. Mom's OK, the job's boring. I'm waiting for my new black-and-white portfolio."

"You *are* going to start auditioning again."

"I think so."

"That's good. That's very good."

"I understand you talk to Rachel sometimes."

"Yeah."

"I guess you know about my, uh, deal."

"I've heard."

Be cool.

"Are you seeing anyone?"

"No."

"Oh, sure."

"A few dates, more bar-buddy stuff than anything. Nothing serious. How about you? He's nice to you?"

"He's there for me right now. We spend time together. He just got out of a long relationship, too. It kind of…works for both of us, right now."

"But you *are* sleeping with him, right?"

"Let's not discuss that."

"Yeah, OK." *Grr.*

"Is it hard for you?"

I checked my anger, my pleas for forgiveness, the expletives and apologies I wanted to blurt out. I held it all back. There was no point in letting my rabid barrel of monkeys explode in her face. "Yes, it's hard for me."

"I miss you so much."

"You shouldn't be talking like that. You're seeing someone. Not nice."

"He's got this ex-girlfriend..."

"Let me stop you right there. While I'd like to support you in any way possible, I don't think I can listen to petty details of your love life."

"I'm sorry. You're right. I wouldn't either."

"It's OK."

"I miss you, Lamb Chop."

"I miss you too, baby." I hesitated, knowing the probable response to my next question. "Maybe we could have coffee when I'm down in DeeBee over spring break and talk?"

"Maybe."

"It'll be the last time I'm home before graduation."

"Did you get into any grad schools yet?"

"San Diego State's master's program, and UC San Diego's doctoral program. Haven't heard from any others yet."

"Oh, that's wonderful! Have you decided on anything?"

"I was kinda waiting...I was considering all my options."

There you go. Play it cool. Even though you haven't accepted admission anywhere because you're waiting to see if the raven's going to take you back.

"I see."

"Lee...do you want to see me?"

"I...I'm not sure. I don't know if I'm ready yet."

"I don't want to impose on whatever you got going on. I just want to see you." *Like I don't want you to dump this loser and jump into my arms.*

"I don't know. I'll have to think about it."

"It's only me."

"Daren, *don't.*"

"OK. I didn't mean to push it."

"I should go now. Hearing your voice has been nice. In a torturous kind of way."

"I know what you mean."

"I'm not sorry I called, though."

"Neither am I."

"OK…I love you, Daren."

"I love you too, Lee."

"Bye."

"See ya."

She hung up. Had I known it was the last time I would ever speak to her I might have discussed more pressing issues.

27

I struggled with my jeans. They were tighter than usual. I had gained some weight, no doubt thanks to a few too many midnight munchie runs. I chewed on a piece of dry toast, thinking about which books I needed for class. I filled my backpack with the day's texts and went downstairs, breathing in odors of WD-40 lube and milk. Keith sat at the kitchen table slurping down a bowl of Cheerios. In the living room, Tim greased up bike chains for his morning ride, oil-streaked rags strewn across the floor.

"Mornin," Keith mumbled between spoonfuls of cereal.

"Urgh," I said.

"You were up late watching the tube," Tim remarked.

"Couldn't sleep," I replied.

The phone rang. Keith picked it up. "Hello? Hey, what's up? Yeah, he's here." He threw the phone to me. "It's Alex."

"It's a little early, isn't it?" I said into the phone.

"I haven't slept yet. Me and Valerie were up all night."

"I'm not up for a post-slopes ramble, Alex. I've got to get to class."

"Are you sitting down?"

"I *hate* it when people say that. What's the problem?"

"Fuck. I don't know how to say this." I heard Valerie's voice in the background. "No, I'll do it. Daren...we live just down the block...um, from the guy Lee's been seeing."

Oh no.

"And last night we heard shots from up the street."

"Gunshots?"

"Yeah. There's police all over the place. We're not really sure, but... oh, fuck. I'm sorry, man, but we think that...that..." His voice faltered. "We saw the coroner's car. It looks like somebody shot the guy...and Lee...last night."

My God, no, he didn't just say that.

"Wh...what?" My knees gave way. I collapsed in a chair. Keith and Tim looked at me curiously. "Are you *sure*? Is she OK? Did they take her to the hospital?"

"I don't know. We talked to the cops...they've been talking to everyone on the block...and they won't say straight out what happened. It *might* have been a murder-suicide, we don't know. But they think it was the dude's ex-girlfriend."

"Alex, how do you know anyone is dead?"

This can't be right, this can't be happening.

"We saw them...uh, fuck...we saw them carry out a couple of body bags."

My fingers and hands grew cold. Dizzying pain burst inside my head. Reddish-black haze settled over me, thick and damp and sticky.

"Daren, we shouldn't jump to any conclusions. There's a possibility she killed one of them and then killed herself. The cops aren't saying one way or another yet. They're taking statements from other neighbors right now. We told them everything we heard last night. We figured you'd want to get down here."

"Did you call Lee's mother?"

"The cops said *they* would."

Not a good sign.

"Alex, *find out what the fuck happened!*"

"I will. I promise. Either way you should get down here right now."

"I'm out the door. Can you call my mother and tell her?"

"Sure. Look, a plane from Sacramento will get here faster. We can pick you up at the airport in Santa Crisca."

"No…it won't matter. By the time I check in and wait for a flight, it won't make that much difference. This has gotta be a mistake. Oh, fuck. This can't be right."

"Just get down here. Don't kill yourself on the way, either."

"Can't be right. I didn't feel it."

"What?"

"I didn't *feel* it. I'd have felt it. If she died."

"There's no use in thinking about that now. We don't know shit yet."

"I'm out the door."

I put the phone back in its cradle.

My body quaked.

"What's up?" Tim asked.

"Um…I gotta run home right now."

"Why? What happened?" Keith asked.

"Ah…he said that maybe, um, Lee…and her new boyfriend… were shot last night."

"*What?*" Keith demanded.

"I dunno. Might have been a murder-suicide by an ex-girlfriend. They don't know. I have to go find out. Jesus."

Keith put his hand on my shoulder. "Anything you need."

"Ditto that," Tim said.

"I'm gone."

They watched me leave, my wobbly footsteps betraying my fluttering mind. I hopped in the truck, lighting a smoke. It shook in my mouth, ash dribbling on my clothes. I rounded the turn to the highway. I floored the gas pedal.

This can't this be right. Those sorts of things don't happen in Durango Bay, that's why every good whitecrust family settles there—because it's not like the big bad city, because it's fucking sterilized Disneyland. Maybe that girl offed the dude in front of Lee, maybe she almost got caught in the crossfire, she could be OK, scared outta her mind, but OK.

Maybe maybe maybe.

Jesus, oh my God, no.

I passed the outer limits of northern Sacramento. I'd made it in under an hour, usually a two-hour drive from Chico. I'd smoked ten cigarettes, tempered with paranoia and fatalism.

As Alex said. What's on the other side of the line? Let's find out, kids. It can't be right. I didn't feel her go. She's my raven, my soul mate. I would have felt her go. Did I? Did I feel anything odd last night?

I remembered watching *Star Trek*. That was all.

Let it not be true.

Let this be a huge miscommunication.

Let her light continue on.

I don't even care if I get her back.

Just let her not…be gone.

Please.

The truck flew down Interstate Five at one hundred plus. Too slow. My mind raced much faster. Black thoughts barraged me, ranging from motley bargains with God to condemnations of myself. If in fact it had all been misconstrued, if when I arrived and she was alive and apoplectic at my hurried tour downstate, I would never, ever let her go. *Scratch that, screw that noise, fuck reconciliation with me, if she never speaks to me again I'll cherish the fact she lights up the world somewhere, anywhere. The universe needs her a lot more than I do.*

The four hundred miles between Sacramento and Durango Bay were a blur. By the time I turned into the driveway to the ranch, the usual eight-hour trip had taken under five hours and I was a thousand years older. The proof would be irrefutable if my friends were congregated at my parents' house, and indeed, through the road dust, there they were: Alex's new Jeep Cherokee, Rachel's Mercedes, Jim's Ford F-150, and Valerie's Cabriolet.

The sunny afternoon grew senseless and unsubstantial.

I parked the truck behind the Mercedes. The engine sputtered and spat and coughed from the severe overexertion I had put it through. I lit another smoke, tasting foul road sweat and anguish, not wanting to go inside, not at all. I sucked on the Marlboro until it was one long ember and stubbed it out. I got out of the truck and walked to the front porch. The screen door was shut, the main door open. I crept up and peered inside the living room window. My family and friends were gathered inside watching the local news channel. Alex, tight-lipped and cross-armed, paced back and forth. Valerie sat on the couch next to my parents. She cried, my mother too, my father's arm around her shoulders. Rachel sat on the floor, her face wet and red. Jim stood in the kitchen drinking a beer. A news reporter's voice droned away. TV always told me the deal, a regal ambassador of red shift. I owed it much allegiance. "Detectives say they are unaware of the whereabouts of the suspect. An APB has been put out statewide, and citizens are reminded not to approach the subject, as she is considered armed and dangerous. The two victims…"

And then they posted video images of some guy and Lee, photo-copied from DMV records. My heart sank. What was left of what I had been melted away, dispersing to destinations unknown.

"…the first double homicide in Durango Bay's history." Stay tuned for further details."

Rachel wailed. Valerie too. Alex swore. My father shook his head in disgust.

She killed them.

She fucking killed them.

Son of a bitch.

No no no no no no no no no no no no no no…

I swallowed what was rising up in my throat. I managed a step. Then another. I opened the door. They looked at me as one, a gang of puppy-dog sorrowful eyes.

"I saw the news report."

My mother rose, came over, and embraced me, crying.

"I'm so sorry, sweetheart."

I held her for a moment. Val and Rachel came to me, and I turned away. "Uh…can't be here right now. I appreciate you all being here, but I must be somewhere else."

I walked outside and headed off toward The Ponds. I wasn't sure if my childhood playground would help. Seeking out sacred ground seemed appropriate. I passed the first two ponds. They had run dry from drought.

You coward.

It's your fault.

If you had been a little less selfish…
If you had been a little more compromising…
She wouldn't have been with him.
And she wouldn't have gotten shot.
KILLED.
She's dead.
Oh God, she's dead.
I killed her.

I hopped a fence, wrenching my hands until blood seeped from my palms. Shotgun shells littered the trails where me and mine had lived and breathed and played so long ago. I shuddered and shrunk away from the spent bullets. I made it to the last pond, walked to the middle of its dried bed, dragging my feet over dried mud, rubbery shards of old tires and inner tubes, remnants of shipwrecked rafts. I kneeled down at the parched center of the desiccated watering hole and screamed. I cried. I ranted. I raved. My tantrum was interrupted by the appearance of Alex and Jim cresting a nearby hill. I grew quiet, incubating my derangement. They probably had heard me wailing en route. I didn't care. I wanted to die. I wanted to be *wherever* she was, so that we could be together. It was a pragmatic consideration. Conveyance from *here* to *there*, wherever *there* was—simple enough, no hopelessness or suicidal depression required; quite the opposite in fact, perhaps even brave.

But first I wanted to find this girl before the cops did.

I wanted to kill her.

It was a unique feeling to seriously consider the relief of violent vindication; of sticking knives inside someone's chest, crushing someone's larynx, blowing someone's head off, to be *contemplative* about the satisfaction of revenge. Then I could off myself, and the four of us, the estranged couples, would work it out in heaven or limbo or hell or wherever star-crossed lovers quibbled in the afterlife.

A crime of passion.
How else could the raven leave this world?
Why are you so surprised, Daren old bean?
Love and other indoor sports.
That's how she always signed off her letters and cards.

"I miss you and love you and can't wait to see you."
"Love and other indoor sports, Lee."
I killed her.
Oh God, I'm so sorry baby, I'm so sorry.
By the time Alex and Jim reached me, I was unhinged, delirious, and incoherent.
I'd decided. A razor blade would be put to my wrists soon.
Jim knelt down and put his hand on my shoulder.
Alex looked on, furious.
"Love and other indoor sports. That was her signature mantra, ya know. Catered to me. The real guy she loved. Something none of you knew. Lots of things you guys don't know, you oughta know, but you don't know. Tell me, did you ever notice I have Mom's eyes, Jimbo? I mean the deep ones, deeper than the Mariana Trench. You've got Dad's utilities, cheap and plenty. Lucky bastard."
"Er...OK?" Jim said.
"Stupid, blonde, tabby-eyed bitch. Why didn't she just keep me there? Why send me back if they knew Lee was bailing out a couple years later? Circumstantial primordial pain? Who cares? That's a conceit. A *degree*. Fuck all, serve nothing."
"What?" Jim asked.
"No bust of Pallas required. Shirt and shoes mandatory."
"Dude...calm down. Take a breath. Take two breaths," Alex said.
"Night's Plutonian shore," I murmured. They looked at each other, worried, at a loss as to how to proceed. I laughed aloud, crazed. "You suck, Edgar...and you too, Malibu Barbie. *Especially* you, bitch."
"Daren..." Alex said.
"And *you*...you should've seen the diner, man. You have no idea. No idea at all. Clueless, my brothers, it's all clueless, I am, you are, everyone is, the illuminati pretend they know what's up, but they don't know either, they're all clued out, everything's clued out. Game over, she took the ball and went home. God has left the building, Jim Morrison decomposes eternally in his Parisian bathtub, Jimi and Janis and Bon Scott are doing the backstroke in the Olympian vomit pool, and Elvis's rotting corpse still sits on the toilet."
"Jesus," Jim whispered.

"*Still nailed to the cross, altar boy!*"

"Daren," Alex said.

"*Hey, Mom, pick up the pieces of the president's brain!*"

"Daren," Alex repeated.

"Nevermore, never more, never fucking more."

"Stop it, Daren," Alex commanded.

"*Fuck you!*" I roared.

"That's more like it. No time for the asylum. Wanna kill that bitch?"

He was dead serious.

It brought me back, a little.

"Where is she?" I whispered.

"They dunno yet. We could go try and find her."

"What happened?"

Alex and Jim sat down cross-legged, wary, as if I'd reach across and claw their eyes out. Alex lit three smokes and passed two to Jim and me. We smoked. "There was a call to 911 last night. Guess that chick rang 'em after she did it, freaked her out. The cops think she busted in there close to midnight, not much warning. They don't have much to go on. They don't know where she is," Jim said.

"Uh, they wanna question you just to be sure," Alex said.

"*What?*"

"They're at the house right now," Jim added.

"You're kidding me. I was upstate."

"They know that. It's routine, I guess. We told them you probably weren't in the mood. They said they'd wait 'til tomorrow," Jim said.

"I'm a suspect?"

"No…they want to know your side of the story," Jim said.

"I have no side to the story. Engaged couple on a break, decide to date other people in the interim. End of story."

End of story.

Nevermore.

"Do you even own a gun?" I asked Alex.

"Oh, fuck going vigilante. Like we need that on top of this?" Jim spat.

"I got a forty-five my dad gave me," Alex said.

"Shut your trap, Alex. Think Lee would approve, college boy?" Jim asked.

My eyes blazed, hating him for that.

"Yeah. That's what I thought," he said.

Crows jabbered from oak trees. I acknowledged them with a curt vibe. How many knew Lee for what she was, a raven in beatific human form? It was my firm belief I'd been the only one. Lee herself had not known, not really, chalking up my occasional off-the-cuff birdie comments as charming poetic license.

Much later, I followed them home. Rachel had left. Keith was supposedly on his way from Chico. Valerie drank wine with my mother. My father tried to talk to me about how life had to go on. My ancestral home was dark. I excused myself to the bathroom, locked the door. I opened the medicine cabinet and took out my father's straight-edge razor. I brought it down to rest on the skin on the inside of my right forearm. The blade pierced the skin. A small stream of blood ran down my arm.

Two slashes—vertical, remember, not across—a half hour, and I'll be with you, and then we can figure this out.

It's not suicide.

I just want to be where you are.

Easy, easy, I can do this.

No, Daren.

This is wrong.

Who...who was that?

That's just me, my conscience, not Lee, no, some idiot in the cast of thousands, that's all.

Daren.

Remember the ring.

No, that's me, that's just me being chickenshit. Do it, do it now, get it over with.

Yet I took off the silver ring Lee had bought me in Mazatlan and looked at the writing inside, the inscription engraved in the semi-precious metal.

(I love you always)

Tears poured from my withered eyes now jaundiced and bloodshot.

I don't care. I need you. I am lost without you.

No.

You have to be strong.

You would expect no less from me.

I don't care.

You have to care.

I will always love you.

That will never change.

I pushed the razor harder into my wrist, running it lengthwise down the vein. Blood came freely then.

It's MY fault you're dead.

It's my fault.

It is not your fault.

It is.

You have to go on.

No.

Curtains drew. Another shift. Again I doubled, like the raven wing premonition dream predating our trip to Mexico. There I was, watching another version of me lying in a pool of blood, sprawled in my parents' bathroom, gray and lifeless, and then my mother, screaming, and her horrific burden of burying a child, her glass-bottom mirror sinking to irretrievable depth.

Oh, fuck.

No, fuck you!

No, no, no!

I hated Lee in that moment, and the angels, Malibu Barbie, my conscience, the cast of thousands, deific birds or gods, chastising all of them with X-rated epithets. Whoever or whatever had shown me the domino effect was a reprehensible force.

And then I was back, the razor at my wrist, blood flowing down my forearm.

It's not always about you, is it?

But I love you.

And I love you.

I dropped the razor in the washbasin. I turned on the faucet and ran cold water over the wound, opened the medicine cabinet, took out a roll of gauze, and wrapped my wrist.

28

My legs buckle with each step. The metallic taste in my mouth is sour. I am soaked to the bone. The deluge from above is preternatural in its persistence and intensity. Something tremendous, somewhere, weeps. I am unsympathetic. I slosh forward.

Haunted, I stare at passersby braving the storm. A young mother hums to her infant as she wrangles with an uncooperative rain poncho. An old man shrouded beneath a black umbrella's canopy peers inside a bookstore window. A couple of kids careen past on skateboards, risking life and limb in the unseasonable wet weather, zigzagging through puddles of rainwater. I want to scream at all of them. I don't understand why everyone isn't more concerned. *How can you be so normal today? Don't you know what has happened? Don't you know what I'm doing here? Has the world not stopped turning for all humanity?*

The door is mahogany, lacquered. Its shiny brass handle gleams. I open it and enter. Thick brown carpet, white patterned wallpaper, plush sofas and easy chairs, overt efforts to make the bereaved comfortable. I have never been in a funeral parlor. Why they are referred to as parlors escapes me at the moment.

A woman sits at a desk at the far end of the lobby. She inquires about who I am and how she can help me.

What am I doing?

I can't do this.

Anything but this.

"Excuse me? Sir? Sir?" I think she's addressed me a few times already. Everything is so vital, vibrant, kaleidoscopic, but it's also like reality is stuck in amber. My head's scrambling eggs. The secretary exhibits all the compassion of a great white shark. She is used to seeing the expression on my face. She has seen it many times before.

"Uh…yeah. I'm here to see the raven."

Who said that? So far away, it sounds so far away.

"Excuse me?"

Then I must give her a look that either frightens her or reminds her of my visitation exception, because she rises and leads me to see some guy, the guy in charge of the joint, I guess. He's a bearded fellow, fat with horn-rimmed glasses, in a dark blue suit. He extends his hand and various condolences. I manage to grasp it with some effort (not the condolences, just the hand). He looks at the bandage on my wrist, sticking out from under my sleeve, and makes the obvious conclusion. It can't be the first time he's seen such reactions to loss. For the last two days I've managed to conceal my failed "experiment" with long-sleeved Oxfords and jackets while I endured the wait over the weekend for the coroner's office to finish their investigation and release her to the mortuary.

I had to beg her mother to give me permission to see the body. Nobody else wanted to view her in her current condition, not a single person, except when I insisted I was going, that I had to go, and then all of them, family and friends, either tried to talk me out of it or demanded to accompany me. The ridiculous groupthink hadn't subsided right up to the moment of my departure. None of it ever had a chance of swaying me. They ought to have known better.

No, I'm doing this alone. It's the only way. An hour ago I left the house, my parents looking on, at a loss, Alex standing in the driveway arguing with me. *Screw your Quixote shit,* he'd said. *She wouldn't want you to torture yourself, and you know it.* It'd be just like my mother to assign a covert shadow to me given the circumstances. Especially if Alex or Jim had relayed my state of mind they'd witnessed a few days before. Having my father, or brother, or Alex, follow me to the mortuary in Santa Crisca and observe from afar would be right up her alley, the wily bitch. I didn't notice a tail on my way here, not that I was looking for one, nor do I care if hidden supervision is indeed in play, as long as they keep their distance and stay away from me while I attend to what needs doing.

Beard Guy takes me down a white hallway, explaining how I'm the only one who wanted to view her, asking me if I've ever seen a dead body. I don't answer. He pauses, clears his throat and goes on, tells me what to expect, how they removed her from the body bag and covered her in blankets as if she were at rest. How they "prettied" her up some for me, a little rouge on the cheeks, washing her hair and the like.

How considerate.

"We only got the body just this morning, after the coroners finished their autopsy…"

Not talking about her, no way, no way, no way.

"Her mother told us to cremate the body as soon as you're, ah, finished paying your respects. Take as much time as you need. And let me again express my utmost sincerity…"

"That'll be enough of that shit," I say this to him with *utmost sincerity.*

He grunts, beckons at a sliding wooden door, and leaves me.

I step into what must be a viewing room. Vases with cloth lilies and silk roses, that thick chocolate carpet, white folding chairs. A marbled dais, atop which…

My eyes fix upon her…lying there…silent.

Still.

Too still.

It is her…right?

I walk a few steps closer.

I see her head. Her body is covered in white linens.

Sit up, honey, joke's over, you got me. Any second everybody's going to jump out and laugh. I was really duped, wasn't I? We really gotcha, didn't we? April Fool's, wiseass!

Sit up.

Please sit up.

Oh no, oh Christ no...

My legs give way now. I fall to the floor, a few feet from the pallet. I bury my head in my hands. I cry, I sob, I heave like never before. To someone else it might look as if I'm bowing to a shrine. I guess I am. My eyes are a life of their own, burning. I struggle to my feet, lurching nearer to her. I see all of her face now. Crow's feet wrinkles in the corners of her seemingly sewn-shut eyes, gray pallor, waxy skin, and her lips, those beautiful perfect lips, blue and cracked from spending three days on ice in the county morgue's fridge.

She's really dead.

Gasping for breath now.

My left hand reaches out. Strokes her right hand peeking out from under the blankets.

So cold...

The same body that I made love to so many times...

It was always so warm.

The same lips that kissed so sweet...

The same hair that I ran my fingers through, silky soft calico-mane...

(Just washed, nice and clean, remember?)

It looks greasy, not her hair, not at all.

Her hand...

Is so cold.

"I love you, I love you. I will always love you..."

I touch her face.

It's cold too.

Like stone.

I look at her chest.

Where the bullet entered.

Go ahead, lift up the blanket.

Come on, what's the matter?

You want proof?

All you gotta do is...

Look.

236

Just above her left breast, there'll be a small thirty-eight-caliber-sized hole.

They'll have washed off the blood.

Her heart didn't explode in a flash of gunpowder and metal.

It's all a lie, only nightmare, and to dispel this hellish illusion you have to see past the charade. Do it and wake up. Please.

I'm doing it.

The corner of the blanket peels back.

Don't.

Just a little bit more…

But I cannot.

I let the blanket drop, fearing the destructive impulse to look at her destroyed body will prevail. I collapse on a sofa.

Fists clenched, fingernails digging into palms. Blood seeping through fingers knuckle-white. Head pounding. Face on fire, crackling with rash. Sobbing again. Hysterics. Uncontrollable. Involuntary.

Now…yes. Screaming.

Beard Guy's outside at the viewing room door, asking me if I'm all right. I hush, take a few gasping breaths. "No, I'm not all right. Leave." Footsteps down the hall.

Control yourself, young man, my third grade teacher's voice echoes.

The cast of thousands all start to pipe in. The Catholic Kid barks loudest, above the buzzing din of the rest, selling cheap penance and easy fixes.

I sob anew. The pain, it is arthritic, dry, twisting horror in my bones.

Some time passes.

An hour?

Two?

When I look up, she's still there.

Just waiting to be cremated, thanks.

Could we move it along, honey?

Things to do, places to go, people to see.

My eyes feel like they've been under the Chinese water torture. Alex was right. She wouldn't have wanted this. I wouldn't have wanted her to be here if it had been me.

God, if only it had been me instead.

I stand, trembling, and I walk to her. I wish her eyes would open. They don't. I lean over and kiss her one last time. "See you later."

No goodbyes.

In a dazed stupor, I stumble out of the room and make my way down the hall. I think of smarmy Malibu Barbie, she of the Halloween peepers, and curse her at length.

So this is madness.

Damned satisfying.

The receptionist says something to me on the way out. I only hear the cast of thousands, their raucous chorus bludgeoning me into submission. I exit the mortuary to a world erupting in wet fusillade, rain coming down in torrential sheets. Reality washes away in a furor of gray watercolors, oozing down dank gutters full of rot and wreckage.

29

Unlike the vivid horror of the mortuary visit, the funeral service was a vague event. A silver framed picture of Lee on an easel, a minister trying to illustrate God's mysterious ways to a shocked community, Rachel's hopeful eulogy, mothers' tears, a drunken Valerie wailing in the back of a church.

It was all a fog.

Not a Victorian one.

Going back to school after Lee's funeral was a joke. I was ready to chuck it all, not caring whatsoever about completing my degrees. I heard her voice among the others; only two months to go, why would I want to throw away something I'd worked five years to achieve, a plethora of other meaningless justifications, blah blah blah. Reluctantly I returned to Chico and tried to return to my usual routines. Biking in the canyons, *Star Trek*, poker, video games, smoking weed. I dropped my honors classes and finished with passing Cs and Ds instead of my usual As. My parents drove up and videotaped graduation, me in black cap and gown once again. They congratulated me, trying to steer my derailed track with bargaining tactics if I'd only keep the endgame in sight, but I deferred my acceptances to graduate school. My father was incensed, my mother crushed. I didn't care. I sold or donated everything I owned and wished both Tim and Keith fairer lives (Keith had another year to go before completing an accounting degree). Then I moved home to my parents' house in DeeBee, and there I festered, one day fading into another. I rotted in my old room, chain-smoking cigarettes, jobless, no longer a professional student, the world stagnant and empty.

The murderess remained on the run for a week and then turned herself into the police. At her trial her attorney claimed temporary insanity, and she maintained during cross-examination that in a fit of jealous, unthinking rage, she went to his home to commit suicide in front of her ex and his new companion. She had intended to fire one over Lee's shoulder to scare them, except her aim was off and the shot struck Lee in the heart, after which the fellow attempted to subdue her, and due to fight-or-flight reflex, she shot him twice, in the neck and stomach. Oops. So much for the grand plan.

The sensationalism was abhorrent. Local news programs at six and eleven kept on top of courtroom developments, and being a born-and-bred media neophyte, I couldn't help but watch. It was horrific listening to strangers talk about Lee, so disproportionate, so detached, merely another statistic of violent crime.

I mustered up the courage to attend the trial once, watched the proceedings for a day. I slunk into the back of the courtroom where Lee's killer sat only twenty feet from me. I considered making a scene, hurling myself across the courtroom and throttling her before the bailiffs could get to me. I suppressed my better instincts and went outside when the judge called a break. In the courthouse hall, two officers led her to a waiting room past the onlookers and media cameras. They walked right past me, and she met my eyes. I didn't know if she knew who I was. I wanted to crush her throat, crack her skull, to inflict cleansing, vindicating pain on the psychopath. But I didn't. She burst into tears as they led her away. Maybe she did know who I was. I'd stood face to face with Lee's executioner and didn't flinch. Not much of a saving grace.

In the five months since the incident I'd gotten at best ten, maybe twelve uninterrupted nights of sleep, those only from consummate exhaustion.

I attended a few concerts that summer with Alex, putting on appearances. We saw AC/DC, Boston, Rush. We did coke and drank whiskey. I found the party would soon be ending for me, too little, too late. When I was high, my shattered mind became dangerously unstable, painting grotesque canvases of gun smoke and blood. During social gatherings I tended to avoid everyone, though there was no solace in solitude, as my hands refused to stop shaking and my eyes often squeezed shut, painfully tight, as I hummed to myself trying to drown the cast of thousands, whose white noise had swollen to draconian levels of opera.

30

"You ready for tomorrow?" I asked.

He adjusted his shiny green bow tie. He looked slick in his bolero-style tuxedo. Alex and Valerie were tying the knot, or the noose as it were, and he'd asked me to be his best man.

"He's ready as he'll ever be," Jim said.

"I'm a model of a modern major general," Alex said.

The TV was tuned to afternoon game shows. Val's cats sunned themselves on the patio. Their apartment was cluttered with prewedding paraphernalia, tux accessories, invitation envelopes, boxes and flowers and vases, cards and stationeries and commemorative albums. The similar nature of weddings and funerals, the need to mark endings and beginnings, was soiling the occasion for me.

I slipped on rented black dress shoes. "They're a little small," I said.

"Fucking thing is choking me," Alex said, yanking on his tie. "Let's go smoke."

We went outside. The sky was blue and clear, a beautiful day. We lit cigs and puffed.

"I don't think you should watch it," Alex said.

"Have to."

"Why?"

"Same reason you do, I guess."

"No. You don't have to do it. You're kicking yourself enough as it is."

"Am I?"

"Look, I appreciate your being the best man."

"No problem."

"I know it's hard. I couldn't ask anyone else."

"I would've been plenty irked if you had asked anyone else."

"It means a lot to me. 'Cause I know it'll be a chore for you tomorrow at the altar. Seeing me, and Val, doing what…"

"Doing what Lee and I should've been doing?" I finished.

"Fuck, man."

"Don't sweat it. Hey, as the best man, aren't I supposed to offer a bail-out?"

"Ha. Yeah, you're taking me to Mexico, right?"

"If you have any doubt whatsoever…"

"I *am* sure."

"As sure as you are about everything else in your life?"

"I've been sober two months running, and I plan to keep that way. Now are you going to marry me off, or do I have to ask Keith to step in?"

"Relax, spud. I'll give you away faster than a Tijuana whore's syphilis."

"That's the spirit. But dude…*don't* watch that fucking thing."

What he was referring to was a half-hour syndicated tabloid show, one that had pursued the story of rural Durango Bay's double homicide. Jim called us and we went to view the sordid media. The show started with images of the deceased overlaid with the splashy title *Murder, They Cried*. A deep, foreboding voice narrated, languishing in its concerted dramatization. A reporter interviewed a couple of the ex-girlfriend's acquaintances, her mother, all parties expressing the age old adages: *She was a quiet one, never thought she was capable, such a nice girl in school.* I began to shake. It went on to construct a re-creation of the night of the murders. Some blonde, slutty-looking actress was playing the part of Lee. She was sitting astride another male actor in a compromising position. A woman came in, gun in hand, demanding to know what was going on. The blonde-Lee said he was hers now and that the woman should mind her own business and get the hell out. My body palpitated, all of it, like an epileptic fit. I knew I should stop watching. I could not stop watching.

"Oh, yeah, that's *exactly* how it happened. Jesus Christ on a crutch. Daren, that's bullshit, and you know it. Goddamn, where do they get the balls to do this stuff? Don't they worry about getting sued?" Alex demanded.

The murderess pulled out her gun and shot them. The gunshot sound effects went off like cannonballs in my head. The end of the short segment had the narrator giving a mournful warning about love triangles. My entire body—arms, legs, fingers, and toes—convulsed. I gagged. The blonde actress who'd played Lee had been so smug, so skanky. *So not Lee.* It was disgusting, an abomination.

Jim and Alex observed me, worried.

"Take it easy. It's just a rag show. It didn't mean anything," Jim said.

"I told you not to watch it, goddammit," Alex said.

"B-better take me home, Jim."

"You sure?"

"*Now.*"

"Take him," Alex said.

"I'll b-be there tomorrow. Don't worry," I stammered. My brother walked me to his car. He asked me to stop shaking. I tried to indulge him but couldn't. He rushed me home. I scrambled upstairs. I quivered for another three hours in my room alone.

I made it to the church the next day. I feigned happiness as they exchanged vows in the same church that had hosted Lee's funeral. I toasted them at the reception. *It's easy to fall in love,* I said. *Don't just love each other. Love each other well.* Wedding attendees applauded. We raised our champagne glasses and hallmarked their overdue nuptials.

Valerie filed for divorce sixty-two days later.

Alex hopped off the wagon the same evening.

31

In Angel City, people lived their lives. Some were dying. Some were birthing. Most were in between those grand bookends, existing day to day per mandate. Work, eat, shit, fuck, sleep. Rinse and repeat.

Keith and I sprawled out on Rachel's deck in chaise lounges. He was down from Chico on a four-day break attending to his other half. They'd asked me to spend the weekend with them, taking their turn in keeping tabs on me. Family and friends made stalwart efforts in following my daily routine, not a difficult job as it varied little. I was still considered a flight risk, either disappearing into world underground or actually ending up under real ground. It confirmed that which I'd feared for years; I wore my heart on my sleeve in all its bleeding, palpitating glory.

It was strange at first being at Lee's former domicile. I got over it. It didn't really matter where I was, Angel City, Santa Crisca, DeeBee. Everything had gotten a lot more global. *No more Lee anywhere.*

Autumn had arrived. Every day for weeks, there were wondrous lavender settings of the sun. I wanted to believe they were catalysts, messages from Lee, but I wasn't so far gone to start anthropomorphizing weather patterns. Only in fairyland comforts of hopeful immortality did ghosts of loved ones manage to affect ecology.

Not much was jibing.

"How was that psychic dude? Rachel didn't tell me much. She said I was too Christian to understand," Keith said.

"Aren't you?"

A crow flew overhead, circling the apartment complex's tennis court down below. Strangely it seemed to have red feathers. *Trick of the sunlight*, I surmised.

"Just tell me."

"It was weird."

"He's like...a *medium*, right? Spirits talk through him."

"Supposedly."

"And?"

"He said people were there, I guess. Rachel's grandparents. My grandparents. Um...our spirit guides. Whatever the heck those are."

"Who's your spirit guide?"

"Some dude named Chief Black Eagle."

"What'd he have to say?"

"What you'd expect. I need to go on. I need to find positive out of the negative."

"What about Lee?"

"The medium said she was in the room with us but was having a difficult time communicating. Guess angel powers are still new to her."

"Did you talk to her?"

Keith was doubtful. He wasn't alone. I'd been skeptical of a number of methods I'd explored to find some understanding: psychic fairs, palm readings, tarot, Ouija. None of it had impressed me.

"I tried. I asked her if she still loved me. The guy said she was angry I would even ask such a question."

Rachel came outside. "Oh, don't keep bashing the guy."

"The guy's a kook, Daren," Keith said, rolling his eyes.

"You have a closed mind. Knock it off," Rachel said angrily.

"OK, OK, sorry."

I watched the reddish crow coast away toward the mountains, its wingspread fading in blue sky. "He got *some* things right about our grandparents. Sorta. Stuff that happened to us when we were kids," I said.

"Daren's grandma said she remembered the World War II model airplane they built when he was ten. And my grandfather talked about when he took me and my brother to Disneyland and my brother threw up all over Goofy."

"Really," Keith said, apprehensive.

"Keith, it was a wonderful thing," Rachel said.

"Then why aren't you stoked?" Keith asked me.

"I don't know."

"Yes, you do. You tested him. I was there. You asked the wrong question," Rachel said.

"It wasn't *wrong*."

"You know why he couldn't answer it."

"He couldn't answer it 'cause *he didn't know*."

"No. She's not supposed to tell you things like that."

"What are you talking about?" Keith asked.

"He asked a question only Lee would know the answer to," Rachel said.

"I asked if she remembered my nickname. Big deal."

"It *was* a big deal. Maybe we're not supposed to have concrete answers about the next world," Rachel said.

"Why not? Is it really going to sway our insignificant little lives on this planet? Knowledge of other worlds is somehow counterproductive to our development? 'Cause, you know, our genesis is progressing SO well."

"And what did he tell you?" Keith asked.

"He said he couldn't quite get across her response to that particular query."

"You *tested* him," Rachel repeated.

"Isn't that whole point of mediums? Confirmation of an afterlife? Talking to passed-on souls?" I asked.

"Absolute proof of life beyond? I'm surprised at you. You more than any of us should know all about leaps of faith," Rachel said.

"You know, sometimes I think about time travel and all this. Like being able to go back to that little Daren starting out with Lee, fresh in love, the whole world ahead..."

I stopped mid-sentence.

I miss her so much.

"Uh...and I wonder how I would look to him. How *do* I look?"

"You'd look haggard," Keith said.

"Old," Rachel added.

At least I look the part.

"What would you say to him?" Rachel asked.

"I'd tell him to cherish the ground she walks on and to never let her go no matter what. I'd tell him to make love a priority, not a luxury."

Rachel smiled. "Hmm...but what about the person you've become? Maybe, just maybe, everything happens for a reason."

"*No,*" I snapped. "It was *not* supposed to happen. People are not meant to kill people. Don't give me that destiny crap. I don't believe in determinism."

"But what about the things we've come to understand through Lee's death? Don't they count for something?" she posed.

"All I know is, I would give up everything I am and everything I will ever be for her to walk the earth again."

"I don't think that's the point," Rachel said.

"Probably not. But I know I will never change my mind."

"*Never* is a strong word. You're going to wait for her, aren't you?" Keith asked, a weird, knowing smirk on his face.

"All my life."

"You'll never love again? I wonder if that's what you'd want for Lee if it had happened to you?" Rachel said.

"I'm not her, and I'm sick of hearing that," I said and fell silent.

After a while they went inside and left me to my old tomatoes. The day grew to dusk. I slipped on a sweatshirt and watched Angel City breathe in twilight. I thought about historical logistics, how if I'd gone to college in LA, we'd have lived together and she never would have met that guy and she wouldn't have died. But hindsight was an illusion, people impacting one another's lives, influencing directions and decisions. I studied enough philosophy to know. It was just as probable if

I'd moved to the city, Lee and I might have been driving to a movie in Westwood on a night I originally would have spent in Chico, and we might have crashed the car and she might have died then, or I might have, or we might have died together, or one of us might have become a brain-dead vegetable, the other cursed to live out their days visiting the great love of their life every Sunday at a skilled nursing facility checking for bedsores, watching them become more decrepit with each passing year. It was acrid fodder to chew on, pointless, cankerous morbidity.

The crow appeared again, at high speed, and this time I was sure it was crimson in color. Red ravens? Ridiculous. Twilight was not infusing it with sunset colors. I checked and double-checked. As it approached, billowing, blood-red cloaks replaced its tail feathers, a conflagration of scarlet entrails and capes spiraling backward behind its sleek body. It was an avian from *elsewhere*, or I was hallucinating, exhaustion and grief finally pushing me over an edge, no longer able to distinguish what was real and what wasn't. The red crow circled, retracted its crimson net, and dove into a bank of mustard weed on a nearby hillside. It rose with a squealing gopher in its claws—a contrary action for blackbirds, hardly birds of prey, their usual menu limited to insects and crops, carrion, and roadkill. It flew away to realms unknown. I was unfazed. I stared at everything. I stared at nothing.

Rachel came back outside, in thick fluffy sweats, and sat next to me.

"I'm sorry about before," I said.

"Don't sweat it."

"Where's Keith?"

"Crashed. You feeling any better?"

"No."

"She *couldn't* tell you. It's against the rules, I think, especially for guys like you, smarty-pants, who're supposed to figure it out for themselves."

"I hope you're right, I really do."

"What *was* the name, anyway?"

"Lamb Chop."

Dusty...

"That's cute. That's so Lee."

"Rachel, have you ever read up on quantum theory? I have. In college. One of the few things I latched onto. There's this hypothesis that all possibilities manifest themselves, in an infinite number of universes. You know, that anything that *can* happen, *does* happen."

"That's a big concept."

"The idea being, there's endless versions of ourselves in a countless string of existences."

"Somewhere in an alternate universe, there's a Rachel who didn't meet Keith?"

"That's right. And somewhere there's a Keith who defected to Russia, there's an Alex who's president of the United States, and there's a Valerie who was abducted by aliens and is now living in an intergalactic zoo, and somewhere..."

"Somewhere there's a Daren and a Lee who are happily married and living in bliss," she finished.

"Yes. Maybe. Somewhere."

"And somewhere there's a Daren who never knew Lee in the first place. He never knew what he missed."

"Perhaps."

"*And* there's a Daren and a Lee who are miserable together. You can't keep guessing what-ifs. We'll get through it. We owe it to Lee."

"I hope one of those Darens is doing it better than I did."

"And yet all you have to go on is this universe."

"There's something comforting about picking up the Sunday paper and opening it to a color comic page, isn't there?"

"That was an odd segue. I've never been into funny pages."

"That's a shame. The comics section is of the few pleasures of modern newspapers, since the rest of it is trying to sell you something, tallying up the day's planetary blood count, or offering insipid op-ed articles on celebrities. The weekly Sunday *Peanuts* strip is the watermark of all comic strips. Poor Charlie Brown's continued humiliations, Snoopy's imaginary adventures battling the Red Baron, the codependency Linus has with his blanket—it's pretty much the perfect medium."

"Really," Rachel said, smiling, probably glad I was discussing something other than death, doom, gloom, or glory.

"The annual viewing of *A Charlie Brown Christmas* was tradition. I know it's stupid, but I can't listen to the Mancini theme without getting teary eyed."

"It's not stupid, and I'm beginning to see what Lee saw in you, you big sap. Why are you always such a pompous ass?"

"All part of the dude façade. I'd have thought you'd figured that out by now, seeing as how you're attached to the dude-iest dude who ever lived. Anyway, Lee loved *Peanuts* too. You know she played Snoopy once. I've seen *You're a Good Man Charlie Brown* at least a dozen times by different theatrical companies, and the best Snoopy I ever saw was Lee's version—and yeah, I'm biased, but I also didn't know her yet when I saw that performance."

"That must've been when she was young."

"And I was even younger. See, the thing is, Snoopy is pure, ego-innocent art. He's a male beagle on the comic page of course, but I haven't considered Snoopy in the masculine sense for a long time. Lee *was* Snoopy. But my original point was what is it about Charlie Brown's everyman loser status that provokes such animosity from his peers? Sure, he's a doofus and a lousy baseball pitcher, but he's actually a pretty cool guy. He definitely doesn't deserve rocks in his trick-or-treat bag. He feeds his dog, he helps his sister with her homework, and he's determined and respectful. Most of the rest of the kids are mean little brats taking advantage of the easy target. Why do they persecute him? Why does Lucy have to jerk the football away from him again and again?"

"I think you're reading a bit much into it."

"No, no. Many professional scholars and theologians have studied the Tao of *Peanuts*. Honest. Charlie Brown, the antihero. *He's* the ethics barometer. It's an Alex term. The *Peanuts* gang, with their insecurities, pet peeves, fantasies, and daydreams are fictional symbols for how Charles Schulz sees the world, and if Charlie Brown's friends are representative of reality, the seemingly hopeless, victimized by their own humanity, then where is *our* real-life Charlie Brown? It's not somebody obvious, like religious leaders or politicians. No, a true Charlie Brown would rally more heart and less token-speak. Who will rescue the gang from themselves? Who better to save the un-savable than an un-savior?"

"Downtown Chuck Brown, mercenary for hire?" Rachel posed.

"*She was supposed to sing! She was supposed to keep performing! Doesn't anyone else know that?*" I cried out, and sunk in Rachel's arms and wept.

"Shh," Rachel whispered, cradling me. "Try to sleep."

"Her favorite play was *Cats*, you know. And her favorite song was..."

"*Memory*, yes, I remember."

"Grizabella's journey to the Heaviside layer kinda more relevant these days, methinks. Fucking Christ on a cracker, Lee," I muttered through tears, losing symmetry yet again.

"Shh. Sleep."

"Dreams are no respite."

"Nothing will be, for a while."

It was good, being held by a woman—also alien, her scent lemony, with a touch of coconut lotion. Not a trace of blackberry or cinnamon.

32

Seconds, minutes, hours, days, weeks, months, eternities passed, discombobulated, a polar opposite of the All-Now I'd experienced in the tunnel and beyond. Frames of reference overlapped, angled unnatural like cubist splashes of space-time, rooted in uneven cycles, muddled and anarchic.

The one-year anniversary of Lee's death came. On that inauspicious occasion I shivered from sunrise to sundown. I took no calls or visitors, told my mom to deter anything and anyone until the next day. She left me tomato soup and buttered toast at the bottom of my stairwell. I watched TV all day as I endured anxiety attacks one after another, shuddering through soaps, evening news, sitcoms, on to David Letterman and the late hours of infomercials, succumbing to depletion at four a.m.

Keith and Rachel decided to get married after he graduated Chico. He was nice enough to sport me a ticket to Washington, where they'd relocated after he found a job working for one of Seattle's more prestigious accounting firms, now settled in a pleasant ranch tract home in the western suburbs of Bremerton. I was happy for him. He was good to Rachel. He knew what he'd been lucky enough to find and had given up all our former vices to take a shot at living happily ever after. My envy held no bounds. His bachelor party was at hand; a group of his new work buddies was throwing him a traditional sendoff in the heart of the northwestern hub. I tried to elevate my mood, get in the spirit of things, but my outlook was bleak. Though I'd been in Seattle for a few days and Keith had given me the grand tour, including four-star food and iced teas atop the Space Needle, a Seahawks-Chiefs game at the Kingdome, and cruising the U of W districts, I remained inconsolable.

Our blue ferry, rusted from stem to stern, split through choppy, white-tufted waters of Puget Sound. The water was cold and deep jade green. The non-Cal vibe was refreshing. Brown pelicans and white seabirds picked at scraps and bread crusts on the upper deck. Ahead, the hyaline citadels and high rises of downtown Seattle towered above the waterfront.

"Ten minutes to my last party before oblivion," Keith said. I tried to light a cigarette on the ferry's windblown deck. "Breezy on the Sound, isn't it?"

"*The* Sound. You're so Northwest hip," I replied.

"Alex called me. He said he'd kick my ass if I didn't take care of you. I told him a trip out of state would do you good."

"You were right."

"But how are you *really* doing?"

"Do I look bad?"

"You're not real present, no. It's been over a year. You gotta start moving on."

"Like I haven't heard that before. I'll move on when I want to. You guys have no idea what Lee and I were. Do me a favor and don't give me the same old lecture."

"Yeah, OK."

The ferry approached the terminal's dock.

"I'm sorry, man. I'm a prick. Don't mind me," I said.

"Naw, don't worry about it. You're right. You've heard that stuff enough."

"How is the real deal, anyway?"

"What?"

"Real life. Adult employment. Committing to a good woman. Getting a grip."

A pelican landed on a nearby railing, its beak slimed with fish entrails. The ferry's entourage of tourists and commuters lined up at the gangplank as the boat hauled keel and prepared to dock.

"It's not as bad as we feared," Keith said, chuckling. "I love it up here, but I miss the Cal surf for sure. Too fuckin' cold up here and the breaks are for shit. But why are you asking me about real life anyway? You should know."

"How do you figure?"

"You and Lee set the standard for all of us. Think I was surprised when you hooked up the first long-term babe, a real woman to boot? Nobody was surprised. Not even your mom. You think it's because you were such a hard-ass she didn't call the cops on Lee? Gimme a break. You're a sensitive basket case, and everybody knows it. Nobody was surprised. Except Alex, maybe, and only for a little while 'cause he was jealous."

"No, I blew it."

"You didn't. You fucked up your method, is all. Everyone knew—it was obvious—you two were totally in love. You had it first."

"Like it matters now."

"I think you know it does. Bet I know something about Lee that you don't."

"What's that?"

"She was living the dream with you all along. You just didn't know it. Few things frightened our sagely pal Daren except real life. Problem was, you never quit the game. You always figured you had another turn coming."

Goddamn the Surfcat.

"You saw that?"

"It was too long a game, bud."

His words dropped like stones in my gut.

"I know," I croaked.

"But Daren...it wasn't your fault. Don't be a dumbshit about that. Yeah, you were trying to balance two different worlds, and in the end you didn't manage. I wouldn't have been able to do it as long as you did, and Alex won't last, not without taking the same road as Lee or worse. You knew all this from day one. But you didn't pull the trigger. Lee is gone because of a screwball psycho and only because of that. The world is a dangerous place. Plenty of wife-beating, child-molesting pricks live their lives untouched by the law or karma, and their victims live right alongside them never saying a word. God doesn't play favorites."

"But…"

"Fuck buts. If my aunt had balls, she'd be my uncle. Don't roll those dice."

Goddamn the Surfcat!

"I miss her, Keith."

"I miss her too. Lee was like a sister to me." The ship docked. People began to disembark. He popped his Zippo and lit a smoke. "She loved you, man. If you wanna wait, hey, I respect that. Fuck what everyone else says. Do whatever it takes to come full circle about it."

"I thought I was the appointed think-tank."

"No, you just thought you had the monopoly on the introspection dealio."

"And I don't?"

"Sorry, Charlie. The universe turns with or without your help."

"Impossible."

We scampered down the plank to the terminal and navigated through the lines to the street. Pike Place Market shops bustled with commerce—fresh-caught cod, crab, snapper, and lobster, laden in ice bins, omnipresent odors of perpetual rain and sea creatures, carven wood sculptures and totems of northwest Native American craft— plenty of Raven represented, along with Bear, Turtle, Thunderbird, Wolf. It was not California. It was good being somewhere else. We walked a few blocks toward the Kingdome to the sports bar hosting Keith's bachelor party. The pub was adorned with Seahawks banners and pennants, Sierra Nevada neon logos buzzing in the front windows. We went inside and were greeted by a roomful of Keith's associates. Rubber sex dolls, VCRs loaded with porn, a couple kegs, and a stripper complete with bodyguard and stiletto heels waited in the back room. The boisterous crowd hoisted Keith up on their shoulders, cheering, and carried him away. He looked at me, shrugging. I saluted him. I watched the strip act for the first five minutes (the girl was foxy, with olive skin, dark eyes, and straight black hair, Hawaiian or Polynesian), and then I wandered out to the main barroom, mostly empty for a Friday night. A few couples huddled at corner tables, drinking martinis and Canadian beer. I sat at the long bar alone, its stools all unoccupied. The bartender asked me what I wanted. I ordered a Coke. I put my smokes on the table, slid an ashtray over, and stared at the looking glass behind the bar. Not a pretty sight, an old man, premature wrinkles in his furrowed forehead, streaks of white at his temples, gray hair at twenty-three. Preposterous. The bartender served me my Coke, and I took a swig.

Someone came in the front door. The draft was chilling. I raised the collar of my denim Levi jacket and nursed my soda. The guy who'd come in sat on a stool right next to me, a fossilized man with a stringy beard, topped with a red-striped fisherman's wool cap pulled down to his ears. A yellow scarf, stained with mud, hung around his neck. His slick overcoat was tattered, and his galoshes dripped on the hardwood floor. He stunk of chowder and exhaust, *haute couture* not at the forefront of his priorities. He smiled at me, revealing gnarled yellow teeth and a blackened tongue. Another street druid, I was certain. I scanned the bar counter for pens or other sharp-edged objects.

The bartender considered the man, apprehensive, anticipating a confrontation with one of Seattle's unseemly elements. "What'll ya have, old timer?"

"Let's see now. How about a rum and Coke? Dark rum, that is," the man said. He had an odd accent. Not European, not Russian or Mediterranean, perhaps something akin to Eurasian. I couldn't place it.

"I'll have to see money up front."

"Of course." The man reached into his breast pocket and pulled out a crisp, new hundred-dollar bill. "Can you run me a tab?"

The bartender was taken back. "Ah…yeah. Rum and Coke, comin' right up."

I smiled at the unexpected turn of events. The old man watched the bartender pour his drink. My reflection in the backboard mirror was now buddied up with the druid's own counterpart, whose visage didn't look so old; in fact, his image looked a damned sight younger than mine. He pulled out a new pack of Marlboros, plastic wrapper still unbroken, and set it on the countertop.

"Mind sharing that ashtray?" he asked.

"Not at all." I pushed it between us as the bartender served him.

The druid pulled a pad and pencil out of a pocket in his overcoat. The pad was damp, the pencil a small, chewed-on stub. He began to write. After a while I became curious and stole a peek. What I saw made no sense. Doodles, odd amalgams of shapes and circles and lines, arranged in varying configurations, vague hieroglyphics. I was no linguist, but I had never seen anything remotely similar. I had taken a few classes in archaeology and anthropology in college, and I didn't think any of it was Egyptian or Greek or Celtic. Every few minutes he would stop and appraise his work, nodding, confirming secret conclusions. I became convinced he was a crackpot who'd found a dropped C-note, bent on drowning his woes.

"Yes, that's it," he said to himself, finishing a string of circles juxtaposed with crisscrossing diagonal lines. He was enchanted with his work. "I will tell him."

He turned to me. "How are you tonight, sir?"

"Fine, thanks."

"No, you most certainly are *not* fine. Only truths told between men of character, if you please. You lost someone recently?"

Shocked, I was unable to respond.

"Oh yes, it is clear to people who know such things. Don't be so surprised. You believe you are mysterious, eh?" He cackled, picked up his drink, and brought it to his lips, then set it down untouched. "Arrogance in a broad mind. How delightful. Paradox does become you."

"Yes...I did lose someone. Did Keith send you in here?"

"I do not know anyone named Keith. I am here on my own regard." He picked up the unopened pack of cigarettes and rolled it around in his hands. "You blame yourself for her death."

"How did you know it was a *her*?"

"Still you question. Questions, questions...all of your life is questions. You ask why, and you ask why again, and when the answers are given, you doubt them. You pretend not to have heard. There are more riddles in life than *why*, boy."

"You know me so well?" I said, irked. Something was up. Something was happening. I wished I wasn't alone.

"I have known men like you, who shun life and love for conceits and intellects wrought in fear, or worse, greed. Men like you who tell themselves worlds end when they already know 'tis false. *Nothing* ends. Nothing. You know this."

"You're wrong. She's dead, and it's my fault. God only knows why the hell I'm talking to you about this."

He smiled. "No. More forces than God know."

"It's my fault," I whispered.

"Nonsense."

"I *know* what reality is."

"Do you now? Do you really? You are among a select few who have been given gifts of sight. And they *are* gifts, young one. Why do you still seek those same answers then?"

"They...the answers aren't good enough," I said weakly.

He roared. "Not good enough! Oh yes, this one's a fine one! Not good enough? I had no idea!"

"About *what*?"

"You want to shape the world!"

"The world's not working. Someone should change it."

"Indeed. Yet you are not an almighty power. No one man is. And holding to your expectations is not what you should be endeavoring to do."

"What, exactly, should I be endeavoring to do?"

"You should be forgiving yourself."

"I can't."

"You must."

"I won't."

"Narcissism is so passé. What lovely pride."

Then he wrote one word of English on his pad—**LEE.**

I shuddered. "Who are you?"

He grinned.

"*Tell me who you are!*" I demanded.

"Keep it down," the bartender implored, though the reprimand was pointless considering the catcalls and bellows resounding from the bachelor party in back. I stood and faced the hoary wanderer. Stars and fire danced in his eyes. I felt like both hitting and hugging him. Instead of doing either, I went to the restroom. I relieved myself and then splashed cool water on my face. When I returned, the cryptic druid was nowhere to be seen. I asked the bartender where the man had gone. He told me he'd left. I ran out to the sidewalk, looked up and down the street. Bar patrons, a gaggle of teenage girls, a bus loaded with geriatric sightseers, but no enigmatic, red-capped waif. I sighed and went back inside to my stool. His drink was untouched, his pack of Marlboros full. I drank Cokes, somber and thoughtful.

Keith and Rachel married the next day. All went well.

On the plane ride home, as a stewardess served me inedible chicken dumplings, the revelation finally hit me, a flash of lucidity so simple it was difficult to feel anything other than contempt for myself in not understanding sooner. Embarrassing, really. Lee would've scoffed at my brick-headed stubbornness.

Finding the light of ravens again would only come to pass by finding my own.

And the peanut gallery of my cast of thousands collectively groaned a big, fat *Duh.*

It was a three-hour return flight. I napped, and dreamed, long deprived of REM nourishment, pleasant impressions of tropics and Mexican silver and jade-green waters and tart golden lemonade, and peace. I woke when the landing gear touched down on the tarmac. As never before, Santa Crisca seemed a haven for un-saviors.

33

I came to a crossroads. Accept a shattered permanence or charge back into the breach. I'd tested the waters of each option. The latter was less polluted.

I attained a level of functioning.

An alternate level, rather.

Van Halen toured again. Alex acquired tickets for a small venue in Costa Mesa. Fearing another arena rock debacle, he had forsaken the guys-only mantra and purchased an extra ticket for his estranged ex-wife Valerie, who defrosted her frigidity long enough to attend the show with us. Alex figured adding some estrogen into the mix might help his chances in enjoying a Van Halen concert sans casualties of mind, body, or heart.

I was optimistic.

The band ripped out a terrific set. We rocked hard, the three of us forgetting our respective voids for a few hours. I cheered, nearly close to normal. Halfway through the gig, in the middle of Eddie's solo, I missed Lee, and then...

You look so happy.

It has been too long since you have smiled like that.

I told you I wanted to see the next show with you.

The rest of the concert I was quiet and content, harmonious with the crowd energy. Afterward Valerie asked me why I'd simmered down, and I told her. She hugged me, and the three of us went for coffee and biscuits and gravy, and we were, for a short time, brothers and sister once again.

The next day, Alex and I went to the beach. Sand crabs hopped between our knees as we reclined in the sand. Families scrunched under colorful beach umbrellas with bologna sandwiches and tubes of sunscreen. Kids rode boogie boards and bodysurfed, shouting and laughing and being right where they were.

"Sure you don't want a hit?" Alex asked, toking a smoking bowl of Humboldt green.

"Nah," I said, chugging bottled water.

He was darker than ever, his divorce lingering like a psychic wart. I tried to offer empty counsel, the same crap people always said. Empty platitudes. People came to terms when they were ready and not one second sooner. And some, never. Such was the world as I'd come to understand it. Always ahead of the curve. Lucky me. Right.

"The cast, man. Fuck 'em," I said.

"I married the bitch. Don't trivialize it. Don't get me wrong, I think it's great that you're not having seizures or hiding in closets anymore."

"Yeah. Seattle reminded me of something."

"Keith did that?"

"Yeah, he kinda did, but some random dude even more so."

"And because of a stranger, my buddy has vanished and sent this weirdo in his place?"

"Getting high just messes with what I've got left."

"Wish that would happen to me."

"Surely they taught you similar stuff in all those rehabs you've been to."

"Programs and schedules, sterile. Lots of brainwash. *Au naturale* is the way to go."

"Be careful what you wish for. You don't want it the way I got it. I've got a secret."

"Spill it."

"Lee was a raven."

"Huh?"

"Ever heard tales about the birds of the family *Corvidae*? They're the largest songbirds in the world. Ravens, rooks, crows, jackdaws, magpies. In literature and folklore, they're mostly considered birds of ill omen."

"Do tell."

"Poe's raven was a moody little hack. Even an illiterate like you must remember that poem from sophomore English class. Tolkien's *crebain* were agents of Sauron, the evil lord of Mordor, and one of Gandalf's many names was Stormcrow, which sort of meant *bearer of bad tidings*. Aesop's fables didn't paint rosy portraits of blackbirds. Jewish legend tells tales of Noah sending out a dove *and* a white raven, which got so caught up with the world—some versions have it feasting on a drowned corpse—that it failed to return to the ark and was punished by being blackened and condemned to eat carrion, um... forevermore."

"*Badabump.* A pun, how fun! I'm not that illiterate, bozo. That last bit about corpses and carrion is lovely, by the way. I fail to see how it relates to Lee's being a raven, though I'm going to be pleased to inform your parents you did pick up some knowledge from that hundred thousand-dollar education of yours they bankrolled."

"A large portion of raven mythology comes from the Native Americans, including the Pacific Northwest tribes, who to this day pass on stories and customs about the role Raven played in creating the world."

"Raven...the god bird, yeah? Like on the totem poles?"

"Yup. The tribes believed their world was laden with spirits encased within animals and trees. The raven-god was called *Nekilstas* the Trickster, a shape-changer able to take the form of any animal or human he desired, prone to fickle unpredictability, yet through his cunning Raven brought light, fire, and game to feed on, fashioning ceremonies and magic spells to thwart enemies. They say he saved the animals of the earth when the great flood came, and he held the sun and the moon in his beak—when he *stole the light*. His appetite was matched only by his enthusiasm for causing trouble. He loved to upset the natural order of things."

"Your point is?" Alex said, impatient with my parable. "You think Lee was some sort of reborn shape-shifter immortalized in Indian legend? Come on, man."

"I don't think she was *the* Raven, I think she was *a* raven, in human guise, an undercover angel-type. Maybe there are beings with access to greater realities, or maybe we're *all* archangels or daemons or demigods traveling at different levels and in alternate dimensions and in varying forms, divergent timelines and perspectives, existence an infinite cat's cradle."

"Good god. We're just lowly, shit-for-brains, hairless apes. And Lee was not a goddess. You put her on the pedestal you're building, and you're never going to get laid again."

"Among other definitions, a *murder* is a group of crows. There's a parliament of rooks, a tiding of magpies, and an unkindness of ravens."

I paused, gazing at the Pacific splayed endless on the horizon, suppressing tears.

"It's a strange term. I only knew their kindnesses. "

"Oh, for fuck's sake..."

"I wanna dance around fires, talk to shaman elders, run naked through forests, keep the curtains open, and turn the TV off. Dark light and red shift, they're dug in, but it's possible to reverse the trends. Sooner or later we all reach the bottom of the glass. At school I learned in physics courses that red shift is the color of the spectrum as the universe expands. In the far future, it's theorized, when the universe collapses, blue shift sets in. But red shift is something else too, something much more ornery."

"More ornery than a collapsing universe?"

"That's *blue* shift. You don't remember, do you?"

"Remember what?"

"That day we were running in the back forty, at the ponds, chasing after that king snake. It conscripted us. It mugs everybody."

"You've lost your mind. What was left of it, that is."

"I was pushed off the plank. No choice. You've still got one. And you ought to exercise it. Being forced to do it sucks. We need to get tribal again. Respect nature, give thanks to the universe, dance around fires, all that jazz."

"Spoken like a classic lapsed Catholic boy."

"Everyone is an un-savior, dude."

The sun blazed.

Seagulls squawked.

Surf crashed.

Dolphins breached offshore.

Children frolicked, as yet untouched by red shift.

34

I walk in, a bit nervous, trying to look official.

"Are you a new staff?" A teenage Hispanic girl bars my way, wild-eyed, throwing off attitude as if it were on sale.

"Uh…yeah. My name's Daren. What's yours?"

"Wouldn't you like to know. Another dumb-ass white boy."

Yes, exactly right, cupcake, just another dumb-ass white boy. Bingo. Bango. Presto.

I got a job. I moved back to Santa Crisca, in a small, expensive, one-bedroom apartment on the west side. Hoping my bachelor's degrees might amount to something other than regret, I drew up a resume and applied for a few entry-level positions in the mental health field. In my first interview, I was hired on the spot, at an institution in Santa Crisca serving the needs of developmentally disabled children.

I'm not going to grad school, not right now. Got some catch-up to do, extra ketchup. My parents hold out hope I'll resume graduate studies at some point but are satiated with the fact that my free ride is at last ending and I seem ready to accept some personal and financial culpability.

My mother still wrestles with her Olde Worlde demons. I await her victory. I'm aware of the years under her belt and how much weight they *yield. I talk softer to her these days. It'll happen at her pace, or maybe never. It's a rough understanding. Truth always is.*

Jim's a grizzly bear, buff and dozer-honed, hooked up with a divorcee broad and her four kids, battened down under the Durango Bay code of country living.

Keith and Rachel prosper in Washington, busy and in the black. They have a beautiful baby girl named Charlie, who's inherited her mother's eyes and her father's penchant for nonchalance. They tell me she's cried a few times during the night since her birth but otherwise is an atypical mellow youngster. The world will be enjoying the light of a surf kitten for years to come, a fact that gives me warm fuzzies. I am glad one of us escaped relatively unscathed.

Valerie moved away from DeeBee. She lives at a low-income condominium complex in a ghetto portion of a rundown, central-coast beach hamlet. She's stripping to make ends meet and has become a barfly fixture at the watering holes there. I've heard she's doing soft porn on the side. The dark light in her is more potent than ever, dusky black. When we speak on the phone, she doesn't ask about Alex. She wants to ask for money but is too proud, and I don't offer because I know where she's going to put it. I have become a maverick to her, stepped up—or down—in league. I don't want the role, but she won't reassign me unless I relinquish my persona non grata *status, which I cannot, will not, do.*

The same is true, to a certain extent, of Alex. He still waits tables at the dude ranch, making good money catering to the culinary whims of the rich and famous. He has yet to move out of the place he shared with Valerie, insisting the ancient history interred there isn't a continuing factor in his volatile ides and tides with the fairer sex, which have become unsettlingly numerous. I fail to understand why he disregards the attraction of my bandwagon under new construction. When I bring it up (and I do on a frequent basis—how can I not, he is my twin), it always results in an altercation, and we laugh it off. We play heads-up poker once a month, and when we part I try to pass him some of my true light. Given its low reserves and Alex's static demeanor to date, I may be wasting my time.

I miss Lee. The pain has faded. The need to be near her, to be in her presence, hasn't. It's hard to shed the potentials of all the things we could have—should have—been, next to impossible, but it's that conventional kind of "impossible" you know is actually possible. It's just a bitch to get there.

I haven't forgiven myself yet.

But I'm close.

The dormitory is in sore need of a paint job and a good plumber. Peeling strips of wallpaper flake off the walls, pipes rumble beneath corroded sinks. The common living areas are cluttered with stained furniture and old Atari and Nintendo games hooked up to battered televisions. Poster prints are mounted behind protective plastic sheets slimed in spit and god knows what else. Frayed blue carpet is mottled with black wet smudges. Odors of urine, sweat, and anguish are pungent and palpable.

This place feels right.

I enter a dining room where some residents prepare for dinner. A rotund girl with crossed eyes waddles over. Orange Butterfinger crème smears her stubby crooked fingers. The true light beaming from her is unmistakable.

"Hello. Will you be my friend?"

"Yes, I'll be your friend."

One last thing…it's the crows. At first I attributed their commonality to Mother Nature. It's not as if they're rare in southern California. But perhaps it may be more than that. Each day I chance upon several blackbirds, no matter where I am or what I'm doing. They have sentinels everywhere. Their beady eyes follow me as they caw gossip in their fowl rune language. It seems as if they're keeping watch. I think they take account of me. They *consider* me. Sometimes I respond with inadequate human tongue. I tell them to tell Lee I love her. They often lift wing then. I presume they relay the message.

CPSIA information can be obtained at www.ICGtesting.com
Printed in the USA
LVOW131537160513

334165LV00006B/721/P